CRITICAL PURSUIT

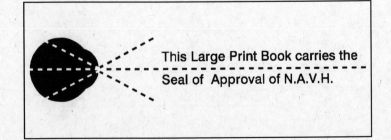

This Large Print Book carries the
Seal of Approval of N.A.V.H.

CRITICAL PURSUIT

JANICE CANTORE

THORNDIKE PRESS

A part of Gale, Cengage Learning

GALE
CENGAGE Learning·

Farmington Hills, Mich • San Francisco • New York • Waterville, Maine
Meriden, Conn • Mason, Ohio • Chicago

GALE
CENGAGE Learning®

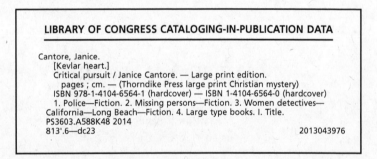

LIBRARY OF CONGRESS CATALOGING-IN-PUBLICATION DATA

Cantore, Janice.
  [Kevlar heart.]
  Critical pursuit / Janice Cantore. — Large print edition.
    pages ; cm. — (Thorndike Press large print Christian mystery)
  ISBN 978-1-4104-6564-1 (hardcover) — ISBN 1-4104-6564-0 (hardcover)
  1. Police—Fiction. 2. Missing persons—Fiction. 3. Women detectives—
California—Long Beach—Fiction. 4. Large type books. I. Title.
  PS3603.A588K48 2014
  813'.6—dc23   2013043976

Published in 2014 by arrangement with Tyndale House Publishers, Inc.

Printed in Mexico
1 2 3 4 5 6 7 18 17 16 15 14

To my aunt E,
who was my inspiration,
but who is now with Jesus.

ACKNOWLEDGMENTS

Thank you to my faithful friends, all the Reunioners: Lauraine, Wendy, Kathleen, Kitty, Marcie, Sue, Bonnie. All of you have helped me more than I can say. And thanks to Geri, Sheri, Patti, Rene, Mary, Sandra, Mark, Lisa, and everyone who encouraged and prayed for me through the years. God bless.

PROLOGUE

The heat of the day evaporated as a curtain of dark descended across the desert floor. Now the breeze had an icy edge, and six-year-old Brinna Caruso shivered. The thin, oversize T-shirt she wore offered little protection. Tears and dirt were dry and caked on her face, and all that was left of her voice after hours of screaming for help was a weak whisper.

She hugged the rough pole to which she was handcuffed and hiccuped sobs, unable to comprehend why she'd been left out in the middle of nowhere, barefoot and terrified.

" 'Jesus loves me; this I know, for the Bible tells me so.' "

She repeated the words over and over, a tuneless song recited between hiccups, wondering if anyone in the dark desert would ever find her.

The roar of an engine bubbled up in the

sky, faint at first and then loud enough to sound to Brinna like something large and vicious, coming to swallow her whole. She craned her neck and sniffled, looking up.

A light blinded her; then dust began to swirl all around, the pings of pebbles hitting the ramshackle building behind her sounding like gunshots. The sting of sand pummeling her bare legs made her fidget, but there was nowhere to hide.

Is the mean man coming back? Where are Daddy and Mommy and Brian? What is happening?

A thousand questions overloaded her six-year-old brain as she squeezed her eyes closed to shut out the dust and sneezed as grit forced its way up her nasal passages. She couldn't run; she couldn't scream.

All she could do was strain at the handcuffs and wait for the monster to attack.

1

Seventy-four percent of abducted children who are murdered are dead within three hours of the abduction.

The grim statistic rumbled around in K-9 Officer Brinna Caruso's brain like a hand grenade without the pin. There was no evidence that six-year-old Josh Daniels had been abducted, yet the statistic taunted her.

Brinna and her K-9, Hero, a four-year-old Labrador retriever, were part of a team of officers fanned out across El Dorado Park, the largest city park in Long Beach, California, searching for Josh. He'd disappeared from an afternoon family picnic two and a half hours ago.

The huge park successfully created the illusion of wilderness, dense in some places, open in others. There were a thousand places to hide — or be hidden. Brinna normally loved the park, the smell of pine trees and nature, the illusion of pristine in-

11

nocence and safety. Today all she could think about was how quickly innocence could be lost or, worse, stolen.

Hero trotted ahead on a well-beaten path, panting in the summer heat. Brinna and Officer Maggie Sloan followed a few feet behind. Maggie had left her partner back at the picnic site with the boy's family.

"You are so intense it's scary," Maggie said.

"What?" Brinna glanced from Hero to Maggie, who regarded her with a bemused expression. She wasn't just another officer; she was Brinna's confidante and best friend on the force.

"I'm just keeping an eye on my dog," Brinna explained, wiping her forehead with the back of her hand. "He's definitely following a scent."

"That's good news, isn't it?" Maggie asked. "It means we should find the boy. Why the frown?"

Brinna shrugged. "I want to find a boy and not a body."

"Harrumph." Maggie waved a hand dismissively. "There's no indication Josh was snatched. The best guess is he got lost playing hide-and-seek. El Dorado is to parks what Disneyland is to carnivals. He could be anywhere. You always imagine the worst where kids are concerned."

Brinna gritted her teeth. "Because you know as well as I do, if a kid is abducted, the chances are overwhelming that they will be a victim of murder."

Jaw set, Brinna returned her full attention to the dog. She'd had this conversation before, with Maggie and others, almost every time a child went missing. The guys on her team liked to say that since Brinna didn't believe there was a God watching out for kids, she'd given herself the job.

"The operative word is *if*. You're such a glass-is-half-empty person." Maggie slapped Brinna's shoulder with the back of her hand. "What about the ones found alive? Elizabeth Smart, Shawn Hornbeck, Brinna Caruso?"

"For every three of us rescued, there're nine who die," Brinna shot back. "You know my goal is 100 percent saved."

Maggie snorted in exasperation. "All the time you spend riding rail on registered sex offenders and monitoring any missing kid case flagged suspicious." She shook her head and wagged an index finger. "You can't save them all."

Brinna said nothing, hating that truth. Hero came to a stop, and like dominoes, so did Brinna and then Maggie.

"Maybe I can't save them all," Brinna conceded to Maggie. "But it certainly won't be for a lack of trying."

Maggie followed Brinna's gaze to Hero, then turned back to her friend and smiled. "You sure earn your nickname, Kid Crusader."

Brinna watched the dog. His nose up, testing the air, Hero trotted off in a more determined fashion than before. When he caught a scent, the hackles on the back of his neck rose ever so slightly. Brinna felt her own neck tingle as if there were a sympathetic connection between her and the dog.

"He's got something stronger." She stepped up her pace after Hero, Maggie on her heels.

They jogged to the left, into an area thick with tall pines and full oaks. After about a hundred feet, Hero barked and sat, turning toward Brinna. It was his practiced alert signal. Brinna's heart caught in her throat. If her dog had just found Josh, the boy wasn't moving; in fact, he wasn't even standing.

She followed the dog's gaze to a pile of leaves and held her breath.

When she heard muffled sniffling coming from the leaves, Brinna exhaled, rolling her eyes in relief. Then she saw the toe of a small tennis shoe sticking out. The boy was hiding. Turning to Maggie, she pointed at the shoe. Maggie smiled.

Brinna spoke to the quivering mass. "Josh, Josh Daniels. It's the police. Is that you?"

A half sob and an intake of breath emanated from the pile. The leaves moved, and a dirty-faced blond boy peered out at her.

"The po-police?" He cast an eye toward Hero. "That's not a coyote coming to eat me?"

Kneeling, Brinna bit back a chuckle. The boy's fear was plausible. He'd wandered into a particularly dense section of the park. The only things absent were dangerous animals. She understood a lost boy's imagination getting the best of him.

"Nope, it's my dog, Hero. Hero is a police dog. He doesn't eat little boys. He helped me find you."

Josh sat up and the leaves fell away, revealing a little boy smudged with sweat, soil, and grime. He sniffled. "I was playing and I got lost. I called and called, but my mom didn't come. Then I heard noises. I was afraid of wild animals, so I hid."

"Well, your mom and dad sent us to find you," Maggie said. "Are you ready to go home?"

Josh nodded vigorously and stood, brushing off dirt and leaves as he did so. "Can I pet your dog?" he asked Brinna, the tears already drying.

"Sure," Brinna said as she stood, ignoring the triumphant smirk Maggie shot her. Brinna pulled out her handheld radio and notified the command post that the situation was code 4, all over and resolved. "We're on our way out."

Brinna smiled as she took the boy's hand. "Do you like Beanie Babies, Josh?"

He looked up at her and nodded.

"I've got one for you in the car," she said with a smile as the statistic tumbling around in her mind disappeared in a poof, like a dud.

"Officer Caruso, Officer Caruso!"

Brinna groaned. Tracy Michaels, the local police beat reporter, was hailing her. Brinna had almost made it to her car avoiding all contact with the press. She wished Maggie were still with her. Maggie always knew how to talk to the press. But Maggie was with her partner, seeing to the happy family reunion.

"Officer Caruso! I have the okay for an interview."

Brinna stopped at her K-9 unit, a black-and-white Ford Explorer, and turned, counting to ten so she didn't say anything she'd regret. Reporters only wanted bad news. They thrived on tragedy. She faced Michaels, a young, eager woman who approached with a pad and pen in her right hand.

"Tracy, we found the kid in a pile of leaves, alive and unmolested — not much excitement in that story."

The reporter shook her head. "I don't want to talk about Josh Daniels. I want to talk about your upcoming anniversary."

"My anniversary?" Brinna frowned.

"Don't tell me you don't mark the day in some special fashion," Tracy said, hands on her hips. "Next week, it will be twenty years to the day that you were rescued after being abducted."

2

"Hey, Hot dog, is it time for the rest of us to retire?"

"Is it Caruso and Hero or Batman and Robin?"

"Hey, John Walsh Jr., when does your TV show air?"

"Do you want to be called RoboCop now?"

The e-mail ribbing began before Brinna left her driveway. As a K-9 officer, she took the Ford Explorer home and left only a few work-related items in her station locker. She dressed at home and logged in before driving to the station for the squad meeting. The messages popped up on the mobile computer as soon as her status showed 10-8, in service. Bracing herself to endure teasing from her coworkers all night, she cleared the screen as the station came into view.

Tracy's article had run in the local paper that morning. With a headline like "Local

Cop Tells Pedophiles, 'Watch Out; I'm After You,' " Brinna knew her fellow officers would have a field day. Collegial teasing was as much a part of police work as writing tickets.

When she'd first read the headline of Tracy's article about her anniversary, a headache tiptoed into her temples. It was the text that made the ache stomp with combat boots. Tracy got the facts right, but the way she'd embellished everything made Brinna sound like a cross between the Lone Ranger and the Terminator.

Brinna climbed out of the Explorer and left the engine running with the AC on for Hero. Her afternoon shift began at 4 p.m., and sweltering summer heat had not yet abated for the night. She stopped at the locker room to see if Maggie was there. Before she was all the way inside the room, she could see that someone had pasted the article and headline to her locker. *Maggie.*

Brinna tore the paper off and tossed it in the trash, trying and failing to think of a witty retort for her friend.

"Hey." Maggie poked her head around the corner, a silly grin on her face. "I was hoping you'd autograph that for me."

"Ha-ha. Go ahead, pile on," Brinna groaned. "You should have seen all the e-mail messages I got when I logged on."

"Come on, it was a great article." Maggie stepped to where Brinna stood and held her arms wide. "Enjoy being the celebrity of the moment."

Brinna snorted. "Tracy made me sound like some sort of Lone Ranger cop, an aberration. That kind of celebrity I can do without." She blew out a resigned breath and leaned against the locker. "Reporters write to entertain, not inform. I don't like being entertainment."

Maggie stepped past Brinna to the mirror and began to pin her long blonde hair up in a bun, off her collar. "Deal with it. You make good copy. The kidnapped kid growing up to help kidnapped kids. What did your mentor have to say about the article?"

"Milo hasn't seen it yet. He's in Mexico on his annual fishing trip. I'm sure a copy will find its way to him when he gets back."

Maggie giggled. "You got that right."

Brinna and Maggie slid into their seats in the squad room with a minute to spare.

"Hey, it's our own local supercop." Rick, Maggie's partner, moved his desk a bit as if to make room for Brinna and gave her a mock bow.

"Stand in line, Rick. I got about a hundred

20

e-mails cleverer than that." Brinna stuck her tongue out just as one of the afternoon sergeants brought things to order.

The sergeant read off the night's assignments and made no reference to the article. But as everyone was dismissed to log on in service, the K-9 sergeant, Janet Rodriguez, called Brinna back to the office.

"Bad news." Rodriguez gave her a look that said *I'm sorry,* and Brinna braced herself, crossing her arms and waiting warily for the hammer to fall. "Press relations just called. They've decided it would be good PR to send a reporter along during your shift tonight."

"What?" Brinna felt like her jaw hit the floor as Rodriguez continued.

"They're fielding a lot of requests and questions about you because of the Michaels article. The reporter they want to send with you tonight will do a piece about being on the job with the Kid Crusader."

"You're pulling my leg, right? This is a late April Fools' joke to get me going." Brinna glanced around the room, expecting other officers to pop out snickering. Rodriguez's expression, however, said it wasn't a joke, and that made her stomach feel like a greasy doughnut just slid down her throat.

"I wish I were kidding," Janet said. "But a

reporter from the *LA Times*, Gerald Clark, is waiting for you at the business desk."

Brinna was only an hour into her shift when she truly wished she'd called in sick. Gerald Clark had questions about everything. He asked Brinna every question Tracy had and more.

Brinna tried to shift the conversation to Hero's work record and away from her plight at the age of six. "You aren't going to reprint everything Tracy wrote, are you?" She stopped the reporter midquestion.

"Of course not. But I'd like to get my own feel for your story. The *Times* is way more in-depth than your local paper."

Maggie had whispered, "Ooh, eye candy" to Brinna when she glimpsed Clark at the business desk. Brinna grudgingly admitted to herself that he was handsome, if maybe a little too *GQ*. A tall, well-built man with stylish glasses and wavy blond hair just long enough to be appealing, Clark had a quick smile that under different circumstances Brinna would have been attracted to. But she hated talking about herself.

He pointed to the flyer taped on her dash. "Like why do you have this missing poster here?"

Brinna glanced to the text she knew so

well. "Heather Bailey is the most recent unsolved missing case from Long Beach. I use my free time to check up on any leads."

"She's been missing a month. Any leads to follow up on tonight?"

"Unfortunately, no." Brinna bit her lip. She'd wanted to go by and check in with the Baileys before dark. No way with this reporter tagging along.

"Statistics say she's probably dead." Clark tapped the dash with both index fingers.

Brinna fought the urge to argue. "I doubt her parents would like to hear statistics right now. And I don't give up until the case is closed."

Milo's voice echoed in her mind. *A body, warm or cold, is the only thing that stops the search.* And the question that always pinched her thoughts when murdered children were the subject of conversation: *Why was I saved when a kid like Heather might not be?*

"Is Hero classified as a cadaver dog?"

With a quick shake of her head, Brinna cursed her luck. She'd wanted the conversation to turn to Hero, not to cadavers or dead kids.

"Hero is scent-trained. I give him a scent and he trails it. He is not specifically a cadaver dog, no."

23

"He's different from patrol dogs?"

"Yeah. They're trained to bite, tackle, chase — that kind of thing. Hero is trained to follow a scent and, once he finds the source, to sit and bark to alert me. He's not paid for out of the same budget as the rest of the dogs. He's paid for by a federal grant, a product of 9/11."

"I've heard he's experimental. You think he's working out?" His tapping was rhythmical now, a tune Brinna couldn't name. "You've only found three kids in two years. Is that productive?"

Brinna felt her face flush. *Three live kids are better than three dead kids.* The emergency beep of the radio cut off her response.

"Any unit to handle, 415 shots, Eighteenth and Magnolia. CP reports hearing screams and then five to six gunshots."

The radio crackled with Maggie's voice as she and Rick stepped up to handle the call in their beat. Brinna pressed the assist button on her computer and started toward the area.

"Somebody get shot?" Clark asked, his voice an octave higher.

"That's what we need to find out," Brinna answered as she planned the approach that would put her in the best position for backup.

Maggie came on the air again to let everyone know her and Rick's position.

"We're at Twenty-Third and the boulevard, so we'll be coming from north of the dispatch location."

Brinna silently thanked her friend for the information. She was south of the call, so between her and Maggie, they formed the start of a perimeter if there was a shooter to catch. She cruised along Tenth Street, waiting for Maggie to position other backup units, intending to cross Magnolia and head north up the next north-south street.

The whine of a revved engine coming her way took Brinna's attention from the radio. She hit the brakes, saving the black-and-white from a broadside collision. A speeding car blew the red light right in front of the Explorer and roared south down Magnolia, barely missing the police cruiser's front bumper.

Grabbing the radio mike, she slammed the accelerator down and turned left after the speeder.

"1-King-8, I'm following a vehicle, high rate of speed, southbound Magnolia. It's a Chevy, possibly an older Monte Carlo, running with no lights, blowing red lights and stop signs."

She saw the reporter grab the dash and

heard Hero slide across the back of the Explorer as her tires barely held the turn.

Clipping the mike back to its holder, Brinna flipped on her lights and siren and glanced at the speedometer. Her speed neared fifty and she wasn't gaining on the Chevy. She heard dispatch question Maggie, asking her to determine whether or not the speeding car was related to the shots call.

Brinna punched the radio's volume button, ramping up the volume as her body ramped up with a surge of adrenaline. *Am I chasing the shooter?* She forgot Clark.

The Chevy narrowly missed cross traffic at Sixth Street. Brinna slowed at the crosswalk, then stomped the accelerator as soon as she was clear. Now the Chevy was careening toward Third Street. For the first time Brinna saw taillights as the driver hit the brakes.

"He's going too fast. He'll never make the turn." She watched as the speeding car cut the right turn too close and smacked the curb, fishtailing westbound onto Third Street.

Brinna winced. Third Street was a one-way street, eastbound.

The tail end of the Chevy momentarily disappeared from sight, tires squealing in protest. Then Brinna heard the bang and piercing squeal of crunching metal as the car crashed.

Skidding to a stop at Third Street, Brinna leaned forward, checked right, and saw stopped headlights. On the south side of the street sat the Chevy, smoking from the impact with a light pole. Miraculously it'd missed oncoming traffic and broadsided only the pole.

Proceeding cautiously, light bar still activated but siren off, Brinna positioned her vehicle between oncoming traffic and the Chevy. She motioned vehicles around the wreck.

"Stay here," she ordered Clark.

Hero stood, ears pricked with interest, waiting for the call to work. Maggie's voice sizzled over the radio confirming that the speeding car did contain the shooter from her call.

Standing outside the open door of the Explorer but behind the door itself, Brinna keyed her handheld radio and explained the crash to dispatch, keeping her eyes on the wreck. The smell of burning rubber and oil hung in the air like an acrid fog. Every couple of seconds something hissed from the wreckage. It wasn't completely dark yet, and as she peered into the smoky mess, she saw no movement, no one visible behind the steering wheel. The light pole had just about cut the Chevy in half between the front and back seats.

Replacing the radio, she sent a glance toward Clark. He was making himself small under the dashboard.

Sirens screamed in the distance as backup and paramedics raced her way. *Has he run?* she wondered, even as she scanned the surrounding area. There was no place for him to go. He'd crashed next to a fenced construction lot, and there was no way he could have reached cover in the time it took Brinna to park her car.

Where is he?

Brinna started for the mangled Chevy, moving cautiously. Halfway to the car, movement near the driver's side caught her eye. A man, outside the driver's door, rose to face her, but she couldn't focus on his face. Her focus zeroed in on the gun in his hand, pointed at her chest.

Brinna jerked to her right as she drew her duty weapon. She saw the muzzle flash of the suspect's gun before she heard the bang and felt the bullet whiz by her ear.

Raising her gun to the target, she continued moving toward cover, pressing the trigger twice as she dove behind a dark-green mailbox, scraping shoulder, elbow, hip. Half on her back, half on her side, she scrambled to pull the lifeline of the radio from her belt.

"998, 998!" Brinna yelled the code for shots fired into her radio and then took a breath. "Not sure if the suspect is down. He's east of me. All units approaching, the suspect is on Third Street, west of Magnolia, and still armed."

After waiting a few beats and hearing nothing but approaching sirens, Brinna pulled herself to her knees and peered around the mailbox. Several units squealed to a stop at the intersection. Before long, Brinna was surrounded by friendly forces. Together they set up a perimeter, certain they had the bad guy encircled and trapped.

"No movement from the car." The downtown sergeant, Klein, was on scene and taking control. He'd come in from the west and Brinna had moved to meet with him behind his black-and-white. "We'll try calling him out. If there's no response, I'll send someone in." He nodded toward her unit. "How's that ride-along?"

Brinna slapped her forehead. "I forgot about him. I'd better check." The safest place for the reporter was in the Explorer, but Brinna wondered if he had the sense to know that.

She made her way to the Ford. There were two other units in front of the K-9 vehicle now, officers at the ready. Brinna heard Klein on the PA, calling the Chevy's driver, ordering him out, as she peered inside the Explorer. She sighed and choked back a smile. The reporter still had his head down, hiding. Hero gave a whine that said he was ready to work, and Brinna flashed a hand gesture telling him to sit and stay.

"You okay?" she asked Clark.

He looked up at her and nodded, face blanched. "What's going on?"

"We're trying to get a fix on the suspect. You stay down. I'll get back to you as soon as I can." She returned to where Sergeant Klein directed the situation. He sent two officers along the ground behind the wreck to get a visual on the suspect.

"He's down, not moving," they reported after a few minutes.

A moment later, they confirmed their suspicion. The man was dead. One of Brinna's bullets had hit its mark.

3

At 4 a.m., Jack O'Reilly awoke from the dream as he normally did, screaming his wife's name and clutching his pillow as if he could somehow use it to drag her back from the dead.

The cries died in his throat as he opened his eyes to the dark living room, and the terror of the dream faded. Since Vicki's death, the couch had become his bed. The bedroom he left untouched, preserving it as it was on the last day his wife left it.

He sat up, breathing deep, heart pounding. For the briefest of moments he imagined he caught a whiff of his wife's scent, and he inhaled deeply, hoping to prolong the illusion, but it evaporated.

The dream was always the same. He and Vicki were walking and smiling. He held one hand while she rested her other on her expanding belly as if hanging on to the life growing there. The first feelings associated with the dream were those of profound happiness. The bleak reality of the last year disappeared in the pleasant subconscious illusion.

But it didn't last.

At some point Jack was aware of an approaching car. He wanted to tell Vicki to watch out, to move, but his voice was suffocated by dream-state paralysis. The car roared by and took Vicki with it. Her hand was wrenched from his as his screams wrenched him from sleep. He awakened to the empty life he'd lived for almost a year.

Tossing the pillow aside, Jack headed for the shower. To sleep again so soon after the dream would be like trying to put toothpaste back in the tube.

Standing in the shower with hot water pounding into his chest, Jack stared at his hands. He clenched and unclenched a fist, touched the cool tiles, and wondered how it was that he was still alive.

I don't feel alive, he thought. *Maybe I'm dead, and I just don't know it. If it weren't for the pain, I'd feel nothing.*

Toweling off, Jack grabbed a robe and padded barefoot into the kitchen to start coffee. He glanced at the calendar stuck to the refrigerator and saw what was keeping him alive. The date circled in red was a little more than two weeks away. It was the date of the sentencing.

Vicki had been driving to an afternoon doctor's appointment in her economical Honda. She'd called Jack before she left the house, bubbling with excitement about how active the child inside her was. "He'll be big and strong like his daddy," she'd gushed, though they didn't know what sex the baby was yet.

Jack knew now. A little girl had died with his wife.

Fresh from a wet lunch, Gil Bridges had started up his brand-new Hummer. Ignoring at least seven vehicles who'd honked a warning at him, Gil got on the 710 freeway going north in the southbound lanes. Investigators estimated his speed was close to sixty when he crested a small rise and hit Vicki head-on. She never had a chance.

Bridges had already been found guilty of gross vehicular manslaughter. All that was left was the sentencing. Jack hated the man as much as anyone could hate.

The hate, he thought. *That's what's keeping me going, keeping me alive. I just need to be sure he gets what he deserves. If the court doesn't give it to him, I will.*

Jack sipped coffee in the kitchen, staring at nothing, until it was time to get dressed and go to work. He put on his suit and tie, clipped his badge and duty weapon to his belt, and climbed into his car.

Hanging from the rearview mirror was the cross he'd given to Vicki on their second wedding anniversary. It had hung around her neck until the coroner removed it and placed it in an envelope for Jack. While Jack no longer believed in what the cross symbolized, he cherished the necklace because it had been near Vicki's heart when it had beat its last.

Half-listening to the radio, Jack would reach up from time to time and rub the cross between his thumb and forefinger as he drove. There'd been an officer-involved shooting last night. If he'd felt alive, he thought, the news would have given him a jolt. Homicide investigators handled all officer-involved shootings. But Jack felt no excitement, no drive to learn the details.

He'd asked six months ago to be taken off the normal homicide rotation. Now he filed paper and reviewed cold cases all day. But not the pictures. Jack couldn't stand the bodies anymore. In every female victim Jack saw Vicki's mangled body and in every dead child the little girl they'd never had a chance to name.

I'm a dead man working homicide, he

thought. *But only for two and a half more weeks. I just need to hang on for two and a half more weeks.*

4

Nigel Pearce read the headline three times before he slid a couple of quarters in the slot and bought a copy of the newspaper. "Local Cop Tells Pedophiles, 'Watch Out; I'm After You.'"

He sat down on a bus bench and unfolded the front page to read the entire article under a streetlight:

Local K-9 officer Brinna Caruso seeks to right twenty-year-old wrong.

Twenty years ago this month, six-year-old Brinna was snatched off a dusty Lancaster sidewalk in broad daylight by a stranger. The man drove her to a desolate section of the desert, molested her, and then left her tied to a railing outside an abandoned building.

Nigel stopped reading and studied the picture of the cop with her dog. It showed a sturdy-looking, dark-haired woman in uniform. She had an olive complexion, brown eyes, and short-cropped hair.

What a determined expression on her face. Nigel figured she was probably attractive to some, but she was way too old for him.

Setting the paper on his lap, he leaned back and tried to remember her as one of his Special Girls but couldn't.

But I did have one or two in Lancaster back then. She must have been one. I just can't place her face. There have been too many girls in between. I never hurt my precious Special Girls. I simply leave them. If they're found, they're found. If not, well, that's up to fate.

Now, he thought, *fate has apparently brought this Special Girl across my path again, twenty years later. There must be a reason.* He picked up the paper and continued reading:

Nearly forty-eight hours after she was left to die in the desert by her attacker, Brinna was miraculously rescued by a sheriff's deputy K-9 officer. Deputy Gregor Milovich, aka Milo, followed a hunch and unleashed his dog, Scout, outside the grid his fellow officers were searching. He came across a purple Care Bear, identified as Brinna's, and kept going, working twenty-four hours with no sleep. He and Scout found Brinna at 5:30 in the morning.

Though cold and frightened, Brinna showed some of the pluckiness that characterizes her now, telling Milovich, "That mean man took my Care Bear."

"I don't really remember everything that happened that night," Officer Caruso says now. "What I do remember is Milo and his dog coming to my rescue. I knew right then and there that's what I would do when I grew up."

Now, at twenty-six, Brinna Caruso has realized her dream. She's been a police officer with Long Beach for five years, two as the K-9 handler for Hero.

Last year she made news when she and Hero found Alonso Parker, the toddler kidnapped by known sex offender Darius Graves. Hero tracked the child to a garage in an abandoned building where Graves was living, before Graves could complete his plan to molest the boy and sell pictures on the Internet.

"It's all about bringing kids home safe," Caruso said. "Megan's Law was the best thing to happen to kids because it allows people access to information about known sex offenders. If we can keep track of pedophiles, we have a better chance of keeping kids safe. I don't believe child molesters are ever cured. Making sure they register with law enforcement and mind their p's and q's is the only way to limit their opportunities to reoffend."

Stopping again, Nigel smiled. *Provided, of course, they are caught and forced to register.* He snickered. *I'm smarter than that. They didn't catch me twenty years ago, and except for that one slip ten years ago, they'll never catch me again.*

He ran his hand over the cop's picture. *Maybe I should plan something to celebrate our twentieth anniversary.*

Something very special.

5

"How do you feel about everything you just walked us through?" Doc Bell, the LBPD psychologist, leaned casually against a light pole. The brightening morning sky had caused the light to click off a few minutes before.

Brinna inhaled deeply and considered how to answer the "soul slicer," as Milo would call him. While she had nothing against psychologists in general, she felt uncomfortable with the probing they did. Brinna preferred asking questions to being asked. At this moment, Bell reminded her of a psychologist she'd talked to twenty years ago after her rescue. Back then, all she'd wanted to do was go home to her Care Bears, but that man couldn't believe anything was so simple. He wanted shades of gray, and to Brinna — back then, as now — the entire incident was black-and-white.

I was snatched and then rescued. Home

*was all I wanted. Tonight I was shot at and I
shot back. And all I want right now is my own
bed.*

What shade of gray is Bell after?

"I'm not sure what you want me to say."
She held the doctor's gaze, unable to read
him.

"Just what I asked. How do you feel?" He
smiled. "It's not a trick question."

"I feel lucky." She shrugged. "It could just
as easily have been me under that blue
tarp." She crossed her arms, conscious that
her hands were shaking. Bell had already
told her that was a normal reaction to the
adrenaline roller coaster she'd been on that
night.

He nodded. "You'll probably replay the
incident over and over in your mind." He
waved a hand at the others still milling
around the scene — the chief, the handling
homicide detective, members of the DA's
shooting team. They'd all participated in a
walk-through of the incident, where Brinna
explained the events while they were fresh
in her mind.

"No one here thought anything seemed
wrong with the shooting. Remember that
when the flashbacks come."

"I'll do that." She relaxed, tension in her
shoulders easing. Bell wasn't going to try to

41

dig for something that wasn't there. She moved him to an okay list in her mind.

"Come see me if you feel the need. Other than that, I think you're fine to return to duty after your mandatory three days off." He shook her hand and walked off to confer with the chief. After a few minutes they both climbed into an unmarked car and drove away.

"I take it that went well." Ben Carney, the homicide investigator, broke her chain of thought.

"Yeah." Brinna exhaled. "He says I'm fine, normal." She arched an eyebrow. "Got him fooled, huh?" She liked Ben. They'd worked together briefly when she'd finished her probationary period, the first year in patrol after academy graduation, and she'd always thought of him as a solid cop.

Ben smiled. "Everything is clean so far, so I have to agree with him. Only thing that will make it cleaner," he added, "is finding the slug the guy fired at you. We're still searching."

"I hope it didn't end up embedded in a car driving by." Brinna followed his gaze down the street.

"This was your first shooting, wasn't it?" Ben asked.

Brinna nodded.

"You did what you had to," Ben said.

"He didn't give me any choice." Brinna sighed. "I'm just glad instinct kicked in. Sorry he's dead. Glad I'm not."

"Me too. You can take off now, get some sleep. Try not to worry about any of this."

"Thanks, Ben." She shook his hand and practically ran to the Explorer. Clark, the reporter, was long gone. After he threw up in the street when he witnessed the scene, an assisting unit had driven him home.

Once inside the car, she hugged Hero, then pulled out her cell phone. Though she knew the shooting was justified and she'd done the only thing she could do, she craved a solid debriefing by Milo. He always knew what to say about any situation, better than any psychologist. But the phone was answered by the click of voice mail. Brinna slapped her forehead even as Milo's recorded voice told her to leave a message. She'd forgotten about the Mexican fishing trip.

She snapped the phone shut and put the Explorer in gear just as the coroner's van pulled up. Brinna watched as an investigator she'd worked with often climbed out and headed toward the tarp-covered body. There'd been no ID on the man, so among other things it would be the coroner's responsibility to determine his identity. That would be the easy part. They'd probably never be able to determine why the mutt went on a shooting rampage.

Brinna shook her head and pulled away from the scene, yawning. She directed the Explorer to the station. When she arrived, the clock on the dash told her it was 9:30 in the morning, seven hours past end of watch or EOW.

She headed for the locker room to drop some stuff off and pick up a fresh uniform. Inside, she saw Maggie dozing on a cot. A well-placed smack to a metal locker with her baton brought Brinna the desired result. Maggie jerked up, the disorientation of an abrupt awakening all over her face.

"Hey, sleepyhead, don't you want to go home?" Brinna spoke in a singsong voice.

Her friend's expression cleared and she stood, yawned, and stretched. "You just ruined the best dream. But since I was waiting for you, I'll let that pass. I never made it to the shooting scene. How're you doing?"

Brinna worked the lock on her locker and jerked it open. "I'm fine, just tired."

She yawned as Maggie had. Though she was physically exhausted, her mind still whirled with impressions of the chase and the shooting. The afterimages played as if

44

she'd watched the incident unfold but hadn't participated.

"I fired from reflex. I guess all that stuff they say when we're training at the range is true."

"About reverting to what you've learned during stress shooting?" Maggie asked. "Muscle memory and all that?"

"Yeah. I reacted." Brinna shrugged. "Hate to say I got lucky, but that's what it felt like. What was the guy's problem? I heard he shot two at your scene."

Maggie nodded. "Neither of my victims was cooperative about identifying their assailant. It was witnesses who saw the shooter split in the Monte Carlo. The victims' injuries are minor. One got hit in the arm, the other in the foot. Some kind of gang beef. They probably want their own retaliation. Homicide will have their work cut out for them sorting it all out."

"Ben Carney is the lead on my end. He'll probably end up with both cases." Brinna stretched, her gun belt feeling as though it weighed a hundred pounds. She closed the locker and hung her clean uniform on the lock.

"Good; he'll be thorough." Maggie stepped to the mirror, groaned, and waved both hands at the mirror as if to make the image go away.

Brinna chuckled. "He helped me relax a lot before the walk-through, and things went okay."

"I saw the chief and Doc Bell when they came back to the station." Maggie rubbed bloodshot eyes. "They didn't seem upset about anything. I'm sure the shooting is clean."

Brinna nodded and tapped the locker with a knuckle. "You know the drill. I've got three days off. Since last night was Monday, I don't have to be at work for six whole days." She held up one open hand and an index finger on the other. Her normal schedule had her working four ten-hour days with a three-day weekend. But the shooting meant that the mandatory three days off would extend her weekend.

Maggie groaned. "Show-off. I'm jealous."

Brinna grabbed her uniform, and then she and Maggie headed for the door.

"Not only is six days off awesome," Brinna gloated, "but I got the interview with Dr. Bell out of the way. I don't have to visit his office unless I want to."

"Excellent. No one wants to visit him during normal business hours." Maggie rolled her eyes.

Brinna nodded as they walked out of the

locker room. Most cops were like Milo when it came to psychologists. "Stay out of my head," he would say.

"By the way, since you keep up with all the department gossip, where is Ben's partner?" Brinna asked. "He was by himself at the scene."

"Jack O'Reilly?" Maggie snorted. "I hear he's a certified nutcase now. Went around the bend when his wife died, hasn't come back. I'm sorry he suffered such a loss, but speaking of the psychologist, I'm surprised he hasn't relieved the guy of duty."

"But I thought I saw O'Reilly walking to the station from the parking structure as I pulled in. He's a tall redheaded guy, right?"

"That's him. He's still in homicide physically. I think he's working Ken Opie's job, reviewing cold cases, until Opie gets back from knee surgery. Mentally, I think he's —" Maggie made a circle around her ear with an index finger — "about five fries short of a Happy Meal."

They'd reached Brinna's Explorer. "So what are you going to do with all your time off?" Maggie asked. "If it were me, I'd be on the beach the whole time."

"Right now I feel like I need to unwind with a short kayak trip," Brinna said as she opened the door to her SUV. Hero stood to

47

greet her with a wagging tail and a K-9 yawn.

"I knew you didn't know how to relax."

"Kayaking *is* relaxing. Besides, I have to burn off the residual adrenaline. Then I'll sleep."

"Okay, just take care. If you need to talk, call me."

"Will do. See you later."

Brinna climbed into the driver's seat. She turned and checked on Hero in the back, who lay curled up on his mat.

"Well, we've got six days off. What do you want to do?" Getting only a tail thump in response, Brinna started the SUV and turned right out of the station lot. The two news vans parked in front of the station didn't escape her notice.

"I know they're here about the shooting," she said as she glanced in the rearview mirror at their shrinking images. "Glad we won't be around for the start of the circus."

At home Brinna shed her gun belt and jumpsuit in favor of shorts and a tank top. She fed Hero first, then made herself a tuna sandwich, taking a seat at her computer to check her e-mail while she munched.

Above her computer screen hung a shelf loaded with Care Bears and Beanie Babies. She made a mental note to grab a couple to put in her car. She still hadn't replaced the ones she'd given to Josh.

While she waited for the computer to power up, she glanced over to her Wall of Slime. Tacked on the west wall of her office were information posters containing the faces and statistics of twenty high-risk sex offenders residing in the city of Long Beach.

Overall, Long Beach was home to nearly eight hundred registered sex offenders. Brinna had chosen the worst of the lot to post in her office and "ride rail on," as Maggie liked to say.

Shifting her gaze to the east side of the room, Brinna perused the Innocent Wall. There, ten missing posters lined up in three rows, the most recent cases on the top, stared back at her. Heather Bailey's smiling face was first — the same poster Brinna kept in her car. The eight-year-old had disappeared without a trace from her front yard a month ago.

A ding from her computer indicating she had mail brought Brinna back to the screen. Four e-mails awaited her. The first message was from Chuck Weldon, the local FBI agent. She paused before she hit Open, anxiety tingling her fingertips at the thought of what news Chuck's message might bring.

The FBI generally took over any missing

case labeled a stranger abduction. Chuck could be sending her bad news about Heather. Sighing, Brinna opened the message. The contents were a mild relief. No news on Heather. Chuck just sent an update on how the last lead panned out: nowhere.

She remembered what a fight it had been to get the department to recognize her as a search-and-rescue specialist, a position that didn't exist anywhere on the Long Beach Police Department. Finding a toddler named Alonso Parker had silenced a lot of opposition and opened a door she'd charged through.

Hero didn't need to be a normal patrol dog chasing criminals, she'd argued. He was scent-trained. He could find kids and he'd proved it.

Chuck had provided the nudge the brass needed. He stepped in and agreed with her. After that, the sergeant in homicide sat down with Sergeant Rodriguez in the K-9 detail and okayed Brinna's freelancing into missing children cases. There was no position in the LBPD budget for a full-time missing person patrol officer. But Hero's grant and the FBI's endorsement allowed Brinna to be the closest thing to it.

She ran her hand over the plaque she kept to one side of her computer monitor, given by her patrol shift teammates: *To the Kid Crusader, Our Search-and-Rescue Stud.*

She punched open the second message, from the Center for Missing and Exploited Children. The text contained an alert about a ten-year-old boy missing in Utah. Brinna checked her watch. The kid had gone missing about the same time she'd been facing off the lunatic in the Monte Carlo.

Ignoring the next two messages, both from her mother, Brinna finished her sandwich and downed the remainder of her Diet Coke. She walked across the hall to her bedroom, where Hero slept curled up on her bed, and pulled a map of western states from her nightstand, tracing the route to Bryce Canyon, Utah, with her finger.

Utah is way out of my hundred-mile radius for weekend searches, she thought, *but very possible with my time off. And the desert is a horrible place for a kid to be lost.*

As often happened when thinking about children lost and alone, for a second Brinna was six again and back in the desert outside of Lancaster, leaning against the post she'd been tied to and crying.

Shaking away the memory, she focused on the facts and went back to her desk. The first hours were the most important. She rubbed her forehead, her gaze running over the audience of stuffed animals. Milo's words again echoed in her mind: *"Never give up until we've got a body, dead or alive."*

She thought about Heather and refused to admit that things didn't look good for the little girl. She still considered the search active, but it had been a month and all leads had dried up.

This kid in Utah had gone missing hours ago. It was fresh. They had a chance to find him. *And a search will go miles toward getting my mind off the shooting.*

Chewing on her lower lip, she thought about the drive — a long one, but doable.

Brinna picked up the phone and dialed Sergeant Rodriguez's number, crossing her fingers in the hope she was awake.

With a sleep-slurred voice, Rodriguez okayed Brinna's off-duty trip to Utah. With the shooting tentatively labeled clean, if any questions came up, they could be asked when she got back, the sergeant said.

Brinna thanked Rodriguez, knowing her sergeant would fight for her if the need arose, and hung up. She looked up the number of the authorities in charge of the Utah boy's search. It took a while to get connected to someone in charge, but when she did, he said that they'd welcome her help. The terrain was rough on the dogs, and they could use another one.

Brinna rubbed her face with both hands, glad she had a mission to complete after all the drama of her shift. The drive, instead of a kayak paddle, would help her wind down. She had six days to devote to the Utah kid . . . if they didn't find him before she got there. She looked at the clock and decided that since she was still amped up, it might be best to leave now and stop some-place on the road for a nap if she needed it. She and Hero could be in Bryce Canyon ready to join the search early tomorrow morning.

"When we join the search, with any luck, we'll be two for two and start a streak," she said to Hero.

6

Jack closed his open files and began to power down the computer for the day when Lieutenant Gary Hoffman walked into his cubicle.

"Afternoon, Jack. How's it going?"

"It's going, Gary. That's about all I can say."

An uncomfortable silence followed. Jack knew people weren't sure what to say to him, but he never tried to make it easier for them.

"I've got some news for you," Hoffman said finally, after clearing his throat. "Not sure if you'll think it's good or bad."

Jack stood and held the lieutenant's gaze but said nothing.

"Opie's coming back. He'll be here on Monday."

Jack sighed and shoved his hands in his pockets. He'd only been filling in for Opie. He'd hoped the position would last until the sentencing. But if Opie was clear to come back to work, Hoffman's visit told Jack that he could no longer hide behind a desk and avoid active police work.

"So where are you going to put me?"

Hoffman folded his arms across his chest. "I don't have much choice. You aren't considered light duty. And unless you tell me you don't want to work homicide anymore, you'll go back to full duty with your partner, Ben."

Jack felt his mouth go dry. Going back to work with Ben was a two-edged sword, both distasteful edges. Ben was a Christian who never stopped preaching. Jack had been like that before he lost Vicki. His faith died in the car with his wife and daughter. Now Ben's empty Christian platitudes choked him like thick flare smoke. And then there were the bodies.

"No other option?" he asked, wetting his lips.

Hoffman shrugged. "Patrol."

Jack blew out a breath. He'd been a patrol officer when he met Vicki. The move to homicide came shortly after they were married; it was the position he'd dreamed of since academy days. A year ago he would have flamed out and fought to keep his spot in homicide. Now Jack looked past Hoffman, out the window, and decided patrol might be the right place to hide for a couple of weeks.

"Afternoon patrol?" he asked.

Hoffman stammered with surprise. "Sure, if that's what you want."

"Yeah, that's what I want." *What I really want I can't have, so this transfer will do for now. I can hide in patrol for two and a half weeks.*

"Okay, I'll work on arranging it. You know you'll have to work with another officer for the first two weeks? It's a retraining policy."

"Whatever," Jack said. "I don't want to rock the boat." *I just want the sentencing to be over so I can quit pretending,* he thought.

Hoffman nodded and turned to leave but stopped at the door. "Jack, I'm not only your boss; I'm your friend. Can I give you some advice?"

Jack shook his head. "I know what you're going to say. Thanks anyway." Hoffman was as deluded a Christian as Ben.

Hoffman sighed. "You need to be back in church. You need the prayer and support of the church family to help you through this rough time."

Stepping to the door, Jack switched off the lights. "No, I don't. I just don't believe that fairy tale anymore," he said over his shoulder as he headed for the elevator.

7

Brinna made it to Mesquite, Nevada, before exhaustion hit like a brick. She had to stop, so she picked a hotel in the little border town. She called the search center in Utah to let them know where she was. They told her they couldn't do much in the dark anyway and advised her to drive safe. The location of Mesquite was a blessing and a curse. A little over halfway to Bryce Canyon, Mesquite was in the middle of barren desert. Brinna hated deserts and wide-open spaces and knew the only situation that could pull her through the desert to a place like Bryce Canyon was a search.

She preferred her neighborhood, crowded with houses, and her city, packed with cars and traffic. The open emptiness took her back to her childhood and memories of crying out for someone to help her when there was no answer but an eerie, empty echo. Sleep for a couple of hours meant she could resume the drive in the dark and any more barren wasteland would be masked by the night.

The sky was turning pink as she entered the park. Mountain time made Brinna adjust her watch — it was an hour later here. She'd looked over a map before she left home and had it open next to her in case she had trouble. But when she told the ranger at the park entrance who she was, he directed her to the staging area. The kid had gone missing in a part of the park called Fairyland Canyon, and the searchers were staging in the parking area at the trailhead. Brinna had to admit the scenery was interesting here. She'd read that the towering geological formations she could see were called hoodoos.

"It would almost be funny," she said to Hero, "to be lost in Fairyland with hoodoos."

But it wasn't. The boy had been out for almost thirty-six hours in the vast expanse Brinna could see all around as she turned in to the parking lot at the trailhead. The search and rescue operation was being run out of a large recreational vehicle. Local law enforcement, park rangers, search and rescue personnel, and people Brinna figured were volunteers seemed to be everywhere.

She could also see a helicopter in the air in the distance.

She checked in with Jase Robinson, the park ranger she'd talked to on the phone. A large map covered one side of the RV.

"The boy, Stevie, was hiking with his family on the Fairyland loop trail." Robinson pointed. "He thought he lost something on the trail and was angry when his father wouldn't go back and look for it. He left their campsite on his bike, they think, around 2300 Monday. We found his bike on the Fairyland loop trail, but he has disappeared." He dragged an index finger across the map of the terrain marked in grids to indicate the grid search. "Shaded areas have been covered, and we do have some rangers camping out in the area where the bike was found. We also had a team head out at dawn. We'll pair you with Ranger Hara and a search and rescue volunteer." He looked her up and down. "You look in shape; terrain's tough."

"I'm prepared. There's no evidence the boy was snatched?"

"None at all. This trail is the least visited in the park and nothing indicates anyone else was here when the boy was. His bike had a flat tire, and initial investigation indicates he left it and walked off the trail and probably got disoriented and lost."

Brinna considered this for a moment, but she didn't want to second-guess them. "You have something of the boy's for my dog?" Though Hero was not a trailing dog, or one that followed a scent with his nose to the ground, he did follow scent on the air, so it would be helpful for him to be exposed to what he was looking for.

He nodded and pointed to the RV. "You're set to leave at 0830. Wait over there, and when Hara gets here, he'll have something with scent on it."

Brinna nodded and headed with Hero to the RV, where she saw breakfast being set up. She still felt a bit groggy but knew that a little coffee and starting her mission would change all that.

The RV bristled with activity as the food was laid out and people began to eat. The activity and the people brought a calmness to Brinna. *I like a crowded universe,* she thought.

The mood was upbeat as it usually was in the early stage of any search. The people around her were confident the boy would be found — and soon. Brinna felt the same way. It never paid to approach a search with dread. The coffee was good and strong, and the fruit and granola satisfied her hunger.

Every so often someone would comment about how beautiful the area was, an observation Brinna didn't agree with precisely. If it wasn't a wet, sandy coastline or a mountain covered with tall, green pines, it wasn't pretty as far as she was concerned. But there was something about the geology and the red rocks that she had to admit was compelling. She also took special notice of the terrain because it would affect scent. Heat and wind could dry scent out, but gullies, rock formations, and these hoodoos could hold scent in. Wind was not an issue at the moment but heat would be, and Brinna would have to be certain Hero was hydrated.

By the time 0830 rolled around, she saw that the thermometer on the side of the RV read eighty degrees. But with no ocean nearby to blunt the heat, it felt a lot hotter. All around, teams were forming up to begin searching. A short, stocky park ranger accompanied by a fit-looking older woman walked up to Brinna.

"Hello." He held his hand out and Brinna shook it. "I'm Ranger Hara and this is Kathleen Wright. We'll be your team today. I have a T-shirt of the boy's for your dog to sniff."

Hara led them back to the map and explained more about the area, making certain they were clear about their search responsibilities. Fairyland Canyon was filled with hoodoos that were relatively young, compared to others in the park, Hara pointed out. They weren't as eroded, so there were places to hide and be hidden.

After he finished, they picked up water bottles and lunch. Hara asked Brinna if she'd mind spending the night at a campsite set up in the canyon if they came up empty in their search. Brinna had packed a backpack with a change of clothes and food and water for Hero for this situation and said she didn't mind. She pulled out a collapsible bowl for Hero and gave him some water before they started out.

"We've had scent and trail dogs out, and none of them have keyed on anything. Your dog is a scent dog?" Hara handed her a small white T-shirt.

Brinna nodded and took the shirt from Hara. "Yes, but it makes no sense to have him smell the shirt here. Let's head for our grid and get away from all these other odors." She waved a hand toward the dwindling breakfast crowd.

Hara nodded and the trio hiked off for the trail.

They spent the day hiking over hot, dry terrain. Once she gave Hero a scent of

Stevie's shirt, she took him off leash. He took off at a leisurely pace and they followed. Hero sniffed and stayed on the trail, telling Brinna he wasn't keying on anything. If he did key on something, it could take them anywhere, but as they hiked and it got hotter, they stayed in the grid designated by the command center. Kathleen and Hara took turns calling Stevie's name.

Searching for scent, whether it be tracking with nose to the ground like a trailing dog or nose in the air like Hero, was tiring for the animal. Just before they stopped for lunch, as they hiked near a ravine, Brinna pulled out her cell phone to check the temperature. When her foot hit a rock, she was able to right herself and keep from falling, but the phone went flying.

"Arghh!" She bit back a curse as it hit the ground and broke into pieces, the battery disappearing down the ravine.

"Wow, that's bad luck," Hara said. "I should have told you that you'd get no signal here."

Brinna blew out a breath and gathered the pieces she could reach. The battery was long gone; she could see it way too far down the gully to waste time chasing.

She turned to Hara. "It's hot. Hero needs a rest and some water."

"Good idea." He pointed. "There's a bit of shade there; let's break for lunch."

They sat and broke out the sandwiches, Brinna seeing to Hero first. He drank water and she wet down his nose and face before she unwrapped her ham sandwich. Hara got a radio message as they ate. The search grid was being expanded because none of the teams were having any success. He'd brought a map with him and pulled it out to show the new parameters. The terrain looked rougher than what they had just hiked over.

Brinna felt an urgency to find the boy. No one knew how much water he had with him and that was not good. The wind picked up a bit as they ate, and that would mean scent being dispersed.

After they finished lunch and rested a bit, they continued their search as they made their way to the camp. Hara and Kathleen spent a lot of the time calling out for the boy. A pair of rangers who were relieved to return to the search center and take a break had set up the camp they came to. It lay on a flat portion of red rock in the middle of impressive hoodoos.

Kathleen and Brinna spent time after dinner circling the camp, calling Stevie's name. It brought a shiver to Brinna when the silence set in. *Deathly quiet* was the phrase that came to mind when she and her partner waited to hear any response to the boy's name. Darkness settled in late and the coolness was welcome. Hara chose to sleep under the stars, so Brinna, Hero, and Kathleen shared the tent.

It was still dark when Brinna awoke in the tent, the ragged edges of a nightmare slicing through her sleep. Her watch told her it was close to 5 a.m. She pulled her shorts and shoes on, keeping as quiet as possible. Hero wagged his tail, anxious to get out and do his business. Grabbing a small flashlight, Brinna left the tent, the dog on her heels.

To the east, a light-pink glow faintly tinged the sky. Hero trotted away from the camp, and Brinna followed, relishing the cool predawn air. In the distance a coyote howled and she shivered. The memory of the nightmare was vivid, and for a brief moment it was Brinna lost in the California desert, six years old and shivering, scared to death a coyote would find her and eat her.

She rubbed her wrists, remembering the biting cuffs that had secured her to a post. The words to the song she'd sung the whole night in the dark desert came back to her all of a sudden: *"Jesus loves me; this I know, for the Bible tells me so."*

I remember singing that song in Sunday school, she thought. *I didn't remember it when I talked to Tracy. Funny I remember it now. My mom sang it a lot when I was a kid. But it wasn't any Jesus who saved me that night. It was Milo.*

She clapped her hands and whistled to Hero, the terror of the nightmare twenty years ago spurring in her an urgency to find the missing boy. He'd been out in the desert for two nights now.

"Let's find him today, boy," she said to Hero as the dog trotted back to her. "I hate to think of him wandering around in this barren wasteland all alone."

Breakfast was coffee, fruit, and protein bars. Brinna gave Hero the order to "find it" as soon as everyone was finished. They had been hiking for about thirty minutes when, to Brinna's surprise, Hero took off south in a hurry, as if he was onto something.

"He have a scent?" Hara asked as they trotted after the dog.

"He's acting like it."

Hero stopped about seventy-five feet ahead of them, nose in the air, and then cut left.

Brinna gave a fist pump. "He's got something."

Hara reached for his radio as Brinna jogged after the dog, Kathleen on her heels yelling, "Stevie!" every few minutes.

Brinna was winded and sweaty when Hero stopped, sat, and gave a short bark, his alert that he'd found what he was looking for. She got to him first, dread forming in her gut because she didn't see the boy. Did Hero find a body?

"He here?" Hara asked as he reached her a moment later. He was as sweaty as Brinna. Only Kathleen seemed unaffected by the heat, but she was breathing hard.

"Stevie?" she yelled, cupping her hands over her mouth.

They all looked down the rocky ravine Hero had led them to and listened. Faintly — oh, so faintly — they heard a voice respond, "I'm here; I'm here."

Brinna knelt down and hugged her dog, letting his fur hide the happy tears.

It turned out that Stevie had started out looking for what he'd lost and ended up angry that his bike got a flat. He'd decided to run away and took off through Fairyland Canyon. In the heat he'd searched for shelter, lost his footing, and fallen down the ravine. He was wedged in between two large boulders and he thought his ankle was broken. His exposed skin was burned a dark red, and his lips were cracked and dry.

We weren't a minute too soon, Brinna thought as she watched rescue personnel from the helicopter that had landed a short distance away assess the boy. They'd had to climb down carefully and pull him back up in a Stokes litter. Aside from his ankle, he was dehydrated, as well as suffering from exposure. His eyes were closed as they carried the litter to the chopper.

"Good thing your dog caught the scent," Jase Robinson gushed as he pumped Brinna's hand. "He wouldn't have been spotted by the helicopter — or anyone else for that matter."

"Glad we could help." Brinna shielded her eyes as the medical chopper powered up, sending a cloud of nasty red dirt everywhere.

"We'd like to do something for you. How long will you be in Utah?" The ranger yelled to be heard over the roar of the chopper.

"I'm leaving as soon as I get my stuff together," she hollered back, thinking she couldn't get away from the god-forsaken open space fast enough.

The hike back to the camp for her things and the hike back to the staging area took the better part of the rest of the day.

The command center was just about completely broken down by the time she, Hara, and Kathleen got back. There was no press anywhere to be seen now, and Brinna patted herself on the back as she quickly loaded up her truck and headed out, happy to have avoided all the pesky TV cameras.

On the seat next to her sat her sad cell phone. First order of business once home would be procuring a new battery.

Brinna's mood soared. She and Hero were now officially two for two.

"We're not just on cloud nine," she told Hero. "We're on cloud K-9." Chuckling to herself, she turned up the radio and sang along when she knew the words of a song, happy to have the Utah desert fading behind her.

8

Jack stood just behind the twenty-yard line, waiting for the range master to check the line's readiness and start the course of fire. Downrange, he imagined Gil Bridges's face plastered to the bull's-eye on his target.

The order given, Jack pulled the slide back and slid the first round into the chamber of his automatic. He stepped up to the line to begin the qualification course. The shooting line was full. Jack had waited until the last day in the quarter to qualify.

Officers on his right and left began to shoot as he sighted the target. He shut out the noise and concentrated. All four of his first rounds went dead center. Into Gil Bridges's drunk face. The remainder of the fifty-round course continued in the same manner. At the fifteen-yard line, the seven, and the five, Jack imagined pumping rounds into the man who'd killed his wife.

When everyone finished firing and the

range master cleared the line, Jack stepped forward to collect his target. The bull's-eye was a gaping hole, Jack's cluster of bullets neatly destroying the center of the target. Officers on either side of him congratulated his marksmanship.

"Good shooting, O'Reilly," the range master said when Jack handed him the target to score. He scribbled *100%* on the cardboard and reminded Jack to fill out a qualification slip. "It's a nice feeling to know you'll hit what you aim at."

Jack nodded and filled out his slip. As he cleaned his gun, he considered the fantasies running through his head. Fantasies of chasing Gil Bridges down and shooting him dead in the street. The closer the sentencing drew, the darker his thoughts became. They fascinated him as much as they disgusted him. For sixteen years he'd carried a badge to protect life, not contemplate taking it.

Somehow his fantasies sent the message that Gil Bridges's death would ease his own pain, make Vicki's death more manageable.

"You have to let go of the bitterness you feel toward Bridges," Doc Bell had told him. "It's eating you alive."

"I can't help it," Jack had said. "Why did Vicki have to lose her life to a worthless drunk?"

"There's no answer to that. No way to change it and bring Vicki back. Grieve, Jack — that's normal — but don't brood. Don't let hate fester. It will poison you. You'll never forget, but you must try for some level of forgiveness. Have you contacted any of the support groups I suggested?"

"No, I'm not ready for that. I just need to work, get out of the house. I think patrol will be a good change." *I'll never forgive.*

When Doc Bell was silent for a minute, Jack had feared he'd failed the interview, feared Bell would see through him and take away the gun, the badge.

"I agree a change will be good for you," Bell had said finally. "And patrol was something you excelled at five years ago." He'd tapped on his chin with his ballpoint pen. "I'm going to approve the transfer, on one condition."

"Condition?" Jack swallowed.

"I want you back in my office after you've been in patrol for a bit, and after the sentencing. I want to hear from you how patrol has been and I want to see how you handle whatever sentence Bridges is given. Agreed?"

Jack had let the thinnest of smiles cross his lips. "Sure, Doc, two weeks."

Now Jack reassembled his gun and loaded

it for duty, wondering what on earth he'd have to say to Doc Bell after Gil Bridges received his sentence.

Brinna stopped again in Mesquite, desperately wanting a long, hot shower. She felt she could take her time getting home. She even had a plan about a place to go before she went directly home. She and Hero left Mesquite early and were back across the California border that afternoon. They stopped for lunch in Baker. Brinna eyed the pay phone and thought about calling Milo. His fishing trip would have ended two days ago.

"How about we surprise Milo?" she said to Hero as he sniffed around a vacant lot. "We haven't done that in a while. I need to talk to him."

Hero responded with a wagging tail.

Milo's home wasn't exactly on the way to Long Beach, but Brinna had plenty of time for the detour. Still pumped with adrenaline after the successful search, she felt like she could drive to the moon and back.

It was a couple of hours before she reached Highway 138, which cut across the Mojave Desert through Palmdale, very near where she'd been found by Milo twenty years previous. The highway connected with the 14 freeway, which took Brinna to Santa Clarita, where Milo lived.

I haven't been out to his house in a while, she thought. In truth, Milo had been distant since his retirement. He'd hung up his badge and gun about the same time Brinna had been partnered with Hero. Brinna got the feeling Milo had a difficult time saying good-bye after his thirty-two years on the job. In the two years since his retirement party, she'd only been out to see him twice, each time on his birthday. His calls were few and far between, and Brinna detected boredom and frustration in his tone when they did speak.

If he had a good fishing trip, his spirits should be high, she decided as she took the off-ramp toward his house. At eight thirty the summer sun had set, and Brinna smiled, happy to see lights on as she approached Milo's small tract home. She parked in front and made a lot of noise as she let Hero out of the truck, wanting to give Milo a heads-up.

Hero bounded up to the front door, sniffing and wagging his tail. Milo's last service dog, a shepherd named Baxter, and Hero were great friends. When Brinna reached the porch and rang the doorbell, the absence of Baxter's bark struck her as strange. The

TV was on, so she knew Milo was home, yet she and Hero stood on the porch for a good five minutes with no response.

Brinna punched the bell again, hearing the tones echo inside the house. "Milo, it's Brinna. You there?" she called out, briefly wondering if she should have called first. Maybe he wasn't home.

About to give up, Brinna knocked a couple of times, then stepped off the porch. The dog kept sniffing the bottom of the door.

"Hero, come," she ordered. He turned and jumped off the porch just as Milo opened the door.

"Hey, you are home." She stood with her hands on her hips. "I almost gave up and decided this surprise visit was a mistake."

"I was in the back of the house. Got home day before yesterday." He covered his mouth and coughed a rib-shattering smoker's cough.

Brinna clenched her teeth, hoping to hide the surprise on her face as she took in Milo's appearance. The ex-Marine, ex-cop used to be meticulous about his dress and personal grooming standards. She noted his normally neat flattop needed a trim as badly as his jaw needed a shave. As he waved her into the house, she didn't miss the blood-shot eyes, the soiled T-shirt, and the odor of

76

cigarette smoke mixed with unwashed body.

"You catch a cold in Mexico?" Brinna asked as she took a seat on his couch.

"I caught something," he wheezed, coughing again before sitting in his recliner and chugging from a bottle of beer.

"Where's Baxter?"

Milo put the bottle down and picked up a smoldering cigarette. "Dead." He took a puff.

"What?" Brinna jerked forward in her seat.

"It happened just before I left for Mexico. Took him to the vet to check out a limp. Doc said he had bone cancer. I had to put him down."

"I'm so sorry. Why didn't you call me, let me know?"

Milo shrugged. "Wasn't anything you could do. Doc couldn't help him, and I didn't want the dog to suffer. He was hurting bad the day I took him in. Doc said he could live on pain pills for a while, but I couldn't dope the guy up, have him live his last days in a stupor. I had too much respect for him." He emptied the bottle of beer.

"Wow. That must have been hard." She absentmindedly scratched Hero's head. Baxter had worked with Milo for his final years on the job. Brinna knew it must have been like losing a kid.

The untidy living room did not escape her notice, and she wondered if Baxter's death had sent Milo into a tailspin. She spotted a pile of books on the table in front of Milo, some open as if he'd been studying.

"Looks like you're doing some homework." She nodded toward the books.

"Passing the time. You want a beer?" He stood.

"You got a Diet Coke?"

Milo nodded and walked into the kitchen. He came back with another beer for him and a Diet Coke for Brinna.

"What brings you out this way?" he asked as he opened his bottle.

Brinna leaned forward in her chair and told him about the kid in Utah. "It was such a great feeling, rescuing that kid out of the desert," she concluded. "Man, it brought back memories. I'm glad you were such a great teacher."

Milo grunted and gulped some beer. "I taught you to trust your instincts."

"Yep." Brinna relaxed in her chair and sipped her Coke.

"What if instincts fail you?" Milo asked.

"What?" Brinna frowned. "Has that ever happened to you?"

Milo set his beer down and picked up a book from the table. To Brinna, it seemed suspiciously like a Bible, but she said nothing and waited for Milo to speak.

"I've been doing a lot of thinking lately."

"That what the burning smell is?" Brinna gibed, grinning.

Milo ignored her. "Your mom always said it was prideful that I trusted my instincts, that a person should trust God. She sincerely believes there is a God up there —" he pointed to the ceiling — "controlling everything."

Brinna squirmed in her seat, suddenly uncomfortable. "My mom means well, but I thought we agreed that was all nonsense?"

"As I get older, Brin, I wonder if it really is nonsense. I'm closer to the end than the beginning, and I wonder what waits for me when I die." Milo turned his gaze to the front window, a faraway look in his eyes.

"Come on, you're going to live forever. Why so morose all of a sudden? Is it Baxter?"

He shook his head. "I miss him, but I couldn't watch him suffer. It's just that . . . Well, what if there is a God and I've ignored him all this time?"

He turned back toward Brinna, but she couldn't read his eyes.

"You know, when I met your mom twenty years ago, she told me that she prayed I'd find you and I did. She was so certain that God led me to you. Even though I didn't believe, she said God used me to answer her prayer."

Brinna waved a hand, searching for the words to get Milo off this subject. Her mother always told people that Brinna's rescue was divine. God had his hand in it, Rose Caruso insisted. Brinna loved her mother, but this was one subject they couldn't talk about without arguing.

"If her prayer was so effective that day, why doesn't prayer work for all the other kids who go missing?"

"I asked her that." Milo crushed out his cigarette. "She talked about God giving man free will. Because of that, there is evil in the world. If God pulled everyone's strings all the time, we'd be puppets."

"I've heard that and don't buy it. If we were put here by an all-powerful God, couldn't he stop the suffering, the murder?" Brinna bit her bottom lip, unable to process her mentor's demeanor and mind-set.

"He will when he returns. That's what your mom says. She also says that heaven is a perfect place, a place without murder and pain."

"You believe that?"

"I want to." Milo covered his mouth as

80

another cough shook through him. "For thirty years I've witnessed the worst people can do to one another. I've always tried to solve things with these." He pointed to his head, his chest, and held up his hands. "Right now, you better believe I hope there is someone stronger and something better somewhere else."

He sat back and took a deep drag on his cigarette, blowing out a plume of smoke. "Your mom makes sense about some things." He nodded to the book in his hands. "I've even been reading the Bible."

Suddenly frustration bit Brinna like a snake. The two people she loved most in the world suffering from the same delusion? What was going on here? "No, Milo, no. You're too strong for that."

Milo sighed as if the world sat squarely on his shoulders, then put the book down. "Am I? All I know is that you and my son are the only people in this world I care about. I've taught you everything I know. But what if some of the things I passed on were wrong?"

9

Nigel didn't miss the next article about the dog cop. She'd actually shot someone. He whistled in admiration. He'd taken the paper to work with him and left it with his lunch. Right now his rent-paying job was in beach maintenance, a fancy name for outdoor custodian. He kept the beaches and marinas clean during the summer months. It was only a seasonal position, but it worked for Nigel.

No one noticed the guy picking up trash from the sand and off the docks. The job facilitated his favorite pastime — little-girl watching. He could snap a surreptitious picture now and again with his digital camera.

It was a great gig.

Careful not to linger because that might arouse suspicion, Nigel couldn't help but notice a group of five little girls playing in the gentle, breakwater-regulated waves Long

Beach was known for. They were all wearing two-piece suits, his favorite, and they were running in and out of the water, squealing with delight. Nigel loved to hear little girls squeal like that.

The two moms weren't watching very closely. One slept while the other had her nose buried in a book.

Nigel emptied his trash bag into a bin without taking his eyes off the girls. He then ventured somewhat closer, picking up trash along the way. When neither mom reacted, he brought out his camera. Very carefully Nigel snapped three pictures, then slid the camera back into his pocket.

Moving away, he kept watching the little girls from the corner of his eye. Would one of them be special enough for his dog-cop plans? he wondered. He doubted he'd be able to snatch one of them today. It'd be too hard to take one out of five, even if the moms were totally clueless. Instead, he decided he'd take his time, snap pictures, review them, and pick the next Special Girl very carefully.

The dog cop deserved his best work.

10

Brinna shut off the AC and rolled the window down as she and Hero neared the coast of Long Beach and home. Taking a deep breath of warm, salt-water-smelling air, she sighed and tried to erase the frown she knew had creased her brow all morning.

Uncomfortable memories of Milo's strange demeanor the night before blunted the good coming-home feeling. Echoes of the conversation bouncing in her brain left her feeling uneasy, as if she'd put a shirt on backward and the tag were scratching her throat.

The image of her hero and mentor reading the Bible and believing it was as incongruous as snow falling on the Hawaiian coastline. Milo had always been so confident in himself and his own beliefs that he'd never needed the crutch of religion. Why did he need it now?

He wants to believe there is an all-powerful being in control of this world, she thought, working hard to wrap her mind around the concept. *If there is such a being, I sure have a bone to pick with him.* Shaking her head to banish the thought, she glanced in the rearview mirror at Hero.

"Well, baby, we're back near the ocean and out of the hot desert." Brinna tapped the steering wheel in rhythm to an upbeat country tune Kenny Chesney sang, trying to force Milo's moroseness from her mind.

She'd been able to lift his mood only briefly. The subject of her shooting had stopped his introspection for a few minutes and he'd been the old Milo. He'd impressed upon her not to worry about it, to stick to the facts as they unfolded before her that night. *"Don't let the fat Monday-morning quarterbacks sack you,"* he'd said.

Brinna was more comfortable with the caustic cop than the reflective retiree. She'd spent the night in his guest room, but he'd been gone when she got up. He'd left a note next to the coffeemaker saying only that he had an appointment.

Still concerned about his state of mind but having no good excuse to hang around and wait for him to return, Brinna loaded up Hero to head home. She found a store that carried batteries for her cell phone on the way out of Santa Clarita. As soon as she powered the phone up, it beeped with several messages. Most were from friends, calling about the shooting investigation and offering support and encouragement. But there was one official-sounding message from Janet Rodriguez. She wanted to see Brinna about the shooting and had a meeting scheduled for Sunday night.

Brinna yawned as she wondered about the meeting and if something about the investigation had gone sideways. *No, not possible,* she thought. It was a pretty clear-cut situation. Smiling, she remembered Milo's football analogy and vowed that she wouldn't let anything about the shooting or investigation get to her.

Once home, she got out and stretched, while Hero did the same. She bent to pick up the newspapers piled in the driveway during her five-day absence. After tossing them in the recycle barrel, she surveyed the yard to see if anything else was amiss.

Her small two-bedroom house had been built in the thirties. The warm Craftsman style, with a welcoming front porch, was to Brinna what the house with the white picket fence was to dreamers in the fifties. Located on a quiet street in an area of Belmont

Shore north of Second Street, the home had a nice-size yard and mature foliage that served to make it all the more comfy and inviting.

For Brinna, being close to the ocean was the best part of the house. Until the age of six, she'd lived in a desert portion of Los Angeles County, on the outskirts of Palmdale in a dust bowl called Lake Los Angeles. If there had been a lake there, it had dried up a hundred years before Brinna's birth. She liked to tell people her soul was as dry as a desert dust storm until her parents wised up and moved to the coast. Stepping onto her small lawn, she never grew tired of inhaling air heavy with ocean moisture.

Brinna picked some weeds, tossed them in the trash, and turned the hose on. She'd sprayed about half the lawn when her cell phone buzzed. Dropping the running hose to water a flower bed, she checked the number before she flipped it open.

"Maggie, what's up?"

"You home yet?" Maggie asked.

"Just pulled in the driveway. What's going on?"

"A lot of nonsense, that's what's going on. Have you read any local papers yet?"

"No, like I said, I just got here. Just tossed a bunch of them, why?"

"Read them. You've been out of the loop. You need to know what's happening."

"Is this about the shooting?" Brinna turned the hose down to a trickle and sat on her front steps.

"You *have* heard, then."

"All I know is that Janet called me and said she wanted to meet about the shooting. She didn't elaborate."

"I'll elaborate. That moron reporter has had diarrhea of the mouth about the shooting."

"Clark? What could he have to say about the shooting? He hid in the car the whole time, and when he got out, he puked all over the street."

"That's not what he's saying. He's teamed up with an attorney and the family of the dead kid. They're saying you shot the kid for no reason."

"What?" Brinna's eyebrows scrunched together, and she reflexively scratched Hero between the ears as he came and sat next to her. "He shot at me first! And why are you saying *kid*? How old was he?"

"I forgot. They identified the dead boy after you left. He was only fifteen."

"Fifteen?" Brinna nearly dropped the phone. "But I saw him. He was a good six feet tall and at least two hundred pounds."

"Yep, he was a Poly High wide receiver. They expected to start him on varsity next year."

"Then what was he doing shooting people and speeding through town with a gun?"

"It's gotten so convoluted. The family retained Hester Shockley — you know, that civil liberties lawyer? They're saying their innocent kid tried to give up, and you shot him in cold blood."

Brinna groaned. Every cop in the city knew the name Hester Shockley. A high-profile attorney who did anything and everything to get in front of television cameras. Suing cops always worked liked a charm. Her last excessive-force case against the LBPD netted her a couple million dollars.

"Ben searched for the slug the kid fired at me that night but couldn't find it." Brinna rubbed her forehead. "What about the kid's victims, the ones you talked to that night? Did they ever say why he shot them?"

"They still won't cooperate. Both of them had minor injuries and long police records. The kid you shot, Lee Warren, had no record. Shockley's MO is to make a saint out of the crook and a sinner out of the cop."

"Wow. I've seen these situations go sideways for other cops, but I shot that kid because he shot at me first. It's so black-and-white."

"Shockley excels at clouding the issue. Rumor is you're going to be reassigned until it all blows over."

"That's why Janet wants to talk to me." Brinna slapped her thigh. "She wants me in her office tomorrow night." She stifled a curse. "Just where do they think they're going to put me?"

"Haven't heard that. What time do you meet her?"

"Five. This is so bogus. I can't believe it. Every time Hester Shockley says jump, the PD asks how high." Fatigue fled, kicked in the butt by anger.

"Call me after you talk to your sergeant. We'll meet for coffee." Sympathy tinged Maggie's voice.

"Will do. Thanks for the heads-up." Brinna snapped the phone shut and groaned.

Are they going to move me inside? Or just to another shift? What about Hero? And what about my Innocent Wall? Will I still be able to search? With each question she couldn't answer, anger swelled.

After a while, Milo's pep talk of the night before echoed in her ears and Brinna calmed somewhat. Milo's advice was like armor. She couldn't believe that he could ever think anything he'd taught her was wrong.

I know what I did was right, she thought. *I won't let them sack me.*

Taking a deep breath, Brinna walked back to the recycle barrel and pulled out three of the bundles. When she opened one, the headline made her gag: "Kid Crusader Turned Kid Killer!"

11

Brinna loaded the kayak on the roof of her personal truck and secured the straps, her movements jerky with anger. From her small house in Belmont Shore, the trip to Alamitos Bay took five minutes. She parked at a meter and fed it enough quarters for an hour and a half.

As she dragged the kayak across the sand to the water, the traditional accoutrements of summer swirled around her and she felt the anger mute. Putting the shooting out of her mind, she let the exhilaration of being back in her crowded, sea-breeze-tickled universe replace it. The shoreline teemed with kids splashing in the gently rolling surf; the smell of salt water mingled with the aroma of sunscreen. It was another scorcher. Heat seemed to roll up off the sand in waves. After Maggie's call, Brinna knew she needed a paddle or she'd go crazy wondering about what was going to happen to her and Hero. A paddle always helped her head to clear.

To her left, the Second Street Kayak Rental Outfit stood open, doing a brisk business. Brinna scanned the beach for Tony DiSanto, the owner of the rental business. Tony, the quintessential New York Italian, even resembled a smallish Tony Soprano. While Milo was what Brinna always wished her father were like, if her father weren't a drunk, Tony DiSanto was the big brother or favorite uncle she'd never had.

She'd met him on the beach. He was the first person Brinna ever rented a kayak from, and he eventually helped her find one to buy. Not generally inclined to open up to people right away, Brinna liked Tony from the first. He and his family were *normal,* unlike Brinna's own and unlike the many dysfunctional families she dealt with at work. She loved the way he talked with his hands and how his expression was always open and friendly.

His devotion to his twin six-year-old granddaughters, Carla and Bella, touched something deep inside. She saw him as he started to walk her way.

"Hey, Brinna." Tony waved. "My good friend, how have you been?" He walked toward her across wet sand.

"I've been good. Where have you been?"

"Back east. My mother is sick."

"Sorry to hear that. Is it serious?"

"Getting old is serious . . . and terminal." He shrugged and jutted his chin toward Brinna. "Look at you — how dark you are for a good Italian girl."

"I was out in the desert for a couple of days. I tan easily."

Tony shook a finger at her. "Be careful you don't get that skin cancer. I'd hate to see them cutting things off that beautiful face." He smiled. "By the way, what's going on with the newspapers these days? A few days ago they were patting you on the back for finding a kid; now I read they're throwing the book at you for a shooting?"

Brinna groaned. "I don't know what to think." Briefly she filled him in on the shooting and then taking off to Utah. "I just got back; I don't know what the problem is with the shooting."

Tony waved both hands dismissively. "Hey, first you were heroic; you'll be heroic again. You care about kids. Kids need people like you on their side."

A bit embarrassed, Brinna sighed and fumbled for something to say. "I hate anyone who takes advantage of the innocent."

Tony stood next to her and they both gazed at the bay. "Hear, hear. If something like what happened to you happened to one of my precious granddaughters —" he clenched his teeth, raised his hands, and sputtered an Italian curse — "I'd be in jail for killing the guy." He turned to face Brinna. "Still, call me old-fashioned, but I worry about you out there. There are too many sick, crazy people in this world. People shooting at you."

"Don't worry about me; I can take care of myself. My worry is always for those who can't. I need to protect kids from those maniacs. That's why I do what I do, my friend. I want to feel useful, like I can help, you know?" *And I want to balance the scales. Someone found me. I owe it to victimized kids to do my best to find them.*

"Just be careful. And on the water today, there are a lot of novices out there." He motioned to her kayak. "Don't run anyone over."

Brinna laughed and it felt good. "I won't. When it's like this, I pretend I'm alone. I shut them out and do my own thing. Want to give me a push off?"

"Sure thing. Enjoy."

Brinna slid the kayak partway into the gentle surf and climbed in, setting a bottle of water in front of her. Once she was set and her paddle ready, Tony shoved until the boat was all the way off the beach and into the water.

Paddle in hand, she used short, strong strokes to move away from the shore. A line of floats roped together separated the beach and swimming area from the channel. Brinna navigated through an opening and dodged a beginner piloting a sailboat poorly.

Out in the bay channel, she steered left to paddle away from Second Street and toward Spinnaker Bay. Brinna would cut across Marine Stadium and around Spinnaker Bay, through the marina and back to Second Street.

The hot sun beat down as she paddled through Marine Stadium, but it was blunted somewhat by a pleasant breeze. Brinna sighed and felt tension drain from her shoulders with each stroke.

As she dug into the water with the paddle, she sought to quiet her mind, drown out the images of the shooting and of the storm that now hung over the shooting.

Reporters like to sensationalize. Maybe that's all this was and it will blow over.

12

"Isn't there an old-timer I can work with?" Jack stood, shoving his chair back so hard it tipped over. For some reason, when Jack's supervisor had said he'd be partnered with Brinna Caruso, Jack immediately felt going back to patrol was a mistake. He'd heard about her. She was a hard charger, and he doubted he'd be able to hide if partnered with her.

"Sorry, no. Caruso happens to need a partner just like you do," Lieutenant Hoffman answered.

"I've just never worked with a woman," Jack said, knowing how lame a statement it was but continuing on. "And ten hours a shift in a car with one . . . I don't know." He bit his bottom lip and frowned, struggling to think of something that made more sense.

"O'Reilly, you don't have a choice. What happened to not wanting to rock the boat?"

the lieutenant countered. "And you can't back out now. The chief has already signed off on this."

Jack sighed, clenching his fists. "I know; this is what I wanted. I just never banked on a woman for a training partner."

"She's been on five years and is a good solid cop. She's being reassigned because the press is all over her case."

"Why?" Jack saw amusement in Hoffman's eyes.

"You really don't read the paper or watch the news, do you?"

"My life is depressing enough. Why do I need to know about the depression in other people's lives?" Realization dawned. "She's the cop who was in the 998?"

Hoffman nodded. "It's become a controversial incident. Kind of like nine years ago when you shot that doctor's kid out east."

A light went on as Jack remembered the incident. "You mean that sixteen-year-old who tried to scalp his mother with a kitchen knife and beat his dad half to death with a golf club? He came at me with both. After I shot him and his parents healed, they insisted he was just misunderstood. Same type of deal for Caruso?"

"Exactly. You'll probably be able to empathize with Caruso."

Jack rubbed his chin. "Well, I came out clean back then; maybe this officer will do the same." And maybe she'd be gun-shy enough to relax and do nothing for ten hours a night.

"In any event, it's only for two weeks. You can handle anything for two weeks, can't you?"

Running a hand over his flattop, Jack blew out a breath. "Whatever you say, Gary. Whatever you say." Resigned but still angry, Jack could think of no valid excuses. And the important fact was that it was only for two weeks.

"Report to the patrol squad room Monday afternoon for watch three."

Jack nodded and turned to leave but Hoffman stopped him.

"I want you to know I'm holding your slot in homicide open for as long as I can. I hope the old Jack O'Reilly will want his job back before long."

Jack grunted and left the office, letting the door slam behind him.

Sergeant Janet Rodriguez poked her head into Lieutenant Hoffman's office.

"I just saw O'Reilly leave. Will he show up on Monday?"

Hoffman shrugged. "Don't know. Wish I

could say I didn't care, but Jack is a good guy. I don't want his career to end with him getting fired or psycho retired."

"You think he can handle patrol?"

"Dr. Bell signed off on it. What about your end? Have you told Caruso what's coming down yet? Can she handle O'Reilly?"

Rodriguez blew out a breath. "She just got back from Utah. I asked her to come in and talk to me tomorrow. I'll break the news then. And she can handle O'Reilly. I'll just have to agree with her when she points out that reassignment sucks."

"Maybe it does and maybe it doesn't. It's best for her to lie low for a while. How do you think she'll take it?"

"Probably same as O'Reilly. But just like him, she doesn't have any choice in the matter."

When Brinna walked into the sergeants' room, Sergeant Rodriguez waited for her. She motioned for Brinna to have a seat across from her.

"Hey, congrats on the Utah find. A park ranger called to recommend you for a promotion."

"Hero found him; I think he'd look great in sergeant's stripes." As soon as the words were out of her mouth, Brinna noticed the look on her sergeant's face. "Uh, they're not taking Hero away, are they?" Fear spread as if it had been dropped by a grenade. Brinna felt sick to her stomach and flushed in the face.

Rodriguez blew out a breath and avoided her eyes. "It's temporary," she said. "And he's not being taken away from you. Hero is just being sidelined, kind of like an administrative leave."

Brinna gripped the arms of the chair. "How temporary?"

"I can't say yet. All I can assure you is that I pressed the chief and he promised that only horrendous circumstances would make it permanent."

"Like me being indicted?" Brinna said with undisguised bitterness.

"That's not going to happen. The shooting was clean; we just have to ride out the Hester hurricane."

Brinna started to rise when the homicide boss, Lieutenant Hoffman, entered the room. The threesome occupied the patrol sergeants' office. A large room off the squad room, it was used by all the sergeants of every patrol watch and was sparsely furnished with old beat-up desks and a few chairs. Hoffman motioned for her to stay, and she sat back down, wondering if he had information about the shooting.

"Evening, Caruso. How's everything?" Hoffman joined Rodriguez on her side of the desk.

"I'm not sure," Brinna said guardedly, looking from one person to the other. "This looks like a double-team."

Janet smiled. "No, you didn't let me finish. You actually have options. You can either ride out the unpleasant storm at the business desk, or you can do some retraining for two weeks for an officer who wants to leave detectives."

Now she understood why Hoffman was there. "A homicide dick wants to leave the detail? That's un—" Maggie's words about an unbalanced detective came roaring back to her memory. "Is it Jack O'Reilly?" Brinna clenched her jaw to keep her mouth from dropping open. Not only were they sidelining Hero; they were assigning her to play nursemaid to a burnout two-legged partner for two weeks.

"He's coming back to patrol?" she asked, her mind racing, struggling to find some excuse to get out of the reassignment. "I've heard he's 5150, ready for a psycho retirement. Is that why they're kicking him out of homicide?"

"Gossip." Sergeant Rodriguez gave a

dismissive wave. "I thought you knew better than to pay attention to that."

"He wasn't kicked out," Lieutenant Hoffman said. "Jack has asked to be reassigned."

Brinna bit her tongue. There were other worries on her mind. A lot of high-ranking officers objected to Hero. They wanted the grant money allocated somewhere else. Would her being reassigned give them ammunition? But would her protests about this "temporary" assignment label her a troublemaker? Milo always taught her to pick her battles. Maybe this was a battle she didn't want.

"Okay, I understand," she said. "It's just for the two-week retraining period."

"Correct." Rodriguez nodded. "Don't worry about Hero. He'll be welcomed back when this is over."

Brinna took a deep breath, relief flooding her veins as Rodriguez read her mind.

"I've heard a lot of stuff about this O'Reilly that isn't gossip." Brinna switched the focus back to the psycho cop. "Will he hold up his end of the unit?"

"Jack has had a rough year." Hoffman stood and walked around the desk, leaning on the corner to face Brinna. "His pregnant wife was killed by a drunk driver. That would be tough on anyone. He's been cleared by Dr. Bell and he needs a change of scenery. Policy says all you need to do is bring him up to speed on everything new in patrol."

Sergeant Rodriguez added, "If he doesn't hold up his end, let me know."

"Oh, I will." Brinna rolled her eyes. "In two weeks I'll be able to work with Hero again?"

Hoffman and Rodriguez exchanged glances. "That's what I'm hoping," Janet said after a minute.

"You've been a cop long enough to know the drill." Hoffman blew out a breath and fixed his gaze on Brinna. "While we don't believe you've done anything wrong, you need to stay under the press radar for a while. No one can say how long that will be."

"But I will get Hero back eventually? We'll get to work cases still, right?" Brinna hated that her voice sounded whiny.

"That's up to the chief. Right now I'd say yes, eventually." Hoffman stood and walked back to the other side of the desk, shoving his hands in his pockets. "I know your rep, Caruso. You're a hard worker. Relax and concentrate on helping Jack get back into the swing of things. I can't promise anything, but maybe the situation will cool down after the shooting board issues official findings."

"You can still train Wednesday afternoons with the K-9 detail," Rodriguez said, "to keep Hero sharp. That should make the pill go down a bit easier."

Brinna blew out a breath. "I don't have a choice." She stood to leave. "I'll make the best of it."

"I knew you would. By the way —" Hoffman smiled as he stopped Brinna at the open door — "congratulations on finding that kid in Utah."

Brinna cleared her throat and kept her eyes on the lieutenant. "Thanks. Hero found him wedged between some rocks in a ravine. Found him just in time too. He was very dehydrated." She shrugged and decided to broach another subject bothering her, turning back to Janet. "What about all the lies Clark keeps spreading about me in print? Is there anything I can do about that?"

Rodriguez sighed. "Right now the circus seems to have the upper hand. These things take on a life of their own, and it will get worse before it gets better. But the truth will come out. Don't read the paper."

"Wait it out patiently," Hoffman added. "No one on the PD is saying it was a bad shooting, but it's political football and it will be messy for a bit. If you remember, last month a cop in LA was on the hot seat after he shot a kid in a stolen car."

Brinna nodded; she remembered the protests and the press. The officer had thought he was going to be run over and emptied his gun into the car. The driver turned out to be a twelve-year-old kid who could barely see over the steering wheel.

"It seems our suspect, Lee Warren," Hoffman continued, "used to be a good kid before he went right rudder. Shockley has lined up a sob story of family members to testify what a sweet, nonviolent brat he was."

Brinna gave a shake of her head and leaned against the door. It never failed. After a creep was killed by the police, everyone had a story about how he wasn't really a bad creep.

"Jack O'Reilly was once sued by Shockley. He may help you out on that score. Besides, he had a great reputation when he worked patrol," Rodriguez said. "He isn't a bad guy."

Small consolation. "Maybe so, but I'd rather have a partner who barks and drools than a partner I'm not certain I can trust."

13

Once a good cop.

Messed up a murder case because he couldn't concentrate.

Investigator of the year two years ago.

Five fries short of a Happy Meal.

All the snippets Brinna had heard about Jack O'Reilly buzzed through her mind like banners pulled by planes. She worked hard to accentuate any positive. There was positive in the mix. Several old-timers had high praise for Jack when he worked patrol. The burnout nickname only came into being in the last year, since his wife died.

How long did it take someone to get over a death like that?

She checked her watch. The meeting had taken all of thirty minutes. This wasn't a battle she was ever going to win. Brinna knew she could have thrown a tantrum and pulled the union into a fight about forced transfers, but that might have gotten her sent to a desk job. She decided to make the best of it with O'Reilly for one reason: they weren't taking Hero permanently. Besides, she thought, she'd only have to put up with Jack O'Reilly for two weeks. Whatever his major malfunction was, two weeks was only eight shifts. Brinna vowed she wouldn't let him cramp her style.

She punched in Maggie's number as she left the building. "I'm done. Where do you want to meet?"

"I'm on my way to Coffee Bean & Tea Leaf. What's the word?" Maggie asked.

"I'll tell you when I see you." Brinna flipped the phone shut and grinned, cutting off Maggie's protest. She hopped in her truck and headed for the coffee shop. Driving down Ocean toward Second Street, contemplating Jack O'Reilly while cursing Hester Shockley and Gerald Clark, Brinna grudgingly admitted to herself that maybe the temporary reassignment was for her benefit. She'd seen good cops destroyed when lawyers like Shockley got to court and twisted the truth. And being destroyed was not a destiny she'd consider.

When she reached CBTL, she shoved worrisome thoughts to the back of her mind, vowing not to let the press turn her into a lame second-guesser — or "zip," as

Milo liked to call anyone whose paralyzed thinking kept them from making decisions or solving problems effectively.

The parking lot at the coffee shop was full. No surprise even for a Sunday night. CBTL sat where Second Street, a busy, six-block section of the Shore, began. Popular bars, restaurants, and shops made up Second Street, and the area always percolated with activity. Brinna found a spot on a side street about a block away and jogged back to CBTL.

Maggie waited at an outside table. She sipped a coffee, and Brinna smiled when she saw a second cup on the table.

"That for me?" she asked as she took a seat.

Maggie nodded, mouth turned down in a pout. "I bought you a latte, though after leaving me in suspense, I should have let you stand in line." She folded her arms across her chest. "So what's the story?"

Brinna sipped her coffee and told Maggie the news.

"Jack O'Reilly?" Maggie's cup stopped halfway to her mouth.

Brinna nodded.

"We were just talking about him," Maggie exclaimed. "I thought he was certifiably 5150, ready for the rubber-gun squad." She

109

shook her head and put her coffee down.

"Apparently, according to Hoffman, O'Reilly requested the move back to patrol," Brinna explained. "He wasn't kicked out of homicide. That should prove he's 5150, as hard as it is to get into that detail." She blew out a disgusted breath. "You think maybe it's really just politics? That homicide wants him out but can't demote him without agitating the union?"

Maggie laughed. "My, how cynical you are. Actually, Rick heard a locker room rumor that it was O'Reilly who wanted out of homicide. He's burned out. You can handle an old burnout. I don't call you Briny for nothing. You're a salty old copper."

"Ha. I like working on my own, with just Hero. He doesn't argue with me about what we're going to work on."

"You're worried about your kids, aren't you?"

Brinna nodded and took a long gulp on her latte. "Rodriguez says we can work a wild car so we won't be tied to one beat. I might still be able to follow leads, carefully."

"But you're the Kid Crusader." Maggie laughed.

Brinna sighed. "I don't even know this guy. He may run and tattle on me. Plus, I have to admit all the stuff Hester Shockley is saying about me shooting an innocent kid is distracting. Remember Pratt and Barker?"

Brinna brought up a pair of Long Beach cops who'd been forced to resign after a use-of-force incident. Hester Shockley accused them of being racist, and the pressure from the community left the pair no other option but to get out of police work.

Maggie shrugged. "That's the game Shockley plays. But the difference is the department deserted Pratt and Barker, left them out to dry. From what you told me, they're supporting you."

"I guess." Brinna sighed and sipped her coffee. "But even Sergeant Rodriguez said these things take on a life of their own. What might happen next week? I love my job."

Maggie waved a hand. "Don't be a glass-is-half-empty person now. You're a good cop. And there is a bright side. O'Reilly's not hard to look at."

Brinna snorted and concentrated on the coffee. "I just want to do my job with a partner I can count on, not a boy toy."

"Boy toys can be fun. By the way, what's going on with Marcus? You two still dating?"

Brinna shook her head, making a circle with her thumb and fingers. "Nada. He told me I'm too obsessed with missing kids and pedophiles."

Maggie threw back her head and laughed. "Much as I don't care for Marcus, he hit that on the head."

Brinna frowned. "Come on," she scoffed. "I am not obsessed." She punctuated her last four words by tapping on the table with an index finger.

"Of course not." Maggie tossed her hair back. "You're in serious denial. I don't know any other cops with a whole wall in their home office plastered with creepy sex offenders."

"I need to know those guys so if I find them in violation, I arrest them on the spot. It is not an obsession. It is a mission." She set her coffee cup down.

"What's the diff?" Maggie clicked her tongue and regarded Brinna with raised eyebrows.

"An obsession sounds twisted." Brinna leaned forward. "There is nothing twisted about wanting to keep kids safe."

"I don't want you to stop helping kids. I just want you to see that this obses— mission — can't consume your life. The last three guys you dated couldn't handle taking second place to missing posters. Sometimes it seems like you hide behind those kids."

Brinna drained her coffee. "When I meet

the right guy, my missings will not be an obsession to him. Let's change the subject. I don't want to talk about my love life."

"Or lack of one? All right, back to O'Reilly. What are you going to do if he's 5150?"

"Hotfoot it back to the station and drop him at the back steps." They both laughed and hit their cups together in a toast.

"Rick and I will be there to back you up if you need it," Maggie promised.

"Thanks. For the first time in my career I find myself wishing for a quiet couple of weeks. At least until Hester Shockley runs out of steam. Don't want to get into anything big until I know I can trust my partner."

14

Jack grabbed his gear and headed out of the house for a workout. It was after 10 p.m. but thanks to twenty-four-hour gyms, he had a place to go. This was the time the walls in the house really began to close in.

The clock couldn't strike ten without Jack feeling Vicki's loss as if it were an abscess on his heart, aching and festering. Ten or ten thirty was the time they used to settle into bed, talk about the day, watch the news, or whatever. He hoped that returning to patrol would relieve some of the despondency he felt. At least he'd be out of the house most of the dark hours and not dwelling on how empty everything was without her.

He found a parking place quickly. The gym was usually pretty empty at this time of night. After flashing his membership card at the receptionist, Jack changed in the locker room and hurried out to the free-weight floor.

Happy to see he had the area to himself, Jack began with squats. He loaded up the bar and cinched his weight belt. Before he stepped under the bar for his first set, someone called his name.

Turning, he saw Ben Carney walking toward him. Jack worked to keep his face neutral. He and Ben had grown up together, gone to school together, and eventually attended the police academy together. After the academy their careers took different turns. Baby-faced Ben had been sucked up to work undercover narcotics while Jack became a star patrol officer.

They were reunited three years ago as partners in homicide. It was a great partnership, until . . .

Jack blinked hard to banish the images that flashed through his head. Ben as best man at the wedding, Ben helping celebrate the year Jack was voted best investigator in the division. Ben stepping into the office to tell him Vicki was dead.

"Jack, buddy, it's me. You okay?"

Jack focused on the man standing in front of him. "Yeah, I'm peachy. What are you doing here? You're not dressed to work out. Are you stalking me?" Ben wore a polo shirt and slacks, homicide call-out dress.

"No, I'm not stalking you. You just avoid me at work, so I tried to think of where I might get a chance to talk to you for a minute. I figured you'd be here. I didn't come to work out. I came to wish you luck back in patrol."

Jack turned away from Ben and back to the bar. "That's right. As of tomorrow, I'm gone. I'm out of homicide. You don't have to worry about your albatross of a partner anymore. Right now you probably have a call-out. Don't let me keep you." He stepped under the bar, hefted the weight off the hooks, and began his warm-up set, ignoring Ben, simply concentrating on his form in the mirror in front of him.

"How can I make you see that I'm on your side? I never saw you as a burden — or an albatross, as you put it. You're the one who didn't want to go on call-outs anymore." Ben stepped beside Jack as he finished the set and put the weight back on the hooks.

"My side?" Jack faced Ben, breathing hard, angry for having his own weakness tossed back in his face. "I made that request with you in mind. All I got as thanks was preaching."

"I'm sorry you thought it was preaching. All I wanted to do was impress upon you that you weren't alone."

Jack waved him away and slammed more weight on the bar, pushing Ben out of the way to get to that end of the bar. "So I'm supposed to thank you? You and Gary can continue being deluded by religion. I want nothing to do with it. God deserted me. I've returned the favor." He turned away and stepped back under the bar to complete his second set.

Ben sighed. "God will never leave you, no matter what." Ben moved in front of Jack, blocking the mirror. "Whether you want to believe it or not, I am your friend. Ever since Vicki died, you're a shell of the Jack O'Reilly I used to know. All I can think of is how it would break her heart to see you like this."

Jack grunted and shoved the weight onto the hooks. The hard clang reverberated through the empty gym. Face flushed, seeing red, and breath coming in gasps, he came out from under the bar and grabbed Ben by the neck, shoving him against the mirror.

"Don't talk to me about what Vicki would want! Don't even say her name!"

"Okay, okay. Hit me if it will make you feel better." Ben's calm eyes regarded Jack. His words made Jack realize he'd raised one hand in a fist, as if he were going to slam it into Ben's face.

Immediately ashamed, Jack dropped his hand and let go of Ben's neck. He stepped back under the bar and to the bench-press station, where he sat down heavily, shoulders sagging. "I'm sorry. I don't know what got into me," he mumbled while staring down at his shoes.

Ben walked around and knelt in front of Jack. "Forget it. I know it's been a rough year. But I don't think isolating yourself and shutting out your friends is helping. You've stopped going to church, to studies. You've shut yourself off from the world. This isn't healthy."

"Church isn't healthy," Jack said bitterly. "All I got there were empty platitudes. I was a Christian all my life. So was Vicki. And what did it get us?" Jack shook his head. "You want to help me? Leave me alone."

Ben stood and sighed. "I'll keep praying. As much for you as for me. I want my partner back, and I'm praying that your working a beat car will do the trick." Ben stayed there for a moment. Jack felt him watching but refused to acknowledge him, saying nothing. After a long silent minute, Ben turned and left the gym.

Jack sat on the bench for a long while before resuming his workout. When he finally did return to the squat rack, he studied his reflection in the mirror. Blood-shot gray eyes glared back at him. Six-two, two hundred pounds of solid muscle, thanks to all the weight workouts of the past few months, Jack was a big, strong man. But he took no pleasure in his physique or reflection.

"Pray all you want, Ben," he whispered. "Someday you'll find out just like I did: all prayer is, is talking to the wind — nothing more."

15

Brinna fidgeted and paced her small living room on Monday afternoon. She watched the clock tick closer to the time she'd have to leave for work. As if worrying about the reassignment to work with Jack O'Reilly weren't enough, the morning's headlines had screamed with Hester hype attacking Brinna's actions.

Though Brinna had been warned not to read the paper, she'd glanced over the current edition, read the headlines, and turned the page only to find letters to the editor running three to one against her. Everyone seemed inclined to believe Hester Shockley's latest rant, calling Brinna an out-of-control maverick cop.

As it usually was with cops, Brinna felt people perceived her guilty before any charges were filed. When she tried to shut Hester out of her thoughts, concern about her new partner weighed heavily. She loved her job but knew that riding around in a car for ten hours with someone you didn't like was hard work.

"Hero, how about a run? I can't relax, might as well do something active."

Hero jumped off the bed, tail wagging.

Brinna grabbed her running clothes and changed quickly. She picked up Hero's leash and started for the door as the phone rang. Groaning, she checked the caller ID and recognized the homicide office extension. Dread pricked her heart like a hot fireplace poker. *What if they found Heather?*

She answered the call. "Caruso."

"Brinna, Ben Carney here. Hope I didn't interrupt anything."

"No, you didn't. I was just heading out for a run." Brinna tensed. "What's up? The shooting? Or did one of my kids turn up?"

"Neither. I just wondered if you'd be able to meet me for coffee before your squad meeting."

"This afternoon? And it's not about the shooting?"

"Nope. Just a friendly chat is all I'm after."

Brinna relaxed but frowned as she tapped on the counter with an index finger. What could Ben want? She thought about their short time as partners. He'd been friendly but very devoted to his wife. Once he went

121

to detectives, she hadn't heard a word from him until the night of the shooting. Curiosity got the best of her. "Sure, where do you want to meet?"

"Someplace close. I don't want to make you late to squad. How about Starbucks on Pine? About three?"

"I'll be there."

"Great, see you then."

"Wonder what's up with that?" Brinna asked no one but Hero, sitting quietly, eyes on the leash in his mistress's hand. She bent down to click the leash on, giving the dog a hug. "Guess I'll find out soon enough. Let's go run."

Brinna parked in the PD lot, then jogged the two blocks to Pine Avenue. It was impossible to miss the huge signs posted across the street from the station: *Stop police brutality, No justice, no peace,* and *Justice for Lee Warren. Fire Caruso!*

She hoped the extra jog would ease her anger and frustration. Besides the signs, it had been difficult leaving Hero. He knew it was time to go to work, and it broke her heart to leave him behind. This would be a long two weeks.

Pine Square throbbed with busy afternoon activity. Trendy restaurants and cute shops kept things hopping and parking places full. She nodded to a pair of bike officers she saw patrolling the square.

Ben Carney stood outside Starbucks. Brinna saw him scanning the street. He held his suit jacket tossed over one shoulder and seemed out of place on the very warm afternoon wearing suit pants, a short-sleeved shirt, and a loosened tie.

Ben brought to mind good memories. He'd been a solid partner when they'd worked together, if a little heavy into religion.

"Hey, Ben, over here."

Ben turned her way and smiled. They shook hands and Ben patted her shoulders. "You look great, as usual. Doing a lot of paddling, I see."

"It's been a great summer for it. You aren't hard on the eyes either. I noticed that the other night. You haven't put on the infamous detective spare tire."

Ben laughed and patted his stomach. "No, but it hasn't been easy. Squeezing in work-outs between call-outs and regular cases takes skill." He jammed a thumb toward the coffee shop. "What can I get you?"

"You're buying?" Eyebrows raised, Brinna grinned. "An iced mocha and a banana-walnut muffin."

"Grab a table. I'll be right back."

Brinna found a table on the sidewalk and checked her watch. She had about twenty minutes with Ben and grew more curious by the minute. He came out shortly, carrying two drinks and Brinna's muffin.

"Here you go," he said as he sat down. "So how are you doing with all the nonsense that's swirling around you?"

Brinna tore off a bit of her muffin and chewed on it before answering. "I'm angry. Hester Shockley's three-ring circus is a huge distraction. But I remember being told in the academy that bad things would come from incidents that seemed the cleanest. Can't get any cleaner than shooting someone who shot at me first."

Ben played with a napkin. "Yeah, I agree. Hester loves the spotlight and she'll milk this. It'd help if we could find the slug Warren fired. We're still checking nooks and crannies, by the way." He shrugged. "I'm certain, in spite of all the press right now, it will come out okay."

"Thanks." Brinna sipped her drink. "Thought this wasn't about the shooting."

"It's not — just making small talk. I know you like direct, so I'll get to the point. Jack O'Reilly." He raised his eyes from the napkin and held Brinna's gaze.

Brinna snapped her fingers. "Your ex-partner in homicide."

Ben sipped his coffee, nodding. "Partner and friend. I'm worried about him."

"That makes me feel good —" she shook her head — "since I have to work with him. Just what is his major malfunction?"

"He can't get past his wife's death. It's destroyed his faith. Without faith, he has no hope. I'm praying you'll help him."

"Me?" Brinna pointed both thumbs back at her chest. "I'm not a Bible-thumper or a social worker. He a churchgoer like you?"

"Used to be. He stopped going to church after Vicki died." Ben rolled the coffee cup back and forth in his palms. "What about you, Brin? You still an avowed atheist?"

Brinna nodded. "I have faith in me. That's always been all I've needed. My mom took me to church until I was thirteen and then she said I could choose. Church never did for me what it seems to do for you and my mom. I can understand O'Reilly not wanting to go anymore. I'm not sure how you want me to help him."

"It still amazes me —" he leaned back in his chair, rubbing his chin with one hand — "that after what you went through as a kid, you don't believe in God. You've been on the job a few years now. You've seen first-

125

hand what we deal with. Don't you find your rescue even a little miraculous?" He held his hand up, thumb and forefinger a few millimeters apart.

"We went down this road when we were partners." Brinna drummed on the table with both hands. "You and my mom sound like you read from the same script. I don't believe there's a God who led Milo to me. If I did believe that, then I'd have to believe that same God lets hundreds of kidnapped kids be murdered every year. Why would I want to believe in a God like that?"

"Why not believe that God rescued you for a reason? Maybe so you could do what you're doing now?"

Brinna sucked in a breath, Ben's words reminding her of the strange conversation with Milo. With people like her mother and Ben pushing God stuff, Brinna couldn't fathom Milo being on their side.

"I was rescued by Deputy Gregor Milovich, a good cop who followed his instincts. Period. I don't believe in God or miracles. Now —" she spoke matter-of-factly, with no rancor, and stood, glancing at her watch — "I have to get to work."

"Okay, okay." Ben rose from his chair. "Just be patient with Jack, please. There's a good cop in there under the grief. Don't give up on him too soon. As a favor?" His tone pleaded a bit but Brinna was not offended or annoyed. Ben was being a good friend, she decided.

"I'll do what I can. I'll follow my instincts."

16

Brinna hurried back to the station and dressed for work. Without her K-9 unit now, it made more sense to dress at work rather than home. It felt strange climbing into an itchy wool uniform after wearing her cotton K-9 jumpsuit for two years.

"At least I haven't put on weight," she mumbled as she zipped her trousers. Once finished, she double-checked her reflection in the mirror. Her dark-brown hair was cut short enough to stay off her collar and thick enough to stay where she put it. She glanced at the clock. Fifteen minutes to roll call and no Maggie.

Maggie's absence was only a brief distraction because Ben's words still echoed in her mind: *"Why not believe that God rescued you for a reason? Maybe so you could do what you're doing now?"* She'd heard that argument before, from her mother. It didn't surprise her that Ben thought the same thing. What still muddled her thoughts was Milo.

As she stared at her reflection without really seeing it, the question she knew she'd never get an answer to blazed through her mind: *If there is a God, why does so much bad stuff happen?* Why did Milo want to find such a God? Shaking her head, she pushed the questions away and snapped the leather belt keepers on her Sam Browne.

Maggie or no Maggie, it was time to head to the squad room, not ponder the existence of God. Maggie would probably roll in at the last minute.

Brinna wasn't even certain what Ben wanted from her concerning Jack O'Reilly. She stopped in the break room and purchased some Life Savers, the disturbing thoughts about Milo and Ben leaving a bad taste in her mouth.

Her assignment was to bring Jack up to speed on new procedures in patrol, not heal his hurts. Jack had sixteen years under his belt to her five. Neither of them were rookies. And she fully expected the man to carry his weight.

Brinna slid into the squad room ten minutes early. Rick was already there.

He lifted his chin in greeting. "Seen my partner yet?"

"Nope. I'm sure she'll be along shortly."

"She told me about you being partnered with O'Reilly. Know what you'll be working yet?"

Brinna nodded. "Sarge is putting us in a wild car." As an all-city backup unit, they wouldn't have an assigned beat to patrol. Brinna was about to ask Rick if he'd seen O'Reilly, but Maggie's breathless arrival as she jogged to her seat, still pinning her hair up, interrupted the question.

"I wondered why you weren't in the locker room." Maggie spoke with hairpins in her mouth. "Awfully early . . . A little excited?"

Brinna didn't rise to the bait. "Those of us with short, manageable hair don't need twenty extra minutes to make ourselves presentable."

Maggie grunted and took a seat. The rest of the watch filed in and Brinna found herself searching for O'Reilly.

"By the way —" Rick tapped her on the shoulder — "I saw O'Reilly in the locker room. Shiny new vest and uniform."

"Who cares about the uniform," Maggie gushed. "What's he look like shirtless?" She shot Brinna an evil grin.

Brinna snorted. "Settle down. All I care about is how he handles his end of the unit."

"Like you're a nun or something. He may

be a nut, but he's gorgeous; enjoy the view."

Brinna turned her attention to the front of the room. Sergeant Eddie Klein walked in and checked the clock. There were two minutes left till four o'clock. He took his seat and studied paperwork in his hand.

While the second hand ticked through the final minute, Jack O'Reilly strolled into the room and took an open chair near the door.

Brinna regarded him for a minute as the sergeant began the meeting by reading some current in-service training.

O'Reilly kept his eyes on Klein. Brinna had to admit that Maggie was right. The guy was handsome. With his dark-red hair in a tight crew cut, he reminded her of Damian Lewis in *Homeland.* He wore a neat mustache and had a build like a jock, with broad shoulders and trim hips. Her gaze wandered to his hands and noted that they appeared strong and calloused.

As she tore her eyes away from him, she decided he did fill out the uniform nicely. Sighing, she tuned in to the sergeant and wondered if she was paying too much attention to Maggie.

Klein read each assignment. Brinna and Jack would be unit 4-Frank-8, a generic wild-car designation. When everyone was dismissed to log in to service, a couple of older guys walked up and greeted Jack.

"Want to meet for dinner?" Maggie asked as Brinna stood.

"Sure, as long as you promise not to drool on my partner."

Maggie stuck her tongue out and Brinna chuckled. "That's grown-up." She dodged the slap and caught O'Reilly before he left the room.

"Hey, Jack O'Reilly, I'm Brinna Caruso." She held her hand out and for a minute didn't think he'd take it. When he finally did, the grip was firm and the shake brief.

"I guess we're partners for now. I hear things have changed a lot in the years I've been out of patrol." He smiled, but there was no warmth in it.

"Things around here change on a daily basis." Uneasiness smacked Brinna like a baton thrust. O'Reilly's eyes were so empty. They weren't cop eyes. They weren't dead. They were empty. They were a victim's eyes — a lost and hopeless victim's eyes. A shiver went through her.

"I've already got a car," she said as she turned to the door. "Ready whenever you are."

"I'm ready," he said. "At least as ready as I'll ever be."

She waved for him to follow, and together

they walked up the stairs and out to the parking lot. All the while Brinna wondered how she could spend ten hours working with a partner who had Stephen King–character creepy eyes.

17

Monday afternoon into early Tuesday morning was generally a quiet time to work. The weekend had ended and people usually slid passively back into the workweek. But as she and Jack headed for their vehicle, Brinna listened to the busy radio traffic of the day units and knew tonight would be an exception.

"Here's our sled." She tapped the back of a black-and-white. "I'll pop the trunk so you can store your kit." She opened the driver's door and hit the trunk release. Then she took a seat and waited for Jack to join her. She clicked on the mobile data terminal and let the computer boot up.

Jack climbed into the passenger seat after a few minutes. He sighed and nodded toward the MDT screen. "We use the same password here as in the station?"

Brinna shrugged. "Same. We might have access to more searches for the car than when you were in patrol, but that's all that's different."

"I hope that's all."

"Well, it's still the passenger officer's job to operate the MDT, so you'll have plenty of time to catch up on any changes."

She started to point out all the buttons he was likely to utilize during the course of the shift — the 10-97 button when they arrived on scene, the 10-6 button when they stopped for investigation, the 10-8 button when they were clear of a call, and the emergency button if they were in trouble — when he held up a hand.

"Hey, I'm not a keystone cop. I do know how to use a computer."

"Just trying to help." She rattled off the identification numbers to her radio and the car. He'd need to enter them all when he logged the unit on.

As she watched him work, face illuminated by the glow of the computer, he seemed at ease with the keyboard. Hopefully he'd slide into every other aspect of patrol as well.

Jack met her gaze with those vacant eyes after he'd entered the needed numbers. "I'm ready to hit the in-service button."

Brinna gave the go-ahead sign with a wave of her hand.

Right off the bat they were assigned to assist on a domestic violence call. A day unit already on scene requested another unit to stand by while paramedics assessed the victim.

Brinna made a left out of the police lot and headed for the address given. On her mind was what the dispatcher said regarding the call. Neighbors reported a loud, violent fight. The victim stumbled out into the courtyard bleeding and begging for help.

Jack interrupted her train of thought with a question. "Aren't you the girl they gave the search-and-rescue dog to?"

Brinna cast him a sideways glance. "I'm the cop who earned the right to work with the dog, yeah." The edge in her voice was unmistakable, but O'Reilly didn't seem to notice.

"They took the dog away from you because you got some bad press?"

"They didn't take Hero away. They just reassigned me until things calm down." She stopped at a signal and turned to regard Jack.

"Did you shoot a juvenile?" he asked.

"Yeah, one that was at least six feet tall who shot at me first. Haven't you read the papers or listened to the news?" Brinna focused on the road again. "Hester Shockley got involved. She has microphone radar;

136

she finds one everywhere she goes."

Jack harrumphed. "I don't get the paper or watch the news. I'm just trying to determine how you feel about this partnership. I'm guessing you don't want it any more than I do."

"No, I don't. Nothing personal, but I like working with my dog." She jerked the car to a stop at the dispatch location. "But we both have to live with it, so I expect you'll carry your weight."

Brinna threw the car door open and headed to the apartment complex, not waiting for Jack's answer.

Everything was just too tight.

Jack squirmed to get comfortable in the stiff new Kevlar vest and rigid Sam Browne gun belt. Compounding the physical discomfort was the situation he now found himself in — working patrol with someone who didn't want to work with him.

He watched Caruso do a job he'd handled with equal grace six years ago but now felt as inadequate to perform as someone who was deaf, dumb, and blind.

Six years ago radio traffic was like a second language to him. Now it sounded like gibberish. The computer was one bright spot. No different from his desktop. But he couldn't do police work only on the car computer.

The knowledge that Caruso didn't want to work with him rubbed his ego as raw as the stiff wool shirt collar rubbed his neck. Everyone had wanted to work with Jack O'Reilly. He was a cop's cop. Who was this female to think he wasn't a worthwhile partner?

Finally starting to feel comfortable when they arrived at the dispatch address, he relaxed. *What does it matter?* he wondered. *What does anything matter?* He followed Caruso to where paramedics tended the victim, and every step of the way he wondered why he even bothered. There was no Vicki waiting at home for him.

He'd never imagined her loss would hit him so hard all over again. He was so sure patrol would be his salvation now. But as he watched Caruso talking to the handling day unit, it felt as though he were detached from the situation, viewing everything from above but not actively involved.

As Brinna reached the crime scene, she forgot Jack. The young woman on the gurney took her breath away. Her face resembled raw hamburger, and while the paramedics tried to assess her condition,

138

her breathing rasped and rattled.

"What did he beat her with?" she asked the day guy, an officer named Nugent.

He pointed to a wooden figurine of a horse, stained with what appeared to be blood, on a bench next to him. "That. Might be a homicide. Not sure if she'll pull through; medics are having a hard time stabilizing her for transport. Thanks for rolling." He waved his hand around the apartment complex. "We've got a ton of neighbors to interview and a large scene to secure. I guess we're thin all over the city. It's just the four of us right now."

Brinna contemplated the courtyard and all the people watching the police activity. Jack was standing to one side, out of the way, but not jumping in to help. Nugent's partner had a roll of yellow police tape, and he was stringing it around the perimeter of the courtyard crime scene.

Children hung over the railing staring at the bloody victim. Brinna felt sick to her stomach, not wanting the youngsters to view the carnage.

"Where is the suspect?" Brinna asked, needing a task.

Nugent shrugged. "Not sure. When we got here, the victim was in the courtyard bleeding to death."

"Where'd the 911 call come from?"

"Well, a couple neighbors called in, but the first one came from her apartment." Nugent pointed across the way to a first-floor apartment with its front door open. "It was an incomplete. No one said anything. We figure she dialed and then stumbled out here. He's probably in the wind."

"Right. I'll check it out. If this turns into a homicide, the apartment will need to be sealed and photographed." Brinna left Nugent and walked toward the open door. Jack followed, but she paid him no mind.

Once inside the apartment, it was easy to see a battle had taken place. The TV was busted, the couch overturned, and broken picture frames and glass littered the floor.

"What's in here?" Jack asked from the doorway. "I thought Nugent wanted us to talk to wits."

"A hunch, that's all. Why don't you go talk to wits?" Brinna didn't turn around. She continued through the apartment. Something was nagging; she couldn't put her finger on it.

Milo always says trust your instincts.

She heard water running. Turning left into the bathroom, she saw the top of a man's head sticking out of an overflowing tub of water.

"In here," she called out, rushing to the tub. She grabbed an arm to pull the man's face out from under the water and stretched to turn the water off. He'd cut his wrists across the veins, so when he'd lost consciousness, the hands had flopped down and stopped the bleeding.

As she struggled with the deadweight, she wondered where Jack was and called out again. "O'Reilly, in the bathroom."

Grunting, she grasped the man under the armpits and pulled him backward, out of the tub. He scraped his hip on the shower door, but she figured that was the least of his worries. Once he was on the bathroom floor, the wrists began to bleed again.

Brinna cursed and grappled with her handheld. "4-Frank-8, advise Boy-5 I have a second subject in the apartment and I need medics."

Grasping the hands of the limp form in front of her, she curled them inward and applied pressure to stop the bleeding, then pushed the man's stomach in with the back of his hands. Water poured out of his mouth, and in a second he began to cough. After that he began to breathe, sputtering at first, without regaining consciousness.

"What the — ?" Nugent appeared at her shoulder.

Turning, she spoke to Nugent, keeping her hands clamped on the unconscious man's wrists. "This must be your suspect."

"We were so tied up with the victim, I never . . ."

"Could happen to anyone. Just make sure the medics get in here."

"They're on the way."

"Great. Seen my partner?"

Nugent shook his head. Just then the medics arrived. Brinna apprised them of the situation and moved out of the bathroom to let them do their job.

She lassoed her anger and walked out to the car to get some antibiotic wipes from her kit. There'd been no time to put gloves on, and she had the creep's blood on her hands. Where in the world was O'Reilly?

18

When Jack and Brinna had reached the apartment and she told him to go talk to witnesses, he did.

It was the one thing Jack was sure of. He wasn't going to follow Caruso around like a puppy.

Jack approached an elderly couple. "Hi, did you two see what happened?"

The woman nodded. "Will Adrienne be okay?"

"Uh, I don't know. She's on her way to the hospital." He pulled out a brand-new pocket notebook, the leather cover stiff in his hands. He plucked the pen from his shirt pocket and promptly dropped it on the ground. As he bent to pick it up, he fought the uncomfortable feeling of being out of practice. When he looked back at the couple, he realized they didn't seem to notice. Their faces were a study in concern for the victim. And when they looked at him, he saw trust in their eyes.

He took a deep breath and wrote down their names and other pertinent information, the routine of getting the basics helping his confidence to return.

"So you know the victim and the suspect?"

"Adrienne, yes. Not her boyfriend. He keeps to himself, generally quiet, except when he drinks." The woman gave a disapproving shake of her head, and her husband took over.

"When he drinks, he's crazy. But there's no excuse to hit a woman."

"What happened?"

"I don't know what they was fighting about, but we heard them yelling." She looked at her husband, and he nodded. "I could tell he was drunk because that's the only time you know he's here. Then I heard her scream and the door slam." She pointed to their apartment, which was two doors down from the victim's. "I looked out the window and saw Adrienne running, and all of a sudden her boyfriend tackled her. He was beating her with something."

"I called 911," the man said. "I'm too old to go running around breaking up fights."

"Officer! Officer!"

Jack turned as another man approached him. "Yes?"

"My wife knows something, but she don't want to come outside. She don't want to see the blood." He pointed to the apartment next door to the elderly couple. "Can you talk to her in there?"

"Sure." Jack took a few seconds to be certain he had the elderly couple's information correct; then he followed the other resident into his apartment. There he talked to a sobbing woman who basically told him what the elderly couple had. By the time he finished, he'd begun to feel as though he had his sea legs back. Police work was mostly talking to people, making observations, and recording the observations of others. He did it in homicide and now he was doing it in patrol.

When he finished and stepped out into the courtyard again, he saw everyone rushing into the apartment where he'd left Caruso.

What had happened? He realized he'd turned his radio down. And all the indecision and uneasiness he'd felt before returned in a tidal wave. The deck was tossing and turning, and he had no balance.

Brinna was cleaning her hands with some wipes when the patrol sergeant pulled up behind her unit.

"What happened, Caruso?" Sergeant Klein asked.

Sighing heavily, she told him.

"Where's O'Reilly now?"

Brinna shrugged.

Nugent found them at the curb. He addressed Brinna. "Hey, your partner was in an apartment talking to neighbors."

"Wasn't he listening to his radio?" Klein said. "I heard Brinna ask for help."

Nugent shrugged. "Here he comes. Ask him."

Klein stopped Brinna with a hand on her shoulder. "I'll handle this." Then to Jack, "O'Reilly, I need to talk to you."

Brinna watched the sergeant take Jack aside.

"What's up with that?" Nugent asked. "Isn't that O'Reilly, the guy from homicide?"

"Yeah, tonight's his first night back in patrol."

"I'd heard they were sending him back. I didn't think they'd give him to you. Where's your dog?"

"Long story, and not something I want to get into right now. As soon as the sarge is done, we'll head back to the station and file a follow-up for you."

Nugent shook his head. "No hurry. I'll be

146

out here awhile. Homicide wants to check out the scene. My rook is slower than molasses filing paper. We'll be tied up on this till tomorrow."

Brinna chuckled mirthlessly. "I wonder how fast my rook files paper."

It wasn't until Jack saw Sergeant Klein on scene and the sergeant called him out that he realized he must've missed something.

"I haven't even been in the field for an hour yet. What have I done?" Jack asked.

The sergeant launched into a lecture on listening to the radio. "Your partner needed you," he said, then proceeded to dress Jack down as if he were a first-month rookie.

Jack felt his face flush and hooked his thumbs in his Sam Browne to keep his fists from clenching.

"I had my radio turned down," he explained to the obviously Klein, "so I could talk to people. I figured the primary unit would have already cleared the apartment anyway."

Klein blew out a breath. "Are you all here, O'Reilly?"

"What do you mean?"

Klein stepped so close Jack could smell his cinnamon gum. The sergeant almost whispered. "You know what I mean. It's no shame to quit if you can't handle the job. Why do you want to hang in here and maybe get yourself or someone else hurt?"

Jack stiffened, the word *quit* a trigger. Vicki hated quitters.

"I'm not a quitter. I don't know what your problem is with me. This is my first night out after six years. Why are you on my case about not hearing the radio? Caruso wasn't in danger."

"I'm on your case because I think you're a burnout who needs to hang it up. I don't care what the shrink says." Klein backed off and held up an index finger. "You're on notice. One screwup, one complaint from Caruso and I'm yanking you. Got it?"

Jack glared at the sergeant. Six years ago no one would have ever accused him of being a screwup. "I got it."

Klein nodded curtly and stalked away, leaving Jack standing on the sidewalk.

Quitter. Screwup. Jack felt his mind clear somewhat. The sergeant thought he was finished a a cop, and even though he'd felt like that himself, it infuriated him to hear it from someone else.

He sighed and glanced at the courtyard. Paramedics, in their haste to stabilize the patient, had left trash scattered about. Jack considered the victim, his partner, and the suspect — and the harshness of Klein's re-action.

A domestic violence call. Cops got killed on DV calls all the time. That punk in the tub could have just as easily tried to shoot it out as kill himself. The reality of being back on the front lines hit Jack like the business end of a baton. Out here, people would want to kill him just because he wore a blue uniform.

Something stirred deep inside as he slowly walked to the black-and-white where his partner waited.

He'd floundered whenever he tried to think of life past the sentencing. He'd considered trying to end Bridges's life and then ending his own. Now another solution occurred. He wouldn't have to pull the trig-ger or force another cop to do it. Someone else could do it for him. Patrol might just be the best place to put himself out of his misery.

19

Nigel hoarded every newspaper article he found about the dog cop.

"She got herself in a bit of trouble." He giggled as he read Hester Shockley's quote about Brinna being a rogue cop. Not only had she shot a teenager in cold blood, but Shockley was appalled that Caruso had a prejudice against people who had already served their debt to society. She constantly hounded registered sex offenders.

"Can't be chasing down bad ol' pedophiles indiscriminately, can you?" Nigel tsked.

After pinning the article next to all the other ones he'd collected on a bare wall, he went back to his other passion. Nigel powered up his computer and began to print out digital pictures. Surreptitiously taken candid shots of little girls spit out one by one. They were all candidates for his next Special Girl.

Digital cameras are wonderful. There was no fear of some nosy developer asking why he only took pictures of little girls.

All in all he printed about a hundred pictures. The sooner he had them all laid out, the sooner he could pick his next Special Girl, in honor of the anniversary he had with the cop.

"I think I'll leave you a little hint, Officer Caruso," he said as he held up the first few printed photos. "Let's see if you're bright enough to pick up on it."

20

"Hey, I'm sorry." Jack settled into his seat and slammed the car door. "I didn't hear my radio. Is this how it's going to be? You whine to the sergeant every time you think I'm goofing off?"

"I didn't whine to the sergeant. He came out here and asked me what happened. I told him." Brinna turned and met his angry glare. *At least his eyes aren't empty anymore.*

"Did you also tell him you and Nugent both asked me to talk to witnesses?"

Brinna sputtered. She had told him to go talk to witnesses and then paid no attention to the fact that that was what he'd done. Briefly she wondered if she was jumping the gun, not giving him a fair chance to be a partner.

"I didn't realize that was where you'd gone." She started the car but left it in park. "We're not going to get anywhere until we clear the air. Are you going to be a partner I

152

can depend on or not?"

"Why wouldn't I be?" Jack met her glare with one of his own. "I've been a cop a lot longer than you, and I've probably forgotten more about police work than you know. Just because you need to update me on new technology doesn't give you the right to give me grief."

Brinna held his angry gaze, happy to finally see life there but at the same time irritated by his attitude. "You know as well as I do about gossip around this place," she said, working to keep both voice and tone level. "The stuff floating around about you says you're burned out, unreliable. Tell me what's true. I want to be sure you'll watch my back."

Jack cursed under his breath. "What's true is that I'm not a wet-behind-the-ears rook. Stop treating me like one. I'll do my job; you just do yours."

"See that you do." Brinna jerked the car away from the curb and swallowed harsher words. She felt the heat rise beneath her vest and wondered if she'd last with O'Reilly in her car for two hours, much less two weeks.

They spent the next hours, first, filing paper on the domestic violence call and then in the unit not speaking. The silence didn't bother Brinna. In fact she liked it. Hero never bothered her with useless chitchat or stupid arguments.

When they assisted other units, Brinna did the talking. Jack participated but kept a distance from his partner. It seemed to Brinna that his anger had dissipated and he'd slipped slowly, like a turtle sliding into his shell, back to the spaced-out partner with creepy eyes.

The night passed quickly. It was twelve thirty before the radio quieted down enough for them to think about taking a break. Jack was sitting in the driver's seat, so Brinna answered the computer beep when Maggie's message came through.

Brinna read the message and turned to Jack, keeping her voice as neutral as possible. "How about the Colonial for breakfast?"

Jack shrugged. "Sure." He directed the car to the restaurant and parked. Another black-and-white in the parking lot told Brinna that Maggie and Rick were already inside.

Brinna requested code 7, a meal break, and, after receiving permission, opened the car door.

"You go ahead," Jack said, causing Brinna to pause halfway out of the car. "I'm not hungry. I'll stay here and catch some z's." He leaned back in the driver's seat.

Brinna straightened up and shrugged. "Suit yourself."

She joined Rick and Maggie in the restaurant.

"How goes it?" Maggie asked.

"He's creepy and touchy." She gulped her coffee as soon as it was poured.

"Where is he?" Rick turned toward the door.

"Not hungry." She tilted her head toward the car.

"But is he working out?" Maggie looked down her nose at Brinna with a tell-me-the-truth glare.

Brinna held her coffee cup in both hands and hiked her shoulders. "He hasn't been very talkative the whole night, but he says he'll do his job."

Maggie patted the table with her palm. "Saw Nugent at the station. He said you saved the bad guy tonight." She handed Brinna a menu.

Brinna chuckled. "What a zip. He did a better job on his girlfriend than he did on himself. If she lives, she'll need extensive plastic surgery. He'll only rate a few stitches."

"Nugent said Klein came out there and

reamed O'Reilly because he didn't help at all."

Brinna sucked her teeth. "When I found the suspect in the tub, I thought O'Reilly was right behind me. Turns out he was interviewing witnesses, didn't hear his radio when I asked for assistance. I think Klein overreacted. But then again, O'Reilly is not a rook. He should have heard his radio."

"I sometimes don't hear the radio when I'm interviewing people." Maggie shook her head. "That could happen to anyone, especially when the crime scene is chaotic. And it's his first night out in six years."

"Maybe you should give Jack the benefit of the doubt," Rick interjected. "I've heard he was an awesome cop once. He just needs more patrol time under his belt."

Brinna harrumphed. "I keep hearing he *was* awesome. I'll give him time, but I won't coddle him."

"Trouble is, you've worked with a dog too long. Just remember —" Maggie shook her finger at Brinna — "guys don't sit and stay on command, so go easy if he misbehaves."

21

Jack pulled the cross necklace from his rearview mirror and took it with him into the house, pretending it was a link to Vicki. He opened the door to a ringing phone and let the machine pick up as he stripped down to his boxer shorts and hung Vicki's chain around his own neck.

"It's Mom. Are you home?"

He sat on the couch and let his mom talk to the machine.

"I know it's late, or early, depending on how you look at it, but you should just be getting home from work. Please call me. I want you to talk to Pastor Jenkins. Please. I love you, Jack."

He heard his mother breathing on the line for a few seconds before she finally hung up.

Jack stretched out on the couch and clicked on the TV for the noise. Sitting back, he grasped the cross tightly in his right hand. He had no intention of phoning his mother, and he definitely wouldn't talk to Hank Jenkins.

Pastor Jenkins once said he thought of Vicki as his very own daughter. Closing his eyes, Jack pushed Jenkins out of his mind. Jenkins was like everyone else, asking him to come back to God, to trust in God's will for his life.

Nonsense.

He turned his thoughts to the sentencing and debated whether to call the DA in the morning for a hint as to how things were going. Bridges was in the process of being evaluated by the department of corrections for a sentence recommendation.

There'd be no death penalty for Gil Bridges, but Jack wanted him to get the maximum sentence, which would be many years in prison. Trouble was, Bridges appeared to be repentant. He'd apologized over and over, even donated money to Mothers Against Drunk Driving in Vicki's name. Jack knew that if the judge thought the idiot's repentance sincere, he'd be inclined to be lenient.

Bridges had asked Jack for forgiveness. And Jack had told him to pound sand. Now, lying on the couch, Jack thought about the last time he'd seen the man, and his hands clenched into fists.

I'll never forgive or forget. If it were within my power, I'd kill Bridges with my bare hands.

The clock on the cable box said it was a little after 3 a.m. Jack closed his eyes, hoping to sleep soundly until it was time to make his phone call. As usual, his dreams were shot full of images of Vicki and his sleep fitful. He woke just before nine and spent several minutes watching the red numbers before he sat up and stretched.

He left the couch and picked up the phone to call DA Rivers. The secretary said he was in. Jack only had to wait a minute before Rivers answered the phone.

"Jack, how's it going? I hope you're doing better than the last time we talked."

"I'm still taking things day to day. You know why I'm calling. What's the word? You must've heard something by now about Bridges's evaluation."

Rivers sighed loudly over the phone. "Jack, I'm going to level with you. I doubt Bridges will get the maximum. Not only is Andrews a liberal judge; Bridges himself is truly sorry about what happened. He's apologized numerous times —"

Heat coursed through Jack's body. Even the phone felt white-hot in his hand. "He killed my wife! He can apologize all he

159

wants and it won't bring her back." He pounded the wall with his free hand.

"Calm down." Rivers let a beat pass before he continued. "Consider Bridges's situation objectively. He doesn't have a record. I'm not excusing him, but this is a first-time —"

Jack slammed the phone down and cursed. First-time offender. First-time killer.

Why did Vicki have to be on the road the same day Gil Bridges decided to drive drunk for the first time?

He threw himself down on the couch as the tears began. As a cop, he asked questions and always demanded answers. But demanding answers to the questions he had now got him nowhere. No one heard them. He pictured Bridges in his mind, down on his knees begging for his life while Jack held a gun to his head, ready to deal out the correct punishment, the punishment that fit the crime.

Jack heard the voice of Doc Bell in his mind, asking him if never forgiving Bridges and wishing him dead would bring Vicki back. Then there was Pastor Jenkins asking him to trust God in this difficult time.

Jack rolled onto his side, face buried in a couch pillow, Vicki's cross pressing into his chin.

There's no God to trust. It might not bring Vicki back if Bridges gets what he deserves, but I want him to feel pain, to hurt a little bit like I hurt. He groaned, the sound muffled by the pillow. *I fervently wish I could make Bridges's pain as permanent as Vicki's death.*

22

"Hey, you sure are ready to go! Excited about night two with O'Reilly?" A cheerful Maggie slapped Brinna on the back as she passed her in the locker room.

"Man, did you take a happy pill today or what?" Brinna closed the locker and stepped to the end of the row to check her image in the mirror while she fastened her gun belt.

"Are you a grump today or what?" Maggie's laughter reverberated in the room, and Brinna heard her jerk her locker open. "My parents bought me lunch at my favorite place. We had a good time catching up."

"Oh, I forgot they were coming to visit this week."

"They flew in from the Bay Area this morning. They'll do some sightseeing this afternoon, and my mom will probably stock my fridge and cook me a bunch of food." She stepped around the corner pulling on her uniform pants.

Maggie and Brinna had dressing quickly down to a science. Both of them came to work wearing white T-shirts, regulation for under the uniform shirt. That way, dressing was quick — slip off shorts or jeans, slip on vest, shirt, and pants, and you're almost ready.

Brinna yawned and shook her head. "I can't relate to the relationship you have with your mom and dad. My mom and I don't seem to have common ground like you and your mom do. Sometimes, if we're together too long, we argue."

"My parents are great," Maggie gushed. "Maybe you're too hard on yours. Your mom seems nice enough. And even though you think he doesn't, I bet your dad cares a lot more than you know."

Brinna considered this. "You're right. I love my mom, but my dad is another matter. I sometimes don't understand how they've stayed together all these years. I couldn't be married to a guy who drinks like my dad does. It's probably my mom's religion that keeps her with him."

Maggie pulled her vest on and faced Brinna as she connected the Velcro straps. "I heard O'Reilly used to be quite the religious fanatic as well."

"Not anymore. According to Ben, Jack

gave up on the God stuff. Fine with me. No fairy tales in our black-and-white." She surprised herself with her own vehemence as she spit the words out.

Maggie whistled. "In spite of your parents, you turned out okay. Don't be so bitter."

"Do I sound bitter?"

Maggie made a face and pushed Brinna from the mirror so she could check out her reflection.

"Seriously, I don't think I'm bitter," Brinna protested. "I just wouldn't want my parents spending a week in my house. That would be torture."

"They won't be around forever, Brin. If I were you, I'd make peace." She finished pinning her hair up. "Forgive the past; build a better future."

"Thanks, Dr. Laura. Let's get to squad."

The night started out slow. Jack hadn't changed much since the night before, except that it was obvious he hadn't gotten much sleep. A perceptible tension blanketed the car. Brinna didn't know what to expect from him, and that made her nervous.

She decided to ignore him until she needed a partner and took advantage of the quiet radio to drive up to North Long Beach and Heather Bailey's house. Though

Sergeant Rodriguez had warned her to stay away from any missing cases for the time being, it had been too long since she'd checked in with Mr. and Mrs. Bailey.

At the Del Amo Boulevard exit a huge billboard stood with Heather's picture on it and the words *Have you seen this girl?* The billboard listed phone numbers and websites to contact with information.

"What's up here?" Jack asked.

"I want to check with Heather Bailey's mom, see how she's holding up."

"Heather Bailey?"

Brinna cast a glance his way.

Jack rubbed tired eyes.

"Yeah, didn't you see that billboard we just passed?"

"Nope. I'm struggling here, I hardly slept. Give me a break."

Brinna bit back a mean remark. *Settle down; cut him some slack.* "Working nights takes a little getting used to. By next week you won't have a problem."

Jack grunted and leaned back in his seat.

"Anyway, Heather went missing over a month ago. I try to keep in touch with the family. There's still an ongoing search, but leads have dried up."

"Little brats are always going missing. She run away with her boyfriend?" Jack yawned.

"What, do you want a slap? Heather is eight years old." Brinna stared, slack-jawed, amazed at her partner's insensitivity as she jerked to a stop in front of Heather's house. Shaking her head, she threw the door open before irritation won out and she did slap him.

She heard him mutter, "Sorry," as she slammed the door.

As she knocked on the front door, she willed the anger at Jack's cluelessness to ease. The family didn't need any more drama. Heather's mom answered after the second knock. *She's aged,* Brinna thought. *Her hair is grayer or she's stopped coloring it, and the bags under her eyes seem permanent now.*

"Hi, Mrs. Bailey. I hope I didn't interrupt dinner."

The woman managed a ghost of a smile. "No, no. You didn't interrupt anything. Come in."

"Thanks." Brinna followed her into the living room. A pile of flyers lay out on the coffee table, and in the corner next to the fireplace stood a large poster with Heather's face and eight-year-old, gap-toothed smile watching over the room.

"I came by to see how you were holding up and if Chuck has given you anything

166

new." Brinna took a seat on the edge of the couch Mrs. Bailey pointed to.

Heather's mom sat across from Brinna on a worn love seat. "It seems like the tips, even the tips from the kooks, have stopped coming." She leaned back and closed her eyes. To Brinna it appeared as though the weight of grief draped the woman like a Kevlar blanket, heavy and impenetrable.

"Can you believe it?" she continued after a minute. "It will be six weeks on Saturday. My baby has been away from me for six whole weeks."

"I haven't given up." Brinna clenched her fists. "Whenever I have a clue or a lead to follow, I'm there."

"I know, and I can't tell you how much I appreciate that. It seems like everyone else — my husband included — wants to give up. He says we should have a memorial service and get on with our lives." A scowl crossed her face, and haunted eyes held Brinna's. "How do I get on without my baby?"

"I don't agree with him, but I think the two of you need one another right now. This could tear you apart, and I don't want to see that happen. I know what happened to my family."

"But you came back after a week," the

woman said wistfully. "How lucky your mother was."

"Still, things were never the same." *Dad couldn't cope and turned his back on the rest of us,* Brinna thought. "Don't turn on your husband now. When we do find Heather, she'll need you both together as a unit."

The woman's eyes brightened. "You do believe we'll find her? Alive?"

"I won't lie to you. I can't guarantee we'll find her alive. But we will find her, and you'll know one way or another. I won't give up until we do."

23

Jack felt like roadkill. Like some little rodent flat on the street getting flatter every minute because it keeps getting run over.

He'd watched Brinna walk up to the Baileys' house and wondered why he had no compassion for a missing eight-year-old girl. He didn't think cops should get so personally involved, yet he knew that what Caruso did was something Vicki would have approved of. His partner's obsession snapped him out of his smothering self-pity for a moment.

But her obsession also reminded him of something else. For some reason it reminded him of a lot of Christians he used to hang around with. He struggled to shape his thoughts. Like Caruso trying to save every kid was impossible, so was trying to please a God who didn't exist. *Caruso and the rest of them are all really running on a treadmill, exerting a lot of energy and getting nowhere.*

The bitterness in his heart caused a nasty taste to boil up into his mouth. He swallowed and his thoughts returned to the misery he felt. The hope that working patrol would make it easier to sleep had been shredded like paper in an industrial crosscut shredder. His conversation with DA Rivers hadn't helped his mood either.

He and Vicki got the maximum sentence while the pig who sentenced them might get the minimum. The urge to break something surged through him, and he gripped the end of his baton until his knuckles turned white.

Vicki will never know what it feels like to be a mother, to celebrate another anniversary, to see another Christmas. And that pig gets it all.

He leaned his head against the window and closed his eyes. Vicki was there. Ever present in his mind, Vicki popped into his dreams as he dozed off. There she still lived and the last year evaporated like a bad dream. He reached out to touch his wife, to hold her and banish the bad, lonely year forever. But she stayed just out of his grasp, and he felt as though he were walking through knee-deep peanut butter.

The slam of Brinna's door jolted him back

to the nightmare of consciousness.

"Hope you're ready to get to work," she snapped.

Jack bit back a curse. Why did reality have to continue to intrude on his dream? His heart ached as his mind struggled to keep the image of Vicki from fading away.

Brinna left the Bailey house with a heavy heart. She'd promised Mrs. Bailey she'd find Heather but knew that odds of her being found alive were not in the little girl's favor. But Brinna would not give up. She decided to call Milo in the morning and mull over the situation with him.

Her thoughts drifted to her parents, and she wondered what would have happened to them if she hadn't come home. Would things have been different between them? Would the grief have torn them apart? They still would have had her brother, Brian. Would they have been strong for him? Sighing, she decided she didn't know.

She'd paused at the black-and-white. Jack was sleeping, his head lolling to the side, and irritation had replaced the heaviness she'd felt walking out of the Bailey house.

Brows furrowed, she made all the noise she could getting in the car, slamming the door when she sat down and taking great pleasure in the fact that he jumped awake.

"Think you can stay awake for the rest of the shift?" she said as she started the car.

All she got was a grunt in response.

Brinna settled into a patrol routine she would have used if Hero were still with her. She cruised by the addresses she knew by heart — the sex offenders who lived in the area around Heather's house. If she saw any of the registrants she recognized, she'd stop and talk to them. The quiet radio allowed her to check out most of North Long Beach. In fact, it was closing in on midnight before the radio clicked to life with traffic from Maggie and Rick in 3-Charles-5. She and Rick were tailing a rolling stolen.

Brinna grabbed the mike before Jack reacted. "4-Frank-8. Show us assisting Charlie-5." Adrenaline surged. Rolling stolens, or 10-8-51 victors — the radio code for them — were just about the biggest rush in patrol. They were unpredictable. Would the car thief stop or would he run? Brinna ramped up for a pursuit.

"Wake up, O'Reilly. Maggie's got a victor heading our way. They're at the boulevard and San Antonio, northbound."

"I'm awake and I heard," Jack snarled, sitting up in his seat.

Brinna stopped at Del Amo and Long

Beach Boulevard, listened to the radio, and waited for the 10-8-51, described as a black, late-model Honda, to roll by.

They didn't wait long. The Honda crossed the intersection, and a second later so did Maggie's black-and-white. Per procedure, Maggie wouldn't try to make a stop without backup in position. Brinna turned left to follow and waited for Maggie to activate her light bar. The reds went on as the vehicle passed Fifty-Second Street. And the stolen car failed to yield.

"Hang on," Brinna said as she listened to Rick tell dispatch that the victor wasn't stopping and their speed increased. The pursuit was on.

24

Jack almost hadn't heard the radio and the information on the rolling stolen. But when he tuned in, the info got his attention.

Fully awake as his partner put them assisting, Jack sat up, gratified by the distraction of a pursuit. Vehicle pursuits often ended in foot pursuits, and foot pursuits often ended in fights. Jack wanted a fight — a good knock-down, drag-out one. He'd pound the crook and imagine he was pounding Bridges.

When they pulled in behind Maggie and the lights went on, every muscle in Jack's body tensed, and he felt more alive than he had in a year.

Funny how anticipating a good beating just breathed life into me, he thought. His left hand gripped the seat belt, ready to unclip it in a second. His right gripped the dashboard as he and Brinna flew through an intersection. The crook's speed increased, and his partner crushed the accelerator to keep up.

The victor continued on Long Beach Boulevard, rapidly approaching the city's north boundaries. Sirens screamed in his ears, competing with the pounding of his heart. Jack heard Klein come on the air to approve the pursuit and say that he was en route to assist.

It wasn't long before the crook crossed the boundary into Compton. After a couple of blocks he made a right turn off the main boulevard onto a side street, very nearly losing control and crashing.

"He's trying to lose us. Too bad we don't have a chopper tonight," Brinna muttered, pumping the brakes and leaning toward Jack as she made the turn behind Maggie.

Jack gripped the door, bracing as Maggie's lights veered left ahead of them. Old memories flooded back. Memories of chases and arrests intertwined with a realization that at one time he had loved this job.

His partner had assessed the situation correctly. The crook was trying to lose them, or better, was looking for a place to bail out of the car. Jack hoped for the latter.

The victor led them on a zigzag course through unfamiliar residential streets. Two Compton police units tried to enter the chase but a run through a dirt lot by the crook caused them both to spin out. Compton and Long Beach did not share radio frequencies, so Jack couldn't ask if the Compton cops gave up completely. He kept his eyes forward.

After several near misses with other cars and stationary objects, the crook directed his stolen car back into Long Beach, this time south on Atlantic Avenue. By now just about every Long Beach cop who was able was in line with them, Jack thought. They sped down Atlantic, the victor flying through every intersection. Lucky for all the cars involved, traffic was light to nonexistent.

"He's heading for the Verandas," Brinna announced.

Jack agreed. The Verandas, a federal housing project, happened to be home to lots of thieves and gangbangers.

Works for me, Jack thought.

He watched as the stolen Honda made a wild, out-of-control left turn onto Fifty-Second Street, the housing project access. He might have made the next left into the complex if a private security car hadn't entered the mix. Coming from the victor's right, the security car must've caused the thief to hesitate. He oversteered, then overcorrected and missed the turn, slamming into a retaining wall.

Jack leaped out of the car as soon as Brinna came to a stop.

When Jack reached the smashed car, he saw the driver tangled behind the air bag and unable to run anywhere. No foot pursuit or fight tonight. Heart racing, he tightened his grip on the butt of his gun and cursed his bad luck. The urge to pull his baton and smash the car to bits nearly overwhelmed him.

Maggie, a few steps behind Jack, appeared at his shoulder.

"Man, you were quick. Good thing the dirtbag didn't have a gun." She stepped forward to assess the crook's condition. He was moaning and not moving much. From what Jack could tell, the air bag had probably broken his nose.

About ten other cops, including Brinna and Sergeant Klein, swarmed the car. Jack took a deep breath and willed himself to relax, his adrenaline still pumping. He watched everything going on around him, feeling as detached as he had that first night at the domestic violence call.

After paramedics determined that the car thief was bookable, Maggie and her partner took him into custody. Brinna offered to stand by for a tow truck. With the chase over and the crook gone, everything de-escalated quickly. Klein and the other units returned to service.

He didn't have anything to say to me tonight, Jack thought when the sergeant pulled away. He was sitting in the patrol car again. His fatigue returned fourfold as the adrenaline high crashed. He considered the scene around him.

The commotion had awakened several Verandas residents. Some milled around on the sidewalk across from the wreck, watching the cops. He heard Brinna fishing for something in the trunk.

Jack stared at the Verandas residents, wondering how close he had come to beating that car thief within an inch of his life, wishing with every blow he was smashing Bridges. The hair on the back of his neck stood up and Jack shifted in his seat.

Is that really what I wanted?

He watched Brinna walk around the Honda with her clipboard, inventorying the damage. They had a half-hour wait for a tow truck. Brinna reminded Jack of how he used to be. She had a drive to do a good job, and she believed that by doing her job well, she was making a difference. He wondered if he'd ever feel that way again.

I'm a cop fantasizing about breaking every

regulation concerning the use of force and a few laws besides. Will any bit of my life really be better after the sentencing?

25

Brinna sneezed as the harsh smell of burnt oil from the wrecked car tickled her nose. She carefully observed and recorded the damage, trying to keep her mind off the uneasy feeling rumbling through her like an earthquake aftershock.

When the 10-8-51 had crashed, Jack had jumped out of the car as if he'd been ejected. A thought had occurred to her as she watched him sprint to the victor. *He wants to die.*

She shivered in spite of the warm night. *I could be wrong,* she told herself. *He finally showed some life and I'm jumping to conclusions. But rushing up on a stolen car before it's been cleared?*

The arrival of the tow truck interrupted her train of thought. She embraced the distraction, not liking the direction her thoughts were taking her. She was familiar with suicide *by* cop. But the idea of a cop committing suicide was too right rudder for Brinna. She knew it happened too often, even knew one old-timer who'd hanged himself. But if that was why Jack had returned to patrol — to get himself killed — she'd do her best to stop him.

Brinna chatted with the tow truck driver about different calls she'd heard going out while waiting for him. He regaled her with a story about an overturned vehicle on the freeway he'd had to right when he'd first come to work. Brinna was almost sorry to see him finish hooking up the victor and leave.

A glance at the black-and-white told her Jack wasn't sleeping. He was wide awake and staring into the darkness.

Not knowing what to say, Brinna said nothing. *How do you front a guy off if you think he's suicidal?* she wondered. *I was prepared for lazy or indifferent, but not this.*

She directed the car to the North Division Substation to call auto stats with the stolen vehicle information. Jack came into the substation with her and went to the restroom.

After Brinna made her call, she went outside and waited for him, deciding she'd have to confront him whether she knew the right words or not.

She leaned against the patrol car, arms folded. The north substation was situated on the corner of a large city park. She heard crickets singing in the park, and from time to time a lone car drove down Atlantic Avenue.

As Jack walked across the parkway toward their patrol car, Brinna straightened. "What was that all about?" she asked.

"What?" Jack asked.

"The way you ran to that victor before it was secured. He could have had a gun."

"I thought he was going to run. I was ready for a foot pursuit." He turned away and stepped forward to open the car door.

"I hope that's all it was." Brinna walked around to her door and glared at Jack across the roof. "Just remember, we're partners whether either one of us likes it or not. You get hurt, it puts me in danger. And vice versa."

Jack stared at her for a minute. Brinna expected a denial, a curse, anything. He said nothing, just jerked the car door open and sat down.

Gazing out at the dark, quiet park, Brinna took a deep breath and tried to ignore what her instincts were telling her.

I'm working with a partner who may have a death wish.

26

Save for the occasional crackle of the radio and the squeak of leather when one of them shifted in their seat, silence bathed the unit. Brinna kept her gaze roving the empty city streets and ignored her partner. He simply stared out the passenger window while she drove through dark neighborhoods. Brinna decided to take advantage of the lull and stop at a 7-Eleven for coffee.

"Hey, Officer Caruso, how are you tonight?" Vu, the night counterman, greeted Brinna.

"Good, Vu. How's business?"

"Slow tonight. Where's Officer Hero?" He pulled some dog bones from under the counter and shook the box. "I have his favorite treats."

Brinna and Hero had helped catch a man who'd robbed Vu's store a few months before. Ever since then, Vu treated Hero like a prize show dog every time he walked into the store.

"I'm working with a human partner to-night. Hero's home sleeping."

"Oh." Vu sounded genuinely heartbroken. "I love that dog. I hear he found a little boy a couple weeks ago. You take some treats home to him for me?" Vu poured some treats into a plastic Baggie and held it out for Brinna.

"Sure." Brinna smiled and took the bag. "I love to spoil the dog and he knows it."

"Brinna."

She turned. Jack was at the door, frowning.

"Yeah?"

"An urgent 10-21 for you just popped up on the computer. You're supposed to call Chuck Weldon ASAP."

Brinna blew out a breath and tossed her coffee, fearing the worst. *Chuck found Heather.*

"Thanks for the bones, Vu." She grabbed the package and headed out the door.

"Thank you, Officer Caruso. Be careful."

Brinna dug her cell phone out of her kit and punched in Chuck's number. She strolled with the phone to the edge of the 7-Eleven parking lot as it rang.

When Chuck ignored all pleasantries,

Brinna braced for what she knew was coming.

"Brinna, how quick can you get down to the Crystal Cove mountain bike trail?"

"In Orange County, off PCH?"

"That's the place. I'll meet you at the trailhead and lead you up to what we've found. Of course, it will take dental records for a positive ID, but we're sure it's her. Heather Bailey."

"Heather?" Brinna's heart seemed to stop. She closed her eyes and fought for composure, the image of Heather's haunted mother in her mind. *It's time for a cop face. Milo would say to never let emotion cloud your judgment. I need a Kevlar heart right now.* She pressed the reassuring stiffness of her vest with her palm. Cops with Kevlar hearts were the most effective because nothing could hurt them and nothing would distract them from the job they have to do, Milo said often.

"Chuck, I, uh . . . We're just about EOW. I'll have to get approval to leave the city. And Scranton will probably have a coronary."

"Don't worry about Scranton. I already cleared it with the watch commander. I called him first."

"Well, then, give me thirty minutes."

185

Brinna flipped the phone shut and stared across the intersection. The Don't Walk sign blinked red. Traffic signals never got a break; they were always on duty, 24-7.

So were the busy perverts who preyed on children — always on duty, 24-7.

She rubbed her face and checked the time on her phone. It was close to 2 a.m. She wondered if Chuck had already sent someone over to tell Heather's family. No, he'd wait for a positive ID.

She remembered coming home that day, twenty years ago, after doctors had examined her and given her a clean bill of health. Her mom was very sad. She cried for hours on end and her dad just seemed mad. Later, she remembered him being drunk and mad, all the time. Life was never the same. What would happen to the Baileys with the knowledge that Heather wouldn't come home?

"Caruso." Jack's voice cut into Brinna's woolgathering.

"Yeah." She turned, faced him, and buried the memories. "What's up?"

"What's up with you? What was the phone call about? Bad news?"

"Yep, very bad. Chuck wants me in Orange County. I'm not sure what I'm supposed to do with you."

O'Reilly's face reddened. "I'm not a kid

you're babysitting. What's in Orange County?"

Brinna bit her tongue and walked past him to the car. "Hold on," she began when Jack joined her at the black-and-white. "I'm not trying to treat you like a kid. It's just that the FBI called. They found one of my, uh . . . one of the local missing kids, the one whose house I visited earlier. They want me out there for some reason." She shrugged. "Normally I have Hero and he goes with me no matter what. I'm not sure what you want to do."

"We're partners. What would I do if I stayed here? Work the front desk?" Jack drummed his fingers on the roof of the black-and-white.

"I guess you're right. Let's go." Blowing out a breath, Brinna climbed into the driver's seat.

She didn't want to deal with O'Reilly *and* a dead kid. The car was silent as she drove through North Long Beach south to Pacific Coast Highway and turned left toward Orange County.

Jack didn't speak until they crossed from Long Beach into Seal Beach. "So it's true: the FBI clues you in on missing cases?"

Brinna glanced his way, trying to determine if he mocked her. A blank expression greeted her. "Yes, after Hero and I found Alonso Parker last year, I convinced the department it was a good risk to let us work on missing cases."

"And the kid who lived in North Long Beach has been found?"

Brinna nodded. "Heather Bailey."

"Where'd they find her?"

"Crystal Cove, the bike trail."

"Any suspects in custody?"

"Nope, and no solid leads. No one saw anything the day she disappeared. She just vanished from her front yard." Brinna shook her head. At least Hero never asked any questions. *Shut up, O'Reilly. I just want to get to Heather.*

As if reading her thoughts, Jack stayed silent for the remainder of the trip. Brinna found her mind wandering to her mother. *My mom prayed so many times for Heather to be found alive. It hurts that she trusts so much in something that never seems to work.*

"Believe only in what you can see," the old Milo would say. *"When someone breaks the law, the best, most satisfying remedy is to see him or her pay for it."*

That's what Brinna would tell her mother she believed. Punishing the puke was way more useful than praying to an empty sky.

27

"Officer Caruso, good to see you again. Sorry the circumstances aren't more pleasant." Chuck Weldon met Brinna and Jack in the parking lot at the trailhead for the Crystal Cove bike trail.

The lot was awash in light from four portable floodlights. Two government plain cars and two vehicles belonging to the Orange County Sheriff's Department bracketed a black panel truck Brinna recognized as the OCSD's mobile communications center. Four deputy sheriffs stood off to one side of the lot, smoking and chatting. Brinna knew they were probably wondering about jurisdictional considerations. Chuck would have the final say there.

A stereotypical FBI agent, Chuck stood about six-one and wore his dark hair cut to regulation with a just-as-regulation mustache. His eyes were sharp and quick and his expression rarely, if ever, gave away his thoughts. Tonight he wore agency casual, dark slacks and a light-colored polo shirt, service handgun neatly tucked into a belt holster.

Brinna introduced Jack.

"I'd heard you got a new partner," Chuck said as he shook Jack's hand.

"Long story," Jack said, casting a glance Brinna's way.

Brinna nodded toward the trail. "What have you got, Chuck? I assume you found Heather up there."

"Yeah, and something even more disturbing."

"It's well after midnight. How'd you find her in the dark?" Jack asked.

Brinna did a double take. He was right. She hadn't even considered that. She'd just been consumed with grief that she'd lost one. How in the world *did* they find the eight-year-old this time of the night?

Chuck handed Brinna a piece of paper. "That's a copy of something that came into the office late this afternoon."

Brinna studied the paper. It was a hand-drawn map of the area, arrows leading up the bike path, and off to the side a bit, the paper was marked with a red X.

Jack read over her shoulder. "A map to the body?"

"Yep. It passed through many hands before we realized it wasn't a hoax and we were probably dealing with the killer. That's why we got out here so late. Although, at least at this time of night we know there won't be any looky-loos or press. We climbed up and found the body about two hours ago. Everything has been photographed and combed for evidence, but the coroner's been delayed. Might as well check things out before we bring her down."

Brows furrowed, Brinna handed the paper to Jack and faced Chuck. "Why? I mean, I'm glad you called me out and everything, but what can I tell you about the body your forensic team can't?"

"Let's get in the Jeep and I'll show you." Chuck held his hand out toward the Jeep. Brinna climbed into the passenger seat, Jack hopped in the back, and Chuck took the driver's seat.

"The Jeep will take us most of the way; then it's about a ten-minute hike to the body." Chuck started the ignition and directed the Jeep up the trail.

Brinna held on as the Jeep bounced along. After about ten minutes a glow of light was visible off to the right. She assumed it to be illumination provided by the FBI forensic team. She frowned into the darkness and wondered what the end of the path would bring.

It wasn't much longer and Chuck pulled off to the right of the trail and parked. Two other Jeeps were already parked there.

"You guys have your flashlights?" Chuck asked. Brinna and Jack nodded. "Let's go." He hopped out of the vehicle and clicked his own light on. Brinna and Jack followed him along the path.

It was a narrow deer trail, almost over-grown in spots. Dry brush grabbed at their clothing. The night was warm and humid, the sound of the surf audible in the distance.

Brinna kept her eyes on the ground to keep from tripping and to avoid ripping her wool pants. Her cotton K-9 coveralls would be much better suited to this hike. True to Chuck's word, it took about ten minutes to reach the well-lit clearing where the forensic team waited.

Chuck directed his light to the left. Brinna followed the bright stream, bracing herself for a small, sad body. What she saw was hard to imagine as a lively eight-year-old girl. A month in the wilderness in scorching heat had done its work; plus the presence of animals was evident. Blonde hair and bones, some clothing and some flesh, were testi-mony that a body was there, but it was the sign that took Brinna's breath away.

Above the skull, on a two-by-two-foot wooden sign with bloodred block printing, Brinna read:

OFFICER CARUSO,
   HAPPY ANNIVERSARY!
   THE FIRST OF MANY PRESENTS.

28

"Either the shooting or that article Tracy Michaels wrote about me brought a nut out of the woodwork." Brinna sat in the mobile operations van and rubbed her face with both hands. "I should have known better."

"Don't beat yourself up." Chuck placed a cup of coffee in front of her. "This creep was out there already. Now that he's made his presence known, he'll slip up and we'll catch him." He sat down next to Brinna. "It's obvious the body has been there for a month. No telling if it ever would have been discovered. Yet he came back to place the sign, send us the map, and taunt you."

Brinna gulped the hot — bad — coffee, ignoring the burn in her throat and working to target her thoughts on catching the bad guy, not on how Heather's parents would react to this news. She'd lost this one. She'd failed Heather and her family. The least she could do was hound the guy responsible and get him off the streets.

"He's got to be one of the sex offenders from my Wall of Slime," she said. "He's probably got an ax to grind and he's trying to get to me."

"That's a thought." Chuck rubbed his chin. "How many do you have up there now?"

"Twenty. I'll send you a list as soon as I get home."

"Any stick out in your mind?"

Brinna shook her head. "Nope, but they are all high risk."

"If it is one of them, that will make it easy, but I'll admit I'm not optimistic. I've got a couple pictures to show you." Chuck grabbed a file and opened it. He was about to lay down some photos when the door opened and the coroner's investigator poked his head inside.

"We've gathered the remains and are heading to the morgue. Do you need anything else before we leave?"

Chuck shook his head and the man left. Brinna heard the transmission engage as the coroner's van left the lot. Heather's gap-toothed grin tortured her thoughts.

"Earth to Brinna." Chuck tapped the table and pointed to pictures. "Study these, and check out the MO. We're running a computer search for similar cases."

Brinna blinked and turned her full attention to the photos.

"A serial killer?" Jack asked.

Brinna glanced up. He'd been so quiet she'd almost forgotten he was there.

Chuck nodded. "The way we found Heather matches two others in California so far — one in San Diego a year ago and another in San Luis Obispo two years ago. We've expanded our search parameters, widened them. If it is one of the twenty on your wall, we'll connect the dots quickly." He tapped a photo. "There is one unique aspect to the way he left the kid. Does anything seem familiar, Brinna?"

Brinna set down her coffee and picked up the photo.

"Heather was tied to a tree, most likely alive, and left to die," Chuck continued, "probably shortly after she disappeared. The killer left her and returned sometime yesterday or the day before to place the sign."

"And then he mailed you a note so you'd finally find her," Jack added.

Brinna's gaze bounced from the photo to Chuck and back again. "There is something here."

"What is it?" Jack asked.

Brinna blew out a breath. "The knot, or

loop, he used to secure her to the tree. When I was left in the desert twenty years ago, the kidnapper used the same kind of knot. It's called a perfection loop. Fishermen use it."

"That same knot was found in the other two cases I mentioned," Chuck said. "It's not a difficult or uncommon knot, but in these cases it's always used to secure a victim at some remote spot. This mutt doesn't kill his victims. He leaves them to die from exposure, starvation, or worse, animals."

"Are you saying that the same guy who grabbed Brinna twenty years ago is still out there snatching kids and has been doing that all these years?" Jack asked.

"It's a possibility." Chuck nodded.

"No, it's not," Brinna said.

"Why?" Jack and Chuck asked simultaneously.

"I'm surprised you don't know, Chuck. But maybe you don't because he was never officially charged with what he did to me." Brinna slid the photo across the table to him. "Nigel Pearce — the man they think kidnapped me — was killed ten years ago in a standoff with police. It can't be him; this has to be a copycat."

29

"Wall of Slime?" Jack asked as they passed the newest gleaming resort hotel on PCH in Huntington Beach. It was almost five in the morning before they left Chuck and headed back to Long Beach. Exhausted emotionally and physically, Brinna had turned the driving over to Jack.

"Yeah." Brinna yawned. "I have a wall in my home office dedicated to high-risk sex offenders, guys that mess with kids. It helps me to keep tabs on them. If I catch one anywhere he's not supposed to be, I recognize him right away."

Staring out at the landmarks they passed under a slowly brightening sky, Brinna wished it were Milo next to her and not Jack.

"I guess that's a good idea. You really think one of them is Heather's killer?"

Brinna closed her eyes and leaned her head against the window. "I don't know.

Who else would want to get to me like this? But I went over each of them with a fine-tooth comb after Heather disappeared. They all had solid alibis."

Brinna couldn't remember a time she'd felt so helpless. Some psycho nutbag was out there hunting kids to make a point with her. Milo would know how she was supposed to feel, how she was supposed to handle this. A madman just killed a little girl because of her. And he was hunting more. The thought felt like a punch to the gut.

Jack turned left from PCH onto Second Street as they entered Long Beach and started for the station.

"Hey, are you up for some more coffee?" Brinna asked.

"Yep, I'm hungry too. Hof's?" He yawned and Brinna wondered if she looked as bad as he did. His eyes were bloodshot, and bags weighed them down. Thick stubble darkened his chin.

At least I don't have to worry about stubble, she thought as she dragged a hand across her chin. In spite of the desire to talk to Milo and not Jack, Brinna considered O'Reilly and admitted that he had behaved like a partner at Crystal Cove. There was light in his eyes while they talked to Chuck, nothing creepy.

"Yeah, Hof's is good."

Jack parked at Hof's Hut, a chain restaurant with locations all over the city. It was a favorite with cops because it served good food and stayed open twenty-four hours.

"Wow," Jack said as they walked to the entrance, "I can see it's going to take time to get used to these hours again." He twisted and stretched.

Brinna gave an agreeing grunt. The vest and gun belt felt like cement at this time of the morning. A fleeting picture of Mr. and Mrs. Bailey and a thought about the news that would greet them sometime today tempered Brinna's feeling of discomfort. Swallowing a lump, she heard Milo's words: *"The only salve for the family of the victim is justice. Catch the bad guy."*

The early shift waitress, Molly, had her hands behind her back, tying her apron, as Brinna and Jack walked in. She pointed to the dining room with her chin. "Anywhere you like." The restaurant was empty but for a couple of old guys at the counter.

Brinna yawned again as she slid into the booth and squirmed in the seat to get comfortable, wishing she could shed her belt. Morning breakfast smells stirred her stomach and Brinna realized she was very

200

hungry. The microwave dinner she'd eaten before shift seemed days ago.

"Good morning, Brin. I see you have a new partner." Molly brought coffee and menus.

"Yeah. Molly, Jack; Jack, Molly." Brinna grabbed her coffee as soon as the cup was full, needing a flavorful caffeine jolt after the bitter dishwater taste of the FBI coffee.

"I'll give you guys a few minutes." The waitress flashed Jack a toothy smile and returned to the kitchen.

"You already know what you want?" Jack asked as he opened his menu.

"Yep. I like the plain buttermilk pancakes here. I always get them." She gulped her coffee and then refilled her cup from the carafe Molly had left.

"Pancakes sound good." He closed the menu and yawned, then poured himself some coffee. "You know, the first thing you learn when you make it to homicide is not to let any cases get under your skin. Don't take this thing personally."

"Of course it's personal. He left the note for me." Brinna shot him an irritated glance.

He peered down his nose at her, his eyes still normal, not creepy. "It's not personal. This nut doesn't need you or what you do to be a killer. He's chosen to thumb his nose your direction. It could have been anyone in a blue suit."

"I'm lucky, then?" Brinna responded bitterly.

Jack hiked his shoulders and studied his coffee, saying nothing for a minute. "Maybe you were a target because of your high profile. But I'd bet this guy wants to bait a cop — any cop. He kills kids; he's evil. You can't blame yourself for the evil in the world." Jack sat back in the booth, scrunched up a napkin in his hand. His eyes took on a faraway stare.

"Milo says that. He also says good cops are the antidote for evil. Especially when someone is murdered. We're the last voice a dead victim has."

"Milo?" Jack focused on Brinna, seemingly coming back to the here and now.

"Yeah, he's the cop who rescued me twenty years ago. He's retired now, but when he was on the job, he taught me a lot."

"Even good cops lose one now and then. We fight a war that can't be won. The best we can hope for is a draw."

"And Maggie calls me a glass-is-half-empty person. I won't settle for a draw. I want to win every time."

Jack shot her a glance that Brinna felt meant he thought she deluded herself.

Silence reigned at the table until Molly returned to take their orders. When the waitress left them again, Jack broke the silence. "Mind if I ask you a question?"

"Nope, shoot."

"Brinna is an interesting name. Is there some special meaning to it?"

The question couldn't have surprised Brinna more if it had been an invitation to a date. She stuttered, laughed, and turned away with nervousness. "No, other than it's a testament to how screwed up my family is. My dad is a full-blooded Italian who believes boy children are a sign of his virility. He was determined his firstborn would be a boy. He picked out the name Brian, painted my room blue, and refused to believe a girl was possible."

"And then he had a girl."

Brinna nodded. "My parents never even considered girl names. It took them three days to name me. All they did was switch the *N* and the *A* and add an extra *N* to name me Brinna. Two years later he got his boy and named my brother Brian." She stopped, suddenly uncomfortable talking about herself.

Jack smiled. "It's a conversation piece."

Brinna shrugged. "I've always called it my insurance."

"Insurance?"

"Yep. I'm absolutely positive I wasn't adopted because my parents never would have picked a girl." She gulped her coffee, feeling like an idiot for revealing so much to a stranger. A stranger she wasn't even sure she liked.

Molly's return with their breakfast eased her angst. As soon as her plate was in front of her, Brinna slathered on butter, poured some syrup, and dug in.

She was halfway through her stack when she decided to turn the tables and poke. "Since we're being inquisitive, why'd you ask to leave homicide?"

Jack stared at her a moment, and at first she didn't think he'd answer. Finally he cleared his throat. "Uh, let's see," he began, looking at Brinna like a person in pain but dealing with it. "After my wife, uh . . . passed, I developed queasiness when it came to the bodies. Lieutenant Hoffman let me work a desk job for a bit, but it wasn't permanent."

He blew out a breath and continued. "I didn't want to go back to work as a homicide investigator. I didn't want to be preached to by Ben Carney. I needed a change. Patrol seemed like the place."

"Ben *is* a preacher. He says you also used

to be a Christian."

Jack grunted and rubbed the back of his neck. "Used to be. I can't believe in a God who'd take my wife away like he did. She didn't deserve that." His eyes misted.

Brinna turned away. "We agree on something. I can't believe in a God who lets innocent kids like Heather suffer." For a moment, she thought maybe this was her chance to ask him about her fear that he had a death wish. But it wasn't a topic she wanted to get into right then. Instead, she asked, "Did Heather's body bother you?"

Jack stared at Brinna before he answered. "No." He shook his head slowly as if the answer surprised him. "No, not that way, it didn't."

"Maybe you were right, then; maybe patrol is better for you. Your wife got hit by a drunk driver, didn't she?"

"Yes, she did." Jack's fork stopped halfway to his mouth; then he put it on his plate. "His sentencing is less than two weeks away."

Brinna didn't miss the anger flashing across his eyes and the tightness of his jawline. "I read about it. First-time offender. He'll probably get five years. Bet that ticks you off."

Jack grunted and nodded, slopping more

coffee into his cup. "You got that right. The puke deserves the death penalty."

"At least you have closure. You know he'll be punished and pay for the crime he committed. Even if the punishment doesn't fit the crime."

"That's supposed to be consolation?" Though his eyes burned with anger, Brinna liked it much better than when they were creepy.

"Sure. They never caught the guy who kidnapped me. They think Pearce was good for it, but I couldn't ID him. Other kids are found dead, no one is ever caught, parents never get closure, and perpetrators aren't punished. If I did believe in God, that would be one conversation I'd have with him."

"God." Jack spit the word out and reclined against the booth. "Like I said, this is a perfect example of why there is no God. The wicked get away with stuff and the innocent, like Vicki and Heather, pay the ultimate price."

"So why give up the fight?"

"What?" Jack stared at Brinna, his eyes now bright with surprise.

"You left homicide. Everyone says you're burnt out. Why quit?" Brinna toyed with her coffee cup. "A kid like Heather, she's just as important to her parents as Vicki was to you. In homicide you could help find them justice, yet you want to quit. I don't get it."

"I'm not a quitter," Jack said through gritted teeth. "It's just sometimes, when there is nothing to go home to, I think, what is the point? We are fighting a losing battle — admit it."

"There you lose me. Maybe we don't catch them all and maybe I can't save them all, but I owe every one of them the effort. I may not be a Christian, but I agree with your preaching partner, Ben. We have to fight the good fight. If Milo had given up on me, I'd be dead in the desert. Guys like him, you, me — we owe it to the innocent to keep fighting."

Jack said nothing, just stared. After a minute he looked away. "Sounds like you're trying to pass an oral board. You really believe all that?"

Brinna pushed her finished plate away and took a final swig of coffee. "I don't care if you think it's corny. It's why I'm a cop. And it's why I'll catch the guy who killed Heather or die trying."

Molly's return interrupted Jack's response. They paid their bill and left.

They made the drive to the station in silence. Brinna decided she could probably stand a couple of weeks with Jack if he left the creepy eyes at home.

30

Nigel wandered the beach, his camera always at the ready. He wondered if the dog cop had gotten his message. He'd seen nothing in the paper. But she was still being hounded about shooting someone, and that was a good thing. The last article said that the dead kid's lawyer not only wanted the dog cop fired, but serving time.

The thought of the dog cop in prison made Nigel smile.

He wanted to be sure she got the first message before he sent the next. The next message — the next Special Girl — needed to be stupendous. Something that would make everyone stand up and take notice.

He smiled, finding amusement in the thought that he'd never really wanted attention until he learned of the dog cop. He was smart, very able to vanish when circumstances required he disappear, and he'd been proficient at hiding for years. But the knowledge that he shared a special anniversary with someone changed everything.

He took a picture of some children building sand castles near the surf and quickly put the camera away to avoid the inquiring gaze of a vigilant mom. Nigel sauntered to the pier. There he was able to snap a lot of photos, making it appear like he was only interested in the sand and surf.

He'd be patient. He had time. *Hope you don't think I've given up, Dog Cop. I never give up.*

31

Brinna stopped by the house to pick up Hero, then headed for the beach, striving to keep sorrow from engulfing her. *I need some normalcy,* she thought. The only normal family she knew were the DiSantos. Tony would be either at the kayak rental kiosk or nearby. Brinna needed the loquacious Italian and his family to help mitigate the misery she felt.

The weather had cooled somewhat, but it was still going to be a hot day. With everything that weighed on her mind, it would be difficult to sleep under the best of circumstances.

She parked near the kayak outfitter and fed the meter. Hero bounded out of the truck, full of K-9 energy. Brinna threw a ball for him several times as she walked across the sand. As she'd hoped, Tony was there with a big bonus — both of his granddaughters. Tony leaned against the rental

211

kiosk counter. In front of him, running in and out of the small waves, huge smiles on their faces, were Carla and Bella.

"Hey, Tony, my good friend," Brinna called out. "You loafing?"

Tony turned and grinned. He brushed sand off his hands and waved. "Brinna, my good friend. I'm babysitting."

Hero bounded up to him, tail wagging. The man reciprocated by tumbling with the dog onto the sand in playful roughhouse, much to the delight of the two little girls, who squealed as they watched their grandpa and the dog.

After satisfying Hero with some scratching, Tony pulled a couple of beach chairs from the kiosk, and they sat while Hero trotted to the surf to play with the twins. He sat patiently while they tried to bury him with sand, getting up every once in a while to shake and spread sand everywhere, bringing screams of laughter from the girls.

Brinna watched the two girls and Hero play. "How do you tell them apart?"

Tony laughed. "They are bookends. My joy."

"Have you been training them how to respond to strangers?"

"You bet. We go over and over it. Never, ever speak to strangers, I tell them." He

212

shook his finger. "And if a stranger touches either one of you, scream, I say. That Carla, she's got quite a yell."

"Good." Brinna leaned back on her elbows and relaxed, happy that in this small circle, all was right in the world.

32

"You want to quit."

"We owe it to the innocent to keep fighting."

"At least you have closure."

"A kid like Heather, she's just as important to her parents as Vicki was to you."

Words and images from the night before replayed in Jack's mind as if they were a collage on a DVD in a continuous loop. He lay on the couch, a fan blowing in his face, and stared at the ceiling, jarred to the core not only by Brinna's words but also by his own.

"You can't blame yourself for the evil in the world."

How those words had come out without his even thinking about them was a mystery. The Bible preached good versus evil. He didn't believe that stuff anymore, did he? He'd tried to ease Brinna's angst. She clearly blamed herself for the little girl's death. Why did he care?

The thing was, she'd sounded so much like he used to sound before Vicki died that it scared him.

Jack stood and walked to the bedroom. Opening the door, he stared into the room that was just as Vicki had left it one year ago. The bed was made; the book she'd bought on natural childbirth sat on her nightstand, along with a jar of cream she'd been using on her belly.

"Everything stopped when you left me," he whispered. "How can I ever be the same man I was?"

He knew better than Brinna did what the Baileys would feel when they heard the news about their daughter.

"She accused me of being a quitter. I'm not. It just hurts so much. . . ." He leaned against the doorjamb and tears dripped down his face. "Maybe the secret is going back to the job and working it like Caruso, fighting a losing fight but being in denial about it."

He knew that if Vicki were alive, they'd be on their knees in prayer about now. Jack hit his forehead with his palms, refusing to go there, refusing to admit there was a God to pray to. Instead he steered his thoughts to how good it had felt to be a cop for a short while. He'd functioned with his peers at the crime scene. Maybe it would be possible to bury himself in his work.

Yawning, he walked to the living room and lay down on the couch again.

The little girl. He'd studied the sad, decomposed body like he was a cop and not a broken shell of a man grieving his wife and daughter. There, in the harsh lights of a forensic team, he hadn't just sleepwalked through pain; he'd been involved.

The girl's murder stirred more than a little curiosity in Jack. The urge to hunt the killer bubbled up in the recesses of his mind and he wondered if he should encourage it. All he'd initially wanted out of this patrol gig was survival for two weeks. He'd hung on to his empty life for a year. What did another week and a half matter?

His eyelids were heavy. As he faded to sleep, he decided working patrol would be a good thing if it left him this exhausted every day.

For the first time in a year, Jack slipped into a deep, dreamless sleep.

Brinna shared snacks with Tony and the girls and napped for a bit on the beach before admitting she needed to go home and sleep in her own bed for a couple of hours before work. Fatigue would help her sleep despite the heat. She loaded Hero up, bade the DiSantos good-bye, and directed her truck home.

Her mood was mellow and relaxed until she reached her driveway and saw a familiar sedan at the curb. After pulling into the drive, the uneasiness she felt was confirmed. Her mother sat on the porch.

Sighing, Brinna patted Hero's head and parked. She'd been ignoring her mom's e-mail messages.

"Guess I can't avoid her forever," she told Hero. "I bet she wants to talk about the shooting mess." *I'm just not sure I can deal with my mother with Heather on my mind. When it rains, it sure does pour.*

She opened the door and let Hero out first. The dog bounded out to say hello to Rose Caruso. Brinna studied her mom for a minute before following the dog.

Rose never left the house without being carefully dressed and made-up. Today, she was more than a little disheveled. Her tan slacks were wrinkled, and perspiration ovals showed under the arms of her light-colored blouse.

Rose was dark-haired, like Brinna, but green-eyed and a little thick in the hips. She seemed grayer than the last time Brinna had seen her, and her hair wasn't as perfectly coiffed as usual. Brinna wondered if newspaper reporters had been bugging her mom, not only about the shooting but about the anniversary.

"Hi, Mom." Brinna stepped onto the porch to give her mom a hug.

"I've been trying to reach you for days." Rose's voice was clipped, tense.

"I know; sorry. I've been kind of busy. What's up?"

"It's your father. He's in the hospital. Brinna, he's dying."

33

"He's lived in a bottle for twenty years; what did he expect?" Brinna turned away from her mother and shoved a glass under the tap for water, all the while stalling, wondering what it was she was supposed to feel.

"A little more compassion, Brin. He is your father." Rose sat on the couch, head in her hands.

Brinna carried two glasses of water to the living room and gave one to her mother before sitting down in the chair across from the couch. "But are you surprised?" she asked.

Rose looked up, pain etched in her eyes. "Of course it's a shock. I've been praying he'd change before it got too late."

Brinna bit her lip. "Let's face it. The bottle has always been more important to him than us."

Rose shook her head. "I've seen you show so much care and tenderness for children, strangers. Don't you have any to spare for your father?"

"What do you want me to say?" Brinna bristled, thinking, *All I've ever really known is an angry, drunk father.* "For a short time he was a father to Brian, but he's never been a father to me. Once he climbed into the bottle, he wasn't much of anything."

"That day destroyed him." Rose choked back a sob. "He never forgave himself. Can't you forgive him?"

She wiped her eyes with one hand and Brinna saw the struggle for composure. *That day* hung between them, and Brinna had no words.

"Unforgiveness will destroy you," Rose said after a minute. She stood and hugged her arms to her chest. "The two of you are peas in a pod. He hides in a bottle and you hide in your job. Will you consider this from outside the safety of your uniform?"

Brinna blew out a breath and shook her head, choosing to ignore the peas-in-a-pod remark. *I'm nothing like my father.*

"I don't blame Dad for my kidnapping. I never did. The only person to blame is the kidnapper. The only thing I blame Dad for is not being a dad." She chugged her water and willed herself to stay seated. "What about Brian? Is he coming home?"

Regaining her composure, Rose crossed her arms. "He's flying in this weekend. Will you at least come with him and visit your father?"

Brinna closed her eyes and sighed. "There's so much going on in my life right now." She opened her eyes to find Rose staring at her and felt slapped by the grief and pain reflected in the gaze. Guilt at the attempt to avoid her dad swelled, and she gave up. "When Brian gets here, I'll go with him, okay?"

Rose nodded, then smoothed her blouse. "Thank you. It will mean a lot."

Brinna sat on the porch for a long time after her mother left. Hero dozed at her feet. After trying to call Milo and getting his voice mail, she brought a tall glass of iced tea outside and relaxed in her rocker. Sleep was impossible now. Her mother could make her feel guilty and sappy all at the same time. But her thoughts revolved around the fact that her father was dying and she felt nothing.

34

"So how are you doing with O'Reilly?" Sergeant Rodriguez asked as Brinna and Hero jogged onto the K-9 training field early Wednesday afternoon. After Hero's training ended, Brinna would go into service and finish out her shift.

Brinna shrugged. She'd anticipated the question and still struggled with how much to tell her sergeant. "So far, aside from the fact that neither one of us wanted the assignment, no problems. But it's only been two days. Yesterday we were tied up with Heather all night. We haven't gotten in much patrol time."

"Sorry about Heather. Chuck told me what happened. He wants to keep it all under wraps as long as possible so no panic starts."

"I agree with him to a point. I don't want the investigation to be compromised, but I think parents need to know there's a danger.

This guy has already proved he'll kill." The fact that he chose to kill because of her was what galled her all the more.

Janet nodded. "Chuck said he'd meet with our homicide and talk about how to handle the press angle. He doesn't want the press to sensationalize things and give the suspect who taunted you the attention he apparently wants." She knelt down and patted Hero. "Besides, no one knows how releasing your connection to this taunt will affect all the shooting stories."

"Tell me about it," Brinna agreed grimly. "Shockley is doing her best to paint me as a little Hitler. She'll probably try to pin Heather's murder on me."

"Not even Shockley could make that charge. Besides, the shooting review board will convene soon."

"Really?" Brinna faced Janet as her stomach did flip-flops. "Have you heard something?"

"Just a rumor that the chief wants it to happen right away. He believes official findings will neutralize Shockley."

"I hope so." Brinna sighed and turned to the training field, but Janet stopped her.

"By the way, I got a memo from Officer Nugent. He wants me to write up a commendation for you."

Brinna frowned; she rarely worked with the day patrol officer. "For what?"

"Apparently you pulled some guy out of a bathtub, saved his life."

"The girlfriend beater? I just did what I had to do. It wasn't heroic or anything. Anyone would have done it."

Janet laughed. "I'm not sure about that."

Brinna waved off the idea of a commendation. "What do you want me to do with O'Reilly tonight? I normally flex on Wednesdays and leave a little early. Today I'm really tired."

"You think he's up to working by himself? Klein tells me there's no one else to put him with."

Chewing on a thumbnail, Brinna considered what she'd debated all day telling Janet — that she feared Jack had a death wish. Jack would be yanked from patrol in a heartbeat. If she was wrong, she'd be doing him a huge disservice. But if she was right . . .

After a pause, she held Janet's gaze. "I'm not sure. Like I said, we haven't had much patrol time."

"I'll approve overtime if you want to finish out the shift."

"If I don't collapse, I will." *I'd rather be working instead of dealing with the circus that seems to be going on in my personal life,* she thought grimly.

"Great. Let's go train."

For the next couple of hours, Brinna concentrated only on Hero, working hard to put her exhaustion, Heather, and her own father's situation out of her mind. She ran her dog through an agility course, worked on some tracking drills, and let him run around with a few patrol dogs.

"He's doing great," Pops Davis, a senior K-9 officer, commented to Brinna as they watched Hero handle a timed run of the agility course.

Brinna beamed. Pops had been one of the strongest voices who fought Hero's addition to the team tooth and nail. Very old-school, Pops's objections were different from a lot of other officers'. Most just wanted the money to go elsewhere. Pops thought women were too soft to work with dogs. He'd hated the fact that Hero specialized in search and rescue. It felt great to win him over to her side.

"Thanks, Pops. That means a lot, coming from you."

The grizzled old cop rubbed his chin. "I know I was rough on him at first, but he has more than pulled his weight. So have you. Some old dogs can learn new tricks."

"Glad to hear it." Brinna laughed, feeling a lightness she hadn't felt in a long time. She showed Davis the stopwatch. "Hero just beat his best time on the course by fifteen seconds."

Pops nodded approval and went back to his dog and bite training. Brinna gave Hero his treats and some water. Driving home to drop him off before her shift, she realized how much she missed working an entire shift with her four-legged friend. But she only had a week and a half left to go with O'Reilly.

A fear nagged. What if the circus surrounding the shooting hadn't abated by then? That the brass wanted to hurry the shooting review board to counter Shockley's shrill cries of misconduct was a small bright spot.

O'Reilly himself was another worry. What if he did want to take a bullet? She'd had the chance to address the issue yesterday at Hof's but chickened out.

At home she fed Hero, then climbed back in her truck and headed for the station. Clear skies, pleasantly warm temps. Brinna glanced at the ocean. *Now would be a great time for a long, long kayak paddle, way out in the middle of the ocean . . . away from phones, newspapers, money-hungry lawyers,*

and vicious child killers, she thought wistfully.

35

Jack sat in the squad room listening to the banter going on around him without joining in. The topics of conversation were similar to ones that would have bounced around six years ago. Guys talked about last night's difficult arrest, recounted funny incidents, or complained about something going on in the department.

He still felt like a fish out of water. But he'd slept so well — in spite of the fact that he hadn't gotten to bed until 6 a.m. — that the memories didn't seem to be screaming so loud. And Caruso's drive to be a savior to every missing kid lingered in his thoughts. Even though he'd tried to make her feel corny, her mission impressed him. It made him yearn for the same kind of drive to return to him. Could he ever really be the same cop he'd been six years ago?

"O'Reilly."

Jack raised his head when Klein called his

name. "Sir?"

"Your partner called. She's en route from K-9 training and she'll meet you at the back steps." Klein started to turn away, then stopped. "You and her getting along okay?"

Jack nodded and Klein left the room. He knew the sergeant would probably ask Brinna the same thing, and he wondered what she would say.

Well, the arrangement with Caruso wasn't permanent. Sentencing or no sentencing, this partnership was only for another week and a half. Caruso might be an okay cop, with a lot of ambition he admired, but he didn't have a reason to get close — and certainly no reason to care about her work or life. If she wanted to take every missing kid to heart, it was her funeral.

Brinna pulled into the PD lot and parked her truck. She'd left her Explorer at home, seeing no reason to drive it if she didn't have Hero. She hoped O'Reilly at least thought to find them a good ride.

Her partner waited where she'd wanted to meet him. "I got us a car," Jack said, stepping down to meet her. He pointed to a black-and-white.

"Great. Sorry I'm late. I didn't factor in

the time it would take to drop Hero off at home."

"No biggie." Jack climbed into the driver's seat and popped the trunk.

Brinna stowed her kit and took the passenger seat. She noticed Jack already had the log-in screen filled out, and she pushed Send, hoping for a quiet radio. *Let's see if we get some patrol time in and how he handles it. What kind of patrol cop is he, anyway?*

Sighing, Brinna couldn't relax. She was just too tired. It wouldn't do for the trainer to fall asleep on the trainee. Thinking about Jack as a trainee took her thoughts back to the night before. He'd been a partner for a bit. She wondered what mood he'd be in tonight and what she'd see — lifeless eyes or cop eyes.

"Did you sleep better today?" she asked.

Jack grunted. "Actually, I did. Slept until about two thirty. What about you? I hope you didn't let that kid eat you up."

"I just got a couple hours. Lots going on in my life right now besides Heather." She rolled down her window and turned off the air conditioner vent. Though the fresh air was warm, it made her feel more alert.

Jack seemed to start to say something, then stopped. He slowed to standard patrol speed, and Brinna noted that his eyes were roving the street. The car stayed silent until the first radio call.

As they rolled through quiet residential streets, Brinna wondered if Jack would want to jump on anything. Technically, the driver ran the unit, deciding when to answer calls and when to make traffic or subject stops.

When the radio went quiet, guys had different ways of spending their free patrol time. Some liked to try and snoop, working known dope locations. Others liked to work traffic, and still others prowled streets and alleys checking for stolen cars or miscellaneous illegal activity.

Brinna knew she'd be checking out pedophiles from her Wall of Slime and going over every bit of Heather's investigation. She'd faxed the list of names to Chuck, and he'd promised her he'd scrutinize each one. All she could do was wait for him to call, and Brinna hated waiting.

Jack drove through the roughest section of town, she noted. *So he's not afraid to work . . . or is it something else?*

"Can I ask you a question?" Brinna decided not to put off a direct frontal approach any longer.

"What?"

"The other night, when you rushed the

stolen car, were you trying to get yourself killed?"

Jack stomped the brakes, pulled the car to the right, and stopped at the curb. "Is that what you think?"

Brinna shrugged. "I'm just asking. Car wasn't clear; kid could have had a gun. What should I think?"

"Have you run around telling everyone this theory of yours?" He turned to face her, left elbow up over the steering wheel.

"No. I'm the one working with you, so I'm asking for my information." She held his angry gaze, trying to read his thoughts. She knew his concern. All she had to do was mention she thought he had a death wish and he'd be bounced to the department shrink and out of patrol.

Jack blew out a breath. "Maybe at first that thought crossed my mind. At the domestic violence call. I thought it might be easy to get shot out here. But the thought just crossed my mind; it didn't take up residence." He glared at her for a moment, then turned away.

She had the feeling he wasn't finished, so she stayed quiet. After a minute he spoke again.

"As to the victor . . . well, I wanted a fight." He faced forward and sat back in his seat. "I was angry, thinking about Bridges, the guy who killed my wife. I wanted to beat something or someone, pretend it was Bridges."

Sighing, Brinna relaxed. "Okay. Thanks. That I can understand."

"Can you?" Jack's forehead scrunched. "Can you really understand? I fantasize about killing Bridges all the time." He shifted in his seat and stared out the window.

"I fantasize about killing every creep who hurts a kid. Join the club." She shrugged when he shot her a surprised expression.

They were both silent for a minute. Then Jack laughed. Brinna's jaw went slack with shock. He rarely smiled, and this was the first laugh she'd heard.

"What's funny?" she asked.

"You trying to tell me I'm normal."

"I'm not a psychiatrist, so whether you're normal or not is not my call. I just think we care. We hate to see injustice or the innocent taken advantage of. I consider myself a good judge of character. You worry me for a lot of reasons. That you'd take the law into your own hands is not one of them."

He sighed and pulled back into traffic to resume patrol. "What makes you think I won't act out on my fantasy and kill

233

Bridges?"

Brinna shook her head. "Sad, burnt out, and hurt, you're still a cop. It would completely wipe out sixteen years of being a good guy if you went after Bridges. I'd never act out on any of my fantasies because I have faith in the justice system, flawed as it is. Would your wife have married a man who would take the law into his own hands?"

36

Jack worked hard to regain some semblance of patrol rhythm. Though his body was well rested, his emotions were all over the map. He felt like a drunk trying to walk a straight line. Brinna's question about whether he had a death wish came out of the blue and hit him hard. Confessing to her that it wasn't really his own death he wanted but Bridges's surprised him.

For months I've thought of nothing else but taking care of Bridges. I've lived for the sentencing and a clear shot at him, he thought. Brinna didn't think he would do what he fantasized about.

Just a little over a week until the day. He tightened his grip on the steering wheel, angry at the thought of Bridges's future. It was like ripping the scab off a raw wound. Bridges had a future. And it galled Jack that Brinna was probably right. He didn't think he could kill Bridges any more than she did.

Vicki wouldn't have looked twice at a man who acted like judge, jury, and executioner.

The realization freed him in a way. Maybe the scab was gone and the wound raw, but opening it let some poison out. The pressure had stopped building. Jack felt tension release in his neck and shoulders. It was as if a test deadline had just been removed from his day planner.

He decided to take a flying leap at letting the job consume him and run the unit like he would have six years ago. His partner was still a paradox to him. On one hand, he didn't want to get close to Caruso. On the other, he had the feeling they could do some great work together.

He and Brinna made a few traffic stops, arrested a drunk driver, and Jack watched his uneasiness and anger evaporate. He was a cop again, and it felt great.

"Haven't seen you up here in a blue suit in a while," Pettis, one of the jailers, said when Jack dropped off his prisoner.

"Yeah, it's been a while." Jack took his cuffs from the man.

"Sorry to hear about your wife. That has to be rough."

"Yeah, it is." Jack slipped his cuffs into the cuff case on his belt and waited for the depression curtain to descend at the mention of Vicki. His chest tightened with a familiar tightness, but it wasn't suffocating.

"You done with homicide?" Pettis asked.

Jack shrugged, surprised by the question and by the fact that he wasn't upset at the idea of being done. *Am I?* he thought as he struggled for an answer. "I needed a break" were the words that finally came to him as he stepped into the elevator.

"Good luck, whatever you decide." Pettis gave a mock salute as the door closed.

His partner sat in the break room, sipping coffee.

Jack slipped coins into a machine and bought a cup as well. "I'm finished. You ready to go back to work?"

"Sure." She stood, drained her coffee, and tossed the cup.

Jack took his coffee with him. It was Brinna's turn to drive, so he could take his in the car.

As she pulled out of the lot, Jack fidgeted, deciding to be talkative. "I've got a question for you." He didn't turn her way but kept his gaze out the passenger window.

"I guess I owe you one," she said. "You answered mine."

"Thanks." Jack took a deep breath and dived in. "Have you ever lost someone close to you?"

"You mean to death?"

"Yeah."

"No, I haven't," she said, and Jack thought maybe she had more to say.

"You haven't, but . . . ?" He turned to watch her and saw her frown in the light of the car computer.

"But what?"

"It just sounded like you wanted to say more."

"I, uh . . . well, I found out today my dad has liver cancer. He's dying."

"Wow, sorry to hear that."

Jack saw her shrug in the semidarkness, but she didn't turn his way.

"The thing is," she said, "we're not close. He really hasn't been a father to me. He's been a mean drunk ever since I can remember."

"He's still your father."

"That's what my mom said." She gave what sounded to Jack like a mirthless chuckle. "For as long as my father's been drunk, my mother's been praying for him. She swears God can change a person, turn their life around, make them stronger. I think having a crutch like God only makes a person weaker."

"I used to be that way." Jack sucked down some coffee, anger pricking him like a hype's needle. "Your mom believes God will change your father's heart, get him off the bottle, make him a better man, and their life will become all hearts and flowers." He swallowed back the bitter taste in his mouth.

"Yep." Brinna nodded. "My mom's a true believer. Prayer changes everything."

Everything but death, Jack thought, fist clenched around the end of his baton. "I was raised in the church. Vicki and I were both good, faithful. I don't understand why she had to die." He crumpled his empty coffee cup in his hand and stared out the window.

"I asked Ben, your old partner, about that once. I mean, about why good people get murdered or why I was rescued when so many innocent kids are not so lucky."

"What'd he say?"

"Something about God being in control, that believers must trust he's got their best in mind even when something bad happens. I didn't get it all."

"I've heard that enough to make me puke. Vicki believed that as well. How could it be best in anyone's mind that she be killed by a drunk driver?" Jack said bitterly.

"I'm with you. But my mom believes that Christians go to heaven when they die. What do you think about life after death?"

239

Jack stared at his partner while he processed her question. In all his grieving over Vicki's death, he'd worked to believe she was in a better place, but if there was no God and no heaven, where was she?

"I don't know," he said lamely, his good mood evaporating like smoke in a strong wind. He brooded, keeping quiet until the shift mercifully came to an end.

Jack threw his kit on the kitchen floor and turned on the faucet. He held his breath and stuck his head under the tap, letting the cool water run over his face and trickle down his back.

After a few minutes he brought his head out from under the water and shook like a dog, sending water all over the kitchen and not caring.

God just keeps coming back into this, he thought. *Caruso and her mom, my own mom and her constant preaching, Ben, and now heaven. God, heaven — you can't have one without the other.*

He leaned against the sink and stared at the ceiling. "God, if you're up there, why did you take her away?" He'd asked the question a million times before and knew there would be no answer.

He'd asked his mother the same question,

and when she couldn't answer it, he told her not to bother praying for him. But he knew she was on her knees every day praying he'd come to his senses.

Jack grabbed a towel from a pile of clean laundry in the dining room and rubbed his head dry. Memories of all the messages he'd heard through his life about the mystery of God's will and the privilege of spending eternity in his presence popped into his consciousness.

"We see through a glass, darkly." The verse surprised him. He hadn't picked up a Bible in a year, yet he knew the phrase came from the New Testament. He knew it went on to say that one day everything would be clear. One day believers would *know* without a shadow of a doubt, and one day they would be in the presence of God.

Where does my denial of God put Vicki?

Jack's head hurt and he grabbed a bottle of aspirin. Shaking out three tablets, he swallowed them without water.

Too many questions, not enough answers. All I can do is take one step at a time.

When the phone rang, he ignored it, heading for the shower. The answering machine picked up as he stepped into the shower. He heard his mother's voice imploring him to answer the phone.

"I'm not ready, Mom; I'm not," he said to the pounding water. "Maybe I'm getting there, but I'm just not ready today."

He closed the shower door to shut out the sound and ducked under a strong stream of cold water.

37

Thursday night was the end of the work-week for Jack and Brinna. Their days off were Friday, Saturday, and Sunday. As she got ready to leave, Hero watching her every move, Brinna wondered what kind of partner the last day of the workweek would bring — the quiet, dead-eyed Jack or the Jack who acted like a concerned partner and competent cop.

"That's what I like about this job, Hero — every day an adventure. I certainly hope that when next week is over, I can go back to working with you. You're easy. All you require are treats and potty breaks."

She hugged the dog good-bye and left for work. During the short drive, she thought about her afternoon conversation with Chuck.

"Sorry, none of the guys from your Wall of Slime are a match," he'd informed her. "They all come out clean as far as Heather is concerned, and I can't connect any of them to the other cases I mentioned."

"Thanks for trying. I was afraid you wouldn't have any luck."

"Maybe we're after an old cellmate. Whoever killed Heather must have known Pearce somewhat in order to follow his MO so closely."

Brinna sighed. "But he's been dead for ten years. Why would a copycat surface after so long? And as I recall, Pearce never did much jail time. If he had a cellmate he shared his technique with, why all of a sudden decide to pick on me?"

"Maybe the publicity you're getting because of the shooting gave the creep a bright idea. Based on the cases we've tied together, this guy's a traveler, maybe a transient. It's possible he ended up in Long Beach just in time for your headlines."

"Lucky me. They all end up in Long Beach sooner or later, where the sewer meets the sea."

"Look at the bright side —" Chuck began.

Brinna cut him off. "There's a bright side to this?"

"Yep. He's a traveler, but right now he's here in our backyard. We have a chance to stomp him like the roach he is."

"I hope you're right, and I certainly hope

we stomp him before anyone else gets hurt."

"We will. I'll fill you in when we come across any names."

"Thanks."

Was Chuck right? she wondered. Did they have the best chance to catch this creep now? Whatever the odds, Brinna planned on doing her best to catch him, with Jack as a partner or not.

The night started slowly. Time felt as though it limped along. Brinna drove first, and she cruised neighborhoods near where her Wall of Slime inductees lived. Warm summer nights always brought kids out to play and escape the heat of un-air-conditioned houses and apartments. The possibility existed that she'd find a creep out observing some youngsters, thereby creating an excuse to stop and talk to him.

"Is there anything or anyone in particular you're after right now?" Jack asked.

"No, just looking." She cast a glance her partner's way. He seemed to be a normal man tonight, so she decided to take advantage. "I spoke to Chuck today. He thinks we might be on the hunt for an old cellmate of Nigel's."

"None of the guys on your — what do you call it?"

"Wall of Slime."

"That's it. None of them panned out?"

"No. Can't tie any of them to —"

The radio beeped its emergency tune. "4-Frank-8, copy a call on your MDT, ASAP."

Brinna waited for Jack to read her the call. "Well?" she asked after he stayed silent for a long moment.

"Klein wants us to meet him out east." Jack read off an address on Conquista Avenue.

"What is it?"

"All it says is assist him with an unknown trouble call."

Brinna held Jack's gaze for a moment. His bewildered expression mirrored what she felt.

She made her way to the address. When she turned onto the street, nothing she saw put her at ease. Neighbors milled on the sidewalk, some talking to officers. Four East Division black-and-whites plus one sergeant's unit lined the street in front of the dispatch address.

"What in the world is the mystery?" Brinna asked, mostly to herself.

Jack answered. "Let's go find out."

They got out of the unit and walked to the front door. Klein opened the door before Brinna could knock. Sobbing resonated from somewhere inside the house, and Brinna's stomach tightened.

"Thanks for getting here so fast," Klein said. He motioned them inside. It was a typical East Long Beach tract home. A short entryway led to a small living room. There a woman sat on a couch crying; a man held her shoulders and spoke in low tones.

"Let's go to the back bedroom." Klein led them past the couple and into what was obviously a child's room. Brinna felt her stomach drop as if she'd just stepped off a ledge and was free-falling into a bottomless abyss.

The small bed, decorated in Little Mermaid bedding, was empty but mussed as if it had been slept in. There on the pillow, which should have held a young girl's head, was a cardboard sign with a note written in red block letters:

OFFICER CARUSO:
    ANOTHER CHILD, ANOTHER CHANCE.
    CATCH ME IF YOU CAN.

38

"I was in the communications center when the call came in," Klein explained. "I've tried to keep it quiet because I didn't want the press everywhere. But this will get out, Caruso."

"I don't care about the press and me. I care about finding the little girl. What's her name?"

"Jessica Blake. She's seven." Klein blew out a breath. "Parents put her to bed at eight thirty. Dad thought he heard something around eleven but didn't come check until eleven thirty. He found the note."

"Entry?" Jack asked.

Klein walked into the kitchen. "Lock picked. Lab tech is en route for prints." He pointed at the kitchen door. "He came in through here, walked down the hall, grabbed the little girl, and left the same way. This was bold. It was dark but still warm; people were out and about."

Brinna returned to the bedroom. Jack and Klein followed.

"Anyone see anything — cars, anything?" she asked while her eyes scanned the little girl's room, decorated in pink flowers with dolls and mermaids neatly placed on shelves on the walls.

"Not so far. I've got officers talking to neighbors. How about bringing Hero in?"

"What about Lieutenant Scranton? He said —"

Klein waved her silent. "I'll deal with Scranton. Just get the dog."

"Give me fifteen minutes." She turned and jogged out of the house, Jack on her heels.

"What can Hero do here?" he asked as they got into the car.

"He's an air-scent dog. He might be able to pick up a trail to at least where the car was parked, if they left in a car. If they didn't, we might even get luckier." She punched it away from the curb.

"Won't it all have dissipated by the time we get back?"

"Not necessarily. Humans shed scent at an amazing rate." She slowed for a red light, and when she determined the intersection was clear, accelerated through. It was going on twelve thirty in the morning; traffic was light. "Dogs have such sensitive noses. They can pick up scent effectively, even after time has passed."

"But if he took her away in a car?"

Brinna shook her head. "He'll key on where the car was, but it's likely we'll lose the scent then." She made the turn into her driveway. "I've got to run in and get his gear. You can wait here or come in."

Jack followed her into the house. Hero met them joyfully at the door.

"Hey, bud, we got some work for you." She calmed the dog down before striding into her office to grab a harness for him.

Jack followed her through the house. "Wow," he said when he saw her office. "The famous Wall of Slime. You really do take this seriously."

Brinna followed his gaze. "Yes, I do. Kids deserve protection. They deserve someone to fight for them."

"Your mission?" Jack faced Brinna with a questioning expression.

"You could say that. Like I told you before, each of those kids is just as important to their parents as your wife was to you."

"I heard you the first time."

"Okay. Enough said, then. Let's find Jessica. We're stuck being partners at a time when I really need a good one. I asked you once, are you going to be someone I can count on, or are you going to be a zombie wishing for something you can't have?"

Jack stared at her for a minute, then cleared his throat. "You can count on me."

"Fine, then let's get to Jessica's house." She turned and headed out to the driveway, Jack on her heels.

Brinna loaded Hero into the back of the black-and-white, not seeing any reason for her and Jack to take two cars.

She ground her teeth with determination, vowing to find Jessica before it was too late. Struggling to tune in to her instincts, she reviewed all she knew about Nigel Pearce, hoping it would put her in sync with his copycat. He never killed his quarry. He always left his victim somewhere remote after he was finished with her.

Someplace remote. But where?

Jack hung on while Brinna drove like a woman possessed. She paused only briefly at each intersection before zipping through. He felt as if he'd emerged from a long sleep refreshed and alive with the desire to be a cop again.

Brinna Caruso made him think, made him realize that he was not the only person in

251

the world to grieve over something lost. God or no God, she was right. *I can't waste my life wishing for something I can't have.*

Vicki once said she loved me because I made a difference. I helped people. In Caruso's world I can keep helping people, starting with this little girl. He sucked in a breath and his throat tightened.

I can't have you here again, Vic; I can't. He swallowed a sob, aching with the struggle to accept the finality of her death but knowing deep down he had to face the truth and move on.

He took several deep breaths and focused on the job at hand. The pain still pinched his heart, but like the night before, he felt as though he were moving forward, not stuck and sinking in a deep, dark pit.

This is where the rubber meets the road. I'm in uniform with a job to do. People depend on me to make a difference. I have to be all here, give the job 100 percent. I'm angry now, angry at the man who took my wife and the creep who took those kids away from their parents, but I have to put that aside. My partner doesn't have any problem putting one foot in front of the other. Jack tightened his grip on his seat belt. *I'll follow her lead and trust my instincts.*

Brinna was out of the car as soon as they stopped. She hooked Hero up and started for the door with Jack following. A plain car was present and Jack bet it belonged to Chuck Weldon. The house and front yard were now marked off by yellow crime scene tape.

A local news crew badgered a uniformed officer on the tape's perimeter. Jack recognized Tracy Michaels, a local reporter who often covered the city crime beat. He hoped to make it past without her noticing him, but the sharp-eyed reporter spotted him as he crossed the street.

"Jack! Jack O'Reilly."

Jack groaned. He'd spoken to Tracy at many homicide scenes, but he wasn't up to any kind of grilling right now. *I have no idea what Klein wants to release.*

"Jack, please come give me a comment."

To shut her up, Jack stepped her way. "Tracy, I don't have anything to tell you."

"Come on, Jack. I recognized Chuck Weldon. The FBI is involved. What's going on? And Caruso is here. Was a child abducted?"

"I'm not in charge. You have to wait until the incident commander gives out a press release."

"What's with this?" Tracy frowned and her eyes appraised Jack from head to toe. "I just realized you're in uniform. What gives?"

"A change of scenery. Now if you'll excuse

253

me." Jack turned for the front door of the house as Caruso was coming from the backyard, Hero straining at the leash, nose in the air. Klein and a uniformed officer lifted the tape for Brinna and Hero, and Weldon followed.

Jack stepped aside as the dog came by, Brinna giving the order to find. Hero turned south and went down the street, past one house before he headed to the curb. There he stopped, still testing the air. The dog took a few steps into the street, then walked to Caruso and sat.

"Caruso! You're here with your dog. What is going on?" Michaels pushed past the uniformed officer and shoved a digital recorder under Brinna's chin. "You're the object of a big lawsuit. Can you comment on the kid you killed and the kid you're searching for?"

Before anyone else could react, Jack stepped forward and grabbed the recorder. "Now is not the time, Tracy. We'll give you a statement later."

The reporter turned on Jack. "Stop stonewalling. The public has a right to know about police brutality!"

"Not right this minute they don't." Klein stepped in and waved another officer over. "Escort Miss Michaels to her car."

When Michaels erupted in protest, Klein silenced her. "Meet us at the station and you'll get the first press release about the incident here at this house. Officer Caruso doesn't have anything to say about anything else."

The reporter protested for a few more minutes but eventually let herself be escorted to her car.

Caruso turned to Jack. "Thanks. I didn't know I'd be such a lightning rod. Michaels forgot all about the kidnapping to go after me about the shooting."

"Don't worry about it." Jack gave a wave of his hand. "I've dealt with Tracy on many cases. She can be handled. Did the dog key on something?"

Brinna nodded. "My best guess is that the suspect's car was parked there. He put the victim in the car and most likely took off southbound."

"Did anyone see a car parked there?" Chuck asked.

Klein motioned to the uniformed officer. "Anything?"

The officer read his notes from a clipboard. "One neighbor mentioned seeing a van conversion, large and raised up as if it had four-wheel drive. No one else saw anything unusual."

"A conversion van?" Klein frowned. "That's not exactly a classic getaway car."

Weldon turned to Caruso. "You sure about — ?" He stopped and Jack saw that Brinna's face was white. "What is it? What's the matter?" Weldon asked.

"Hero's right. The car was parked here and it was a conversion van. And I know where he's gone. I know where he's taken the girl."

39

"What?" Chuck stepped in front of Brinna. "How do you know?"

Brinna swallowed as the nasty taste of déjà vu rose in her throat like rancid food. "If this is a copycat, a conversion van makes sense. Pearce took me to a travel trailer. He had a four-wheel-drive truck hitched to a travel trailer. That's what he drove me across the desert in. Chuck, you said it; he's a traveler." She felt sweat pop out on her forehead, as much from anticipation as disgust. "That's one way to travel. We need to get a chopper up, contact the sheriff's office."

When Brinna took a breath, Klein stepped in. "Where do you think he's gone?"

"Don't you see?" She challenged the skeptical male faces watching her. "He's taunting me. This is about me. He's taken her to the desert where Pearce left me."

Chuck and Klein exchanged glances.

"That's a long shot," Chuck said.

"But it makes sense. His beef seems to be with me. He wants me to make the connection." She jabbed her thumb toward her chest. "I've made it. Now I need to get out to the Mojave Desert."

She started around Klein, but he grabbed her arm. "We'll contact the sheriff. They can get personnel out there long before you can get there."

"But this is my deal. He took her because of me." Brinna jerked her arm from his grasp. "I want to find her."

"You're both right," Chuck said. "But, Brinna, admit it — the deputies out in Palmdale can get to the scene a lot faster. Besides, this could be a trap."

Klein agreed. "If he is after you, this could be his way to set you up. They'll have a better knowledge of the area anyway. Have you been back to the site in twenty years?"

Brinna blew out a breath and stepped from one foot to the other, hating to admit they were right. "We're just so close. This is so personal. I want to get this guy."

"We all want to get him," Klein said. "First we're putting out a press release. I'll drop a bone to Tracy on Jessica to get the media machine going. She'll be on the radio right away and make the early morning news broadcasts. At the same time we'll contact the sheriff."

Brinna clenched a fist and hoped with all her might that this girl would be found in time.

Brinna gripped the steering wheel so tightly her knuckles turned white. The desire to direct her car to the desert rather than downtown was so strong it almost won out over common sense.

It had hit like a bullet when the officer mentioned a conversion van with four-wheel-drive capabilities being parked on the street. Memories flooded her thoughts — memories of being stowed in the travel trailer until it stopped in the desert. *He told me he was invisible, that no one else could see him.* The stale smell of unwashed blankets and the portable potty rose up in her nostrils. In her mind's eye she saw Jessica inside the van, crying and frightened.

In spite of the emotions raging within, Brinna made the turn into the station parking lot.

Jack got out first, then bent down and peered in the window. "You coming?"

"Yes," she grunted and opened her door. She leashed Hero and followed Jack to the station's back door.

"Good call," Jack said, turning as he reached the door.

"What?"

"About the desert. I think you were right on about where he'd go. He picked you to torment. It makes sense he'd return to the scene of your victimization."

"That's what my instincts tell me." She raised an eyebrow at Jack as she slid her entry card through the slot to unlock the door.

Jack pulled the door open and held it for her and Hero to go inside. "You have great instincts," Jack said, a smile tugging at his lips.

Brinna turned away. "Umm" was all she said, wondering why it was always weird to see a smile from him.

They rode the elevator up to the homicide office. Homicide handled kidnappings, so detectives had been called from home. Brinna wondered who would respond.

"It's not going to bother you being in the homicide office, is it?" she asked.

Jack shook his head. "Nope. I can hang. My partner talked a lot of sense to me a little while ago — about moving on and being a useful partner, I mean."

"That's me. I'm a regular Dear Abby." She fidgeted, glancing away from Jack, suddenly more comfortable with the creepy, quiet Jack than the smiling, helpful one she now saw. *This isn't a permanent partnership,* she told herself. *I certainly don't want to get attached to Jack O'Reilly.*

Klein sat at a computer, putting the finishing touches on a press release and printing out flyers with Jessica's picture on them. Weldon was on the phone with the LA County sheriff's office requesting officers to respond to the location in the Mojave Desert where Brinna had been abandoned so many years ago. Most if not all of the desert communities contracted with the sheriff for law enforcement services.

To Brinna, the office was too small; the walls felt as though they were closing in. She felt caged and ready to burst with energy and anxiety, knowing the sergeant just wanted her to wait. Chafing at the knowledge that she was just supposed to sit and wait while she wanted to be the one in the field hunting for this guy. Hero seemed to feel her restlessness; his eyes followed her every move.

"You want some coffee?" Jack asked. Brinna nodded and he left the room. She checked her watch; it was almost two in the morning. Debating whether or not Milo would mind being awakened, she got up, walked to a desk at the back of the room, and picked up the phone. Hero followed.

The phone rang several times and no machine picked up. Brinna was just about to hang up when an unfamiliar voice answered.

"Hello, Milo?" she asked while her face crinkled with confusion.

"Who is this?" the voice demanded.

"This is Officer Brinna Caruso. Where is Gregor Milovich?"

"Brinna." Some of the sharpness left the voice. "Sorry, this is John Horn. I used to work with Milo. I met you once or twice. Remember me?"

Nonplussed, Brinna responded, "Yeah, I remember you, but where's Milo?"

"Uh, just a minute."

The line went quiet, and Brinna drummed on the desk. *What is going on?*

"Brinna." John's voice returned on the line. "I'm sorry. I hate to be the one to break this to you, but Milo's dead."

"What?" Brinna went numb. Through a fog as thick as dark wool, she heard Horn explain to her that Milo had killed himself. He'd eaten his service revolver, despondent because he'd been diagnosed with inoperable lung cancer. His note said he didn't want to be a burden to anyone and he didn't

want to live the remainder of his life doped up.

From far, far away, Horn ended the call by saying the coroner had arrived to take custody of the body.

She placed the phone in its cradle and felt like the air had been sucked from her lungs. Gregor Milovich, her idol, her strength, the man who had drummed into her to never give up, had given up in a final, shocking way.

40

"Brinna, you okay?"

Jack's voice cut through the haze and Brinna looked up, struggling to focus on his face.

"You okay?" he repeated, setting a cup of coffee in front of her. "Your face is white. Are you going to barf?"

She shook her head, not sure she could speak without breaking down. Grabbing the coffee, she took a gulp, letting the hot liquid scorch her throat.

"I'm fine," she rasped, then cleared her throat. "Thanks for the coffee."

"No problem." Jack took a seat across the desk.

She could feel his worried gaze on her. The words were on her tongue to tell Jack to get lost, but Brinna couldn't speak them. It took all of the strength in her body to ignore the dagger piercing her heart. It twisted every time she put *Milo* next to *dead.*

Staring at the phone, Brinna wished the conversation she'd just had was a bad dream brought about by a lack of sleep. Then again, she thought, maybe it was a stupid prank. *Maybe Milo will return my call and say it was all a mistake.*

"Klein says deputies are on their way to check out the spot," Jack said, the upbeat tone of his voice grating.

"What?"

"The spot — you know, where you were left."

Brinna willed her thoughts to Jessica. "Then we should hear something soon."

"What exactly happened to you? I mean, all those years ago?" Jack asked.

Fists clenched, fingernails biting into her palms, Brinna answered the familiar question. It was easy to answer without much effort because she'd been asked so many times. "He left me tied to the porch of an abandoned building and drove off."

"Overnight?"

"Roughly forty-eight hours." *Until Milo found me. Why, Milo?*

"They never caught him?"

She shook her head. "Not for what he did to me." Brinna pushed the news about Milo down deep.

"But he was caught ten years later."

"Yep, trying to take another girl." She recognized Jack was trying to drag information out of her, and she worked not to be irritated. "The statute of limitations had run out for me."

"How was he killed?"

Brinna sighed. "He escaped while being transported to the courthouse for the first day of his trial. This was out in San Bernardino. SB sheriff's deputies found him holed up at a hotel in the mountains. When SWAT fired tear gas into the room they believed he was in, the whole place went up like a Roman candle."

"He was verified dead?"

Brinna ground her teeth, struggling with control, hands still clenched in fists under the desk. *Hold it together; hold it together.* "Him and four recovering drug addicts. They did blood typing at that time. One set of remains matched Pearce."

Just then Sergeant Klein waved them to the front of the office. "Bad news," he began as Jack and Brinna joined him. "Deputies are on scene, and they've got nothing. No van, no Jessica."

Brinna groaned and bit her bottom lip to keep it from quivering.

"They'll keep an eye on the area," Klein added. He tapped on a desk with his knuckles and gave Brinna a we-tried expression.

"We'll have Jessica's picture on all the morning newscasts." Chuck put a hand on Brinna's shoulder. "We'll find her."

Brinna could only nod. Emotions inside raged, tearing her apart.

Milo is dead. Is it too late for Jessica? Oh, how I need a Kevlar heart.

41

It was five thirty in the morning before Jack was ready to concede the investigation to the homicide detail and go home. Brinna had checked out a short time before — seemingly shell-shocked, he thought. *She's taking this thing with Jessica too hard.* He hadn't forgotten about the office at her house and the importance finding kids had in her life. It consumed her, made her a crusader.

At first glance it was a healthy obsession. But was any obsession really healthy? Jack wondered. One that did good for people was, he decided. At that point he realized that Brinna's obsession had infected him to a large degree.

It was something Vicki would've liked — a crusade for kids. Jack's mind whirred with ideas about how to help Brinna and maybe, in the process, Jessica, too.

"Here's my follow-up." Jack handed the

paper to Klein. "Mind if I head home?"

Klein shook his head. "Go get some sleep. This is your Friday, isn't it?"

"Yeah, I'm ready for bed." Jack turned to leave but Klein stopped him.

"Good job tonight. You're getting back in the game."

Jack nodded, wanting to tell the sergeant he was more right than he knew. Today, at this moment, he felt more normal than he had in a year. But a lingering feeling that he was still hanging on to life only by his fingernails stopped him.

Nothing in his life would be settled completely until the sentencing.

"I'll do my job" was all he said as he left the office. Jack hurried to the locker room and changed. For the first time in a long time, his investigative instincts roared inside him. As a homicide investigator, he'd loved the hunt, the feeling of putting the right pieces together and closing in on prey. Brinna's tale had stirred something in him. He wanted to find out all he could about Nigel Pearce and the police shoot-out ten years ago.

No van.
No Jessica.
Where has the kidnapper gone?

269

Brinna felt each minute ticking off the clock as if it were a knife jabbing her heart. On top of everything else, today was the day she had to meet her brother's plane and brave a hospital visit to her father.

On the way to the airport, she stopped at a 7-Eleven and bought a roll of Tums, popping half of it into her mouth before she got back to the car. The whole roll was gone by the time she reached the airport. She parked her truck and flowed into the terminal with the crowds at LAX to await her brother's plane.

An arrival screen told Brinna that Brian's plane was delayed. She found a place to sit where she could watch arrivals stream out from customs and contemplated her morning up to that point.

After hearing about Jessica, irritated and antsy knowing she couldn't rush out to the desert and search for the girl on her own, Brinna did the hardest thing she'd ever done in her life: she drove out to Milo's house.

It was the last place she wanted to be because she knew once she got there, the news she'd received from John Horn would be real. She wouldn't be able to pretend she'd never had the phone conversation.

The pressure on her chest when she

thought of Milo was unbearable. But she'd made the trip to Santa Clarita and survived.

Initially, good memories surfaced in Brinna's mind. Her first visit to Milo's house had happened when she was seven. They'd celebrated the one-year anniversary of her rescue. Milo's first dog, Scout, was still alive then, and he had tumbled around on the lawn with Brinna. After that, every year they got together for friendly, fun bar-becues.

The visits were more frequent when Brinna got her driver's license. By that time she was firmly on her way to a career in law enforcement. She became a Police Explorer Scout for Long Beach PD, and she picked Milo's brain constantly. He happily worked with her, answering questions, taking her on ride-alongs, being a mentor and friend.

The happy memories were drenched in a dark cloud by the cold truth of the reason for her visit that day.

John Horn met her on the front steps. "Don't think you want to go in there, Brin. He was dead at least long enough for neighbors to call and complain about the smell."

Brinna sighed, remembering her last visit. *Was his moroseness a signal I missed? All that nonsense about God . . . Was Milo trying to tell me something I didn't hear?* She counted back the days, trying to determine when he pulled the trigger. She also tried not to imagine what several days in hundred-degree heat had done to Milo.

"How long did he know he had cancer?" she asked John as she plopped down next to him on the porch, a place she'd often sat with Milo on warm summer evenings. "I was just here; he never said a word."

"Doctor said he was diagnosed a year ago. He wanted to operate then. Milo said no. And I guess by now the cancer was worse. I was on the fishing trip with him. He hacked and hacked. I thought it was a cold." John spit tobacco juice into a paper cup.

"Yeah, he coughed a lot when I was here. Man, he still smoked." Brinna struggled to keep her voice steady.

"Milo smoked since he was twelve. Even a death sentence couldn't break that addiction. His note just said he didn't want to be a burden or be so doped up he was a spit-drooling moron. Lung cancer is a nasty way to die."

Brinna remembered Milo's comment about Baxter and how he didn't want his pal to spend his last days doped up. Was Milo afraid the same fate awaited him?

"He was a fighter. Why didn't he fight

this?" Brinna's fingernails dug into her palm. "And why didn't he tell me?"

John had no answers. He shoved some more tobacco into his cheek. They sat in silence for a few moments.

"I left a message the other day," Brinna said after a while. "Was he already dead?"

John shrugged. "Probably. We won't know the exact time of death until after the autopsy, and maybe not even then."

"If only —" her voice broke — "I could have helped." She sucked back a sob and wiped away a tear.

"Don't blame yourself. Milo was a very independent guy. He just made his mind up and did the deed."

"I didn't even get to say good-bye."

"We all feel that way. Milo was my first training officer. He's the last guy I would have ever thought would go out this way." John's voice was thick with emotion.

"Thanks for telling me," Brinna said, after she was certain her voice wouldn't break again. "And thanks for meeting me here. It'll be a while before I really believe he's gone."

"No problem." John stood and patted her shoulder. "His son is flying in from Washington to make funeral arrangements. I'll let you know when I hear."

"I'm going to sit here for a few minutes, if you don't mind."

"Take your time," John said. She watched him walk across the lawn to his car.

She'd sat quietly for a long while, tears streaming down her face. . . .

Now, waiting in the international terminal for her brother's plane to land, the pain bubbled back up. Two painful facts pierced her heart: Milo was gone, and he'd left by taking his own life.

Brinna watched travelers arrive, greet loved ones, and for the most part leave the terminal smiling. Occasionally someone would catch her eye, a person who trudged along, half-dead with exhaustion, probably from a bumpy eighteen-hour flight. They'd be disheveled with dark bags under their eyes, and even if their luggage had wheels, it was as if they were barely making it underneath their load.

Heart heavy and physically exhausted from the excruciating reality of Milo's death, she felt like one of those travelers, struggling with a horrible case of jet lag, wrung out and empty.

She wondered if this was how Jack had felt when he lost his wife. It was emptiness so dark and total that at the moment Brinna could understand someone losing their grip and giving up. Something caught in her throat as she remembered one of Milo's lectures about never giving up during a fight: *"The will to survive saves many a cop from death at the hands of a bad guy"* was something he drummed into rookies. *"Never give up."*

But where was Milo's will to survive?

Closing her eyes, Brinna smacked a fist into her palm. *I can't think about this anymore. I will do my job. I'll do it even better. I won't dissolve and fall apart; I won't,* she vowed.

The protection she'd put around her heart kept her standing. Not wanting to let Milo's suicide wipe out years of instruction and advice, Brinna clung to what he'd drilled into her — that when things were the toughest, when stakes were the highest, a Kevlar heart was essential. Personal feelings had to be bulletproof, impervious to emotions that could cloud sound cop judgment.

The ring of her cell phone came as a welcome distraction. She pulled it off her belt, noting the homicide extension. "Caruso."

"Brinna." Ben Carney's voice hailed her. "Deputies found Jessica . . . alive. You were right. He left her in the same place you were left. They were just a couple hours early the first time. A recheck of the area hit pay dirt. According to the little girl, the man drove her around for a long time. She said it felt like they went in circles."

Brinna sighed and closed her eyes as one huge load rolled off her shoulders. "That's great news — great. Is she okay?"

"As well as can be expected. He'd tied her up, left her alone out there. But she wasn't molested. She says he seemed to be in a terrible hurry. I bet he's feeling the heat."

"No sign of the van?"

"No. This guy seems to be able to ghost pretty good. Deputies were all over the place, but there's a lot of ground to cover. Jessica confirmed that they had been in a 'van-like camper,' she called it. She's a remarkable little girl."

"Was she able to give a description?"

"Good enough for a seven-year-old. As soon as she's able, we'll set her up with a sketch artist. You want to be there when that happens?"

"Sure, let me know when. Right now I'm at the airport, waiting for my brother's plane."

"He's flying in from South America?"

"Yeah. How'd you know he was in South America?"

"My church prays for missionaries; your brother is on our list. Is he on furlough?"

Brinna rolled her eyes. "That's right; your type sticks together. I guess furlough. My dad is sick, so Brian is coming home."

"Sick? Is it serious?"

Brinna clicked her tongue. "Yeah, but it's of his own making. My dad's lived in a liquor bottle most of my life. It finally caught up with him."

"Sorry to hear that, for him and for you."

"For me?"

"Sure, you sound bitter. It must be rough."

"I'm not bitter. I'm just telling you the truth. Why? I don't know. It's none of your business."

Ben laughed. "Brinna the direct. Well, I'll be praying for you and your family. By the way, Jack filed a great follow-up this morning; it reminded me of the old Jack. What did you do to him?"

"The usual. I slapped him around a bit." *Jack is the least of my worries right now.*

"Good for you. Take care."

"Thanks for the news." Brinna flipped her phone closed and went back to watching the arrival screen, which now indicated Brian's plane had landed.

With Jessica safe, Brinna had only a

couple tons of worry to deal with instead of several.

Her thoughts drifted to Brian. He'd been out of the country for two years. A missionary. Brinna blew out a breath and shook her head. He always took after Mom. But what choice did he have? Dad never had time for either of them.

The thought that she'd always considered Milo her real dad popped into her mind and she smashed it down, not wanting to go there anymore.

She stood and paced, shoving the pain down deep. Apprehension about seeing her father in the hospital grabbed her gut like a thick elastic band pulling taut. Afraid she'd start hyperventilating in front of all the airport strangers, Brinna concentrated on breathing and watching people file out.

When she saw Brian, an unexpected thrill coursed through her. Though they had their sibling quarrels growing up and had little in common, Brinna loved her little brother with a protective big-sister love. But seeing him now, he wasn't really little anymore.

Brian stood a little over six feet tall, and he'd filled out in all the right ways. He was no longer the scrawny, pesky kid she remembered. Broad-shouldered, tan, dark hair on the long side hitting his collar, Brian broke into a grin when he saw her.

"Hey, Sis, it's super to see you." He dropped his backpack and grabbed her in a hug she gladly returned.

"My little brother!" She gripped his shoulders, standing on her tiptoes to do so. "You look great. I guess South America agrees with you."

"I've been blessed, really blessed. How've you been?"

"Hanging in there. You have luggage?"

"Nope, just the backpack. I've learned to travel light."

"Great. Let's get going."

Later, while they were stuck in traffic on the 405 freeway, Brian talked about his work in South America. Brinna listened, happy to have the noise, grateful for the distraction. And very happy Brian would be with her when she walked into the hospital.

"Do you need to go home first? Or do you want to go straight to the hospital?" she asked when he came up for air.

"Let's go see Dad. I bet Mom is there already."

"Okay." Brinna spoke calmly, but the closer she got to Long Beach Memorial, the tighter her throat got. A thought popped into her mind as she drove: she'd rather face ten hardened criminals than one sick father.

"What's been going on with you? You're awfully quiet," Brian said.

Brinna shrugged. "You know Dad and I have had our differences."

"Yeah, I know. But he's dying now. Can't you forgive him?"

"Mom said the same thing. Forgive him for what? For being an absent, mostly-drunk dad?" She shot an annoyed glance at Brian and saw him roll his eyes. "I've moved on and made a great life for myself. Don't you try to say he drinks because he thinks I blame him for something."

"I'm not saying that. He's just always felt responsible. You know that."

"I can't do anything about how he feels. I never held him responsible for what happened to me, not once."

"You and he are so much alike."

Brinna glared at her brother. "Did you get brain damage in South America? I'm not at all like him."

Brian laughed. "He handles problems by drinking; you by hiding in the work you do. And you both need God in your lives, more than I can say."

Snorting, Brinna made the turn into the hospital driveway. "You and Mom won't give up, will you?"

"Nope. Mom's been talking to your friend Milo."

"What?" Brinna jammed the truck into a parking spot, slammed it into park, and turned to stare at Brian. "What do you mean?"

"Just that he called her a while ago and she shared her faith with him. After all these years he listened. Didn't he tell you?"

Brinna felt the breath go out of her in a whoosh. She sat back in her seat and looked away from Brian. "No, no, he didn't tell me he'd talked to her recently. He talked in general about what she's said for years." She swallowed, conscious of Brian's worried gaze. "Milo's dead. He killed himself a few days ago." The force of the words coming out of her mouth slapped her heart. She couldn't look at Brian and closed her eyes.

"Brin, I'm sorry. I didn't know." Brian grabbed her hand. "I know how much he meant to you."

She let her brother hold her hand for a moment but kept her face turned away. "He had cancer. Didn't want to be a burden. When did he talk to Mom?"

"I'm not sure of the exact date. But she said he asked about God and let her pray for him. She said he sounded at peace when they ended the conversation."

281

Brinna didn't know what to say. Milo had mentioned her mother, but the thought of Milo falling for the drivel Mom always spouted was beyond comprehension.

"You okay?" Brian shook her shoulder.

"Yeah, it just hurts that Milo's gone, you know?" It took every ounce of strength she had to keep her composure.

"I understand. Are you up to seeing Dad?"

"Yeah, let's go. Let's get this over with."

42

Nigel pouted for a while after the Special Girl's quick rescue. He'd made it too easy. But there had been pressure. He'd barely escaped because of all the cop cars in the desert. And while they'd found her, the dog cop wasn't mentioned anywhere in the article.

After he'd left the girl, he made his way back to the coast, very conscious of the need to lie low for a while. All the cops' sniffing around for him was disconcerting but not too worrisome. He'd always been able to slip away before and he'd do it again. He pulled the van into a beachside campground with a wireless signal. Sitting on his bed with his laptop, he scrolled through hundreds of pictures and mulled over his next move.

The game had gotten so much more exciting with the addition of the dog cop. She was someone he could work to impress, to directly affect by his escapades. His audience from afar. For the first time in his life, Nigel relished an audience. But he'd have to think up something more difficult the next time.

After a while, the pictures began to bore him. Nothing exciting in images — he needed to see them in action. He powered the laptop down and got up to take a walk. There was still some light left in the day, so he walked down the concrete path that ran along the beach. Many children frolicked in the surf even this late in the day, silhouetted by a sinking sun. Nigel's blood warmed to the hunt. The perfect Special Girl and the perfect anniversary gift for the dog cop. Nigel felt more alive than he had in years.

43

Jack's first day off from patrol dawned bright, as though someone had finally opened the blinds on his life. His mind was active, alive, as he showered, shaved, and dressed for the day, contemplating the hours ahead of him. For the first time in a long while, the calendar on the refrigerator escaped his notice. He rushed out the door with coffee in a travel mug and headed for San Bernardino.

He'd called in a marker he had with a San Bernardino County homicide investigator. Jack had helped Gabe Lopez with a gang homicide a few years ago. The victim had been gunned down on a San Bernardino street corner. The shooter fled. Jack found the gang member in Long Beach and facilitated his capture.

The drive to the San Bernardino County offices took Jack an hour. Once inside, he showed his ID and was directed to the

285

285

homicide office.

"Gabe, thanks a lot for meeting with me." Jack shook the investigator's hand.

"No problem, O'Reilly. It's been a little slow around here. And I admit to being intrigued that you're interested in this old file. Is this about the federal investigation?"

"What federal investigation?" Jack frowned.

Lopez chuckled. "What, is Long Beach in a bubble, cut off from the rest of the state? Don't you read the newspapers?"

Jack hitched his shoulders up and pleaded ignorance. "I haven't been keeping up on current events. What's going on?"

"We — the county and the PD — were sued last year by a guy who spent ten years in jail for a crime he didn't commit. He was recently cleared by new DNA testing."

Jack nodded. "We had a couple of those ourselves. What does that have to do with Nigel Pearce?"

"I'm getting to that. It seems evidence was tampered with, maybe manipulated in the guy's rape case. This brought the FBI out of the woodwork. There is a possibility that a crooked cop, in league with a lab tech, tainted evidence in a few hundred cases during a two-year period between ten and twelve years ago." Lopez sighed and Jack recognized the expression that fell over his face. Lopez's department was under an uncomfortable microscope, and it was a strain. "Every case from back then is being reviewed, the Pearce case included."

"But Pearce was killed in a shoot-out. How could evidence have been tampered with?"

"I'm afraid to speculate. I happened to be one of the uniforms on scene back then. It was my first SWAT call-out, as well as the first time I saw and smelled human bodies fried to a crisp. Things like that tend to stick with you." He held out a thick manila file. "Read what's here. Will you tell me what you've got going on after you read this?"

Jack took the folder. "You bet."

Lopez showed Jack to a conference room and pulled out a chair. "After you review it all, come back to my office, and we'll talk."

Jack nodded, sat, and opened the file. It took about twenty minutes to read all about the capture, arrest, escape, and death of Nigel Pearce.

Initially arrested in a suburb of San Bernardino County, Pearce escaped custody during transport to court on the first day of his trial. A huge manhunt ensued. Pearce remained at large for two weeks before someone called in a sighting. The caller said he believed Pearce was hiding in the mountain town of Running Springs.

The tipster identified himself as a desk clerk at the Rimwood Hotel, a hotel converted to serve as a halfway house for recovering drug addicts. He reported a suspicion that Pearce was hiding in a resident's room. Turned out that the resident whose room was in question, Kevin Banks, was also Pearce's cousin. Banks was on probation for narcotics charges, and Nigel apparently hid in his closet. They aroused the clerk's suspicion when he saw Banks sneaking extra food into the room.

Shots were fired from the hotel when the first police officers arrived on scene to check out the tip. The clerk and two residents escaped after the volley of gunfire. Communication subsequently established with Nigel confirmed that he held his cousin and three other residents hostage. There was a SWAT call-out and Pearce refused to surrender. In fact, he hung up the phone and would not communicate further with negotiators. After a twenty-four-hour standoff, SWAT fired tear gas into the house and the place exploded in a firestorm.

The entire hotel burned to the ground and nearly took the town of Running Springs with it. The siege occurred during a hot and dry Southern California summer. Embers from the fire caused spot fires to erupt everywhere, and one of the fires burned down a house and two businesses close by. From what Jack read, the fire had caused complete chaos that day and several days thereafter.

After things cooled off, an arson investigation indicated Pearce had purposely opened several gas valves in the hotel, which facilitated the fire.

Five bodies were recovered, all burned beyond recognition. Four were identified as residents of the hotel, including Nigel's cousin. One was ultimately identified as Nigel Pearce. Jack noted that all autopsy reports had been removed from the file.

Jack read everything over a couple of times, then studied the photos. After he finished, he found Lopez.

"So you have questions?" Lopez asked, leaning back in his chair.

Jack nodded. "The autopsies are missing."

"Feds have them. The lab tech being investigated worked for the coroner at the time."

"Do you remember how Pearce was identified?"

Lopez rubbed his chin. "Simple blood typing. There weren't any dental records.

Pearce's parents were off-the-wall survivalists. They didn't believe in doctors or dentists. Pearce grew up in the mountains, just above Running Springs in a place called Green Valley Lake. We visited the Pearce cabin after the fire. It was a one-room hovel with an outhouse in the backyard."

"Is there a problem with the identification? Is that why the Feds are involved?" Jack studied Lopez, and the uncomfortable feeling that there was more to the incident than what was in the report began to tug at his thoughts.

Lopez shrugged. "I can remember thinking something was wrong. But I never questioned anything."

Jack frowned and set the folder down on the desk. Lopez wouldn't meet his gaze. "Sounds like maybe there were a lot of loose ends."

"It was a mess," Lopez said, pulling the file toward him. "First, why are you interested so many years after the fact?"

Jack explained about the copycat.

"Whoa." Lopez folded his arms. "I can't believe what I'm hearing."

"Why? Is there something missing from this report?"

Lopez stood, walked around his desk, and closed the office door. He paced, walking to his window before answering Jack. "Man, ten years ago I was a fresh-faced kid, new on the job with a wife and family to support. My training officer was a lazy old-timer, counting the minutes until retirement."

"I've met my share of those. But what does this have to do with Pearce?"

"The perimeter was never secured properly." Lopez sat, hands folded in front of him. "I always felt there was a possibility Pearce got out. When it was all over and they confirmed Pearce was dead, I relaxed. But you hear things."

"Like what?"

"The bodies. When I saw them, you couldn't tell much. Later, I heard that when they got them to the coroner, all five had their hands and feet tied with wire hangers. And they'd been shot." He stopped as if giving Jack time to understand the importance of what he'd said.

Jack didn't need time. "Pearce couldn't tie himself up like that and then shoot everyone. But if what you're saying is true, how could the coroner identify one as Pearce?"

"That's what the Feds are trying to figure. Ten years ago the coroner's office was a disaster. There was a big case going on at a nursing home where they believed a nurse was murdering elderly patients. A bunch of bodies were exhumed, tying up the entire senior office staff. Right now the wires are whispering that an unqualified tech was performing autopsies, telling cops what they wanted to hear, and if evidence didn't exist, he was making it up."

Jack felt his jaw drop. "So Pearce could have walked away free and clear."

Lopez nodded. "Yep. Not only that, defense attorneys are lining up. Every case this dirty cop and this lab tech touched will be reviewed. Chances are, some other guilty guys will walk simply because of the appearance of impropriety."

"And what is the motive in all this?"

"Best guess is that a couple of people decided they'd be judge, jury, and executioner all by themselves."

Jack felt his face redden as he thought of all the little girls who'd fallen prey to Pearce over the years, girls sacrificed to the god of pride or whatever it was that caused a person to lie and manipulate truth.

44

The smell of antiseptic and disinfectant hit Brinna like a wave of murky water as soon as she and Brian stepped into the hospital.

"I hate hospitals," she grumbled as they boarded the elevator. Memories of being brought to the emergency room after Milo found her jabbed at her through the murk, and goose bumps rippled across her arms. She remembered feeling violated all over again in that place. "Nothing good happens in them."

Brian smiled and threw an arm over her shoulder. "People get better in hospitals, most of the time."

"Dad's not going to get better."

Brian sucked in a breath and removed his arm. "I almost forgot how to-the-point you always are. Maybe he won't get better physically, but we can pray he'll improve spiritually."

"You haven't even been home an hour and

already you start with that. He's dying. Why go in there and fill his head with that stuff?"

Brian smiled sadly and shook his head. "I don't want to argue with you, Brin. I want to give Dad comfort. I firmly believe that if he's at peace with God now, then when he dies, he'll be in a better place."

Brinna shot him a disgusted glare. Thankfully, Brian shut up for the rest of the walk through the hallways.

Their father's room was on the fourth floor. The closer they got, the more claustrophobic Brinna felt. They were halfway to the room when Brinna's cell phone chirped.

Sighing with relief, Brinna stopped and grabbed her brother's arm. "I have to answer this; give me a minute." She turned and fled to an outdoor patio and flipped the phone open without checking the number. "Caruso."

"Brinna, what's going on? I've been trying to get ahold of you for a while." Maggie's familiar voice was like a life vest thrown to a drowning person.

Falling onto a bench, Brinna relaxed. "Hey, sorry. Yeah, there's a lot going on. I don't even know where to start. My dad's in the hospital."

Wanting to delay her entrance into that hospital room, Brinna poured her heart out to Maggie about everything going on in her life.

Maggie listened. That was what Brinna loved and appreciated about Maggie — she was a great listener. It was after Brinna calmed down and came up for air that Maggie spoke.

"I don't know how you're standing. I know Milo was like a father to you."

"I can't think about it right now." She swallowed hard as a lump formed and fought to keep her voice from breaking. Inside, she wrestled emotions overflowing her heart. "Milo was no coward."

"I know. He was a great guy. But things change, Brin. Terminal cancer is a gut shot. I'd bet Milo couldn't deal with losing his independence if things got bad. Lung cancer can do that to people."

"I wish he would have said something." Brinna took a deep breath.

"You want some moral support at the hospital?"

"That would be awesome. You don't mind coming down here?"

"Not at all. I always liked your dad. I'll be there in fifteen minutes."

Brinna flipped the phone shut and stood. The patio overlooked a courtyard in the center of the hospital complex. She paused at a railing and stared down without really seeing anything.

Of all the turmoil swirling around her, it was what Brian had said about Milo talking to her mother that puzzled her the most. There was no rhyme or reason to why Milo would want to talk to Rose and not to Brinna. He'd told Brinna more than once he thought Rose was carried away with religion. True, during the odd conversation they'd had that day she visited his house, he'd mentioned doubts. Doubts about his instincts, doubts about whether or not he'd been correct denying the existence of God all his life.

But to turn to my mom at the time of his most dire need?

A burst of anger flared up in her mind like a Fourth of July firecracker. Anger focused on Milo. Brinna was angry that he confided in her mother and not in her, and absolutely furious that he'd never given her the chance to change his mind or even say good-bye.

"Brinna."

She turned.

Brian stood at the door. "You can't hide out here all day."

Blowing out a breath, Brinna walked toward her brother. "I'm not hiding. Maggie called. Talking to her got me thinking about Milo. I was woolgathering."

Brian nodded. "I know this is hard for you for a lot of reasons. But Dad is weak. He won't be awake much longer."

Shrugging, Brinna pushed past Brian. "Okay, okay."

Once they reached the room, Brinna let Brian enter first, taking a deep breath and reminding herself that no matter what, the Kevlar around her heart would keep her emotions safely in check.

Rocky Caruso had a bed by the window. As Brinna made her way across the room, she wondered if her father's yellow pallor was a result of the sunlight or his sickness. She tried to think of the last time she'd seen him. It had probably been last Christmas, she thought, frowning at her inability to remember seeing him since then.

"Brinna, I'm glad you're here." Rose gave her a tight hug as she approached the bed. "He's dozing right now. The medication makes him sleepy." She leaned over the bed and wiped Rocky's forehead.

Studying her mother, Brinna saw that she appeared to have aged noticeably since just a few days ago. Her hair was impeccable today, but worry lines tugged at Rose's eyes, and there were dark circles underneath. Yet there was vitality in the eyes. Brinna realized it was hope. Her mother probably had hope that Rocky would get better.

Swallowing down unexpected emotion, she turned her attention to her father. He seemed to have shrunk and looked small and frail lying in the bed. Brinna struggled to remember him alive and strong, before the bottle got him, and she couldn't.

"Brian and I prayed for him. I think that gave him some peace, and he slipped off to sleep." Rose reached across the bed and straightened the bedcovers.

"He really wanted to talk to you, Brin," Brian said.

Brinna sucked her teeth and said nothing.

There was a knock at the door and Maggie poked her head in. "Hi. Mind if I come in?"

Brinna deferred to her mother and Rose nodded. "Sure, Maggie. Rocky was always fond of you."

"I'm sorry my visit has to come at a time like this." Maggie stood by Brinna. "I remember some good times with your dad."

"Like what?" Brinna asked, raising an eyebrow at Maggie.

"Remember when he took us down to the docks to watch the circus unload the animals? I think we were about ten or eleven."

Brinna frowned at her dad. "I do remember that. It was fun. Dad was sober for a few hours."

"I remember it too," Brian jumped in. "You two let me tag along. We had a great time."

Maggie and Brian began reminiscing. Brinna stared at her father and wondered about the man she'd been embarrassed by for most of her life. Cancer — he had cancer just like Milo. But her father wasn't going to bail out. Her father was facing the same thing her idol faced, but he was hanging on and he wanted to talk to her. Why hadn't Milo at least extended the same courtesy?

45

Jack paced from one end of his living room to the other. For the first time in a year his restlessness was not caused by dreams of Vicki.

He'd called Chuck and filled him in on what he'd learned from Gabe Lopez. Chuck promised to check into the investigation going on in San Bernardino and call back as soon as he learned anything. Jack felt compelled to call Brinna but hesitated. Finally he picked up the phone.

She answered after one ring. "Caruso."

"It's Jack O'Reilly. Are you busy right now? I've got something new on Nigel Pearce."

"A little. I'm at the hospital with my dad."

Jack slapped his forehead. "Hey, I'm sorry. I forgot. This can wait."

"No, that's okay. What's up?"

"I don't want to go into it over the phone."

"Then I'll meet you somewhere — say in

about an hour down at Second and Bay-shore. You know where people rent kayaks?"

"I do. Are you sure? I don't want to interrupt time with your dad."

"Don't worry about it. I'll see you in an hour."

Jack set the phone down and checked his watch, hoping Chuck had something to tell him before he met with Brinna. He went into the kitchen to make some lunch and opened the refrigerator door to find it empty. When he closed the door, the calendar with the circled date of the sentencing on it caught his eye.

He realized that he hadn't thought about Bridges or the sentencing for quite a while, and guilt stabbed. Chewing on his lip while he gathered his wallet and car keys, he decided that in spite of himself he was emerging from his fog of grief, and he liked the feeling.

46

After Jack's phone call, Brinna caught the accusation on her mother's face.

"What?" Her forehead scrunched and she crossed her arms, matching her mother's glare. "I'll be here for a while longer. Dad's still asleep."

Rose simply shook her head. "I'm going to get some coffee. I'll be right back."

"What was the call about?" Maggie asked.

"Jack said it had something to do with Nigel Pearce."

"The guy who kidnapped you?" Brian stared at Brinna. "I thought he was dead."

Brinna sighed, not wanting to get into everything with Brian and wondering if it was a mistake to meet with Jack. What possible new information could he have?

She stepped closer to her dad's bed and nearly jumped when she saw he was awake and watching her.

"Dad! You're awake. How do you feel?"

Suddenly self-conscious because of the lame question, Brinna fidgeted with the railing on the bed.

Brian and Maggie stepped closer, on either side of her.

Rocky shrugged weakly. "It's always work with you." Watery, accusing eyes held hers.

"Brian's here too," she said, pretending she didn't hear the irritation in his voice and trying to hide the irritation in hers.

"That job — it's no work for a girl," Rocky rasped.

Brinna felt her face flush. *So this is why he wanted to talk to me. To continue a lecture I've heard for more than six years?*

"It's what I do. It's what I love, and it's what I'm good at." Brinna's jaw tightened. The last thing she'd wanted to do with her father when she walked into the room was argue with him.

Rocky raised a hand and waved dismissively. "You're a spectacle in the newspaper; that's what you are." A coughing fit began.

Brinna stepped away from the bed. "It was good seeing you too, Dad," she said as she turned for the door.

"Brinna." Brian grabbed her arm.

She jerked away. "You talk to him. He's obviously proud of you. I've got a meeting to go to." Brinna passed her mother returning with coffee as she left the room, Maggie on her heels.

"That could have gone better," Maggie said as they got on the elevator.

Brinna sighed. "Don't you start with me. You saw how it went. He couldn't wait to get after me."

Maggie held her hands up. "I'm not taking sides. I just made an observation."

"With all the stuff going on right now, the last thing I need is my father berating me again."

"He's sick. Cut him some slack."

The elevator doors opened and they stepped off. Brinna took a deep breath and stopped, holding Maggie's gaze.

"I know he's sick. I didn't go in there expecting to pick a fight with him. He always does that to me." She pounded her palm with a fist. "Why can't I just ignore it?"

"Sometimes the people we love the most are the hardest to talk to. I've watched you for so many years." Maggie stepped close. "All the approval you got from Milo, you really wanted from your dad. Trouble is, now Milo's gone and your dad is not far behind. You do a great job, Brin, whether he notices or not."

Brinna looked away, throat thick. "Since

when did you become a psychiatrist?"

"You're my friend. I can't imagine dealing with what's on your plate right now. I want you to know I'm here for you."

Wiping her eyes, Brinna sighed. "Thanks, Maggie, thanks. Right now I don't want to talk about my father." She started for the door and Maggie fell into step with her.

"Then what's up with O'Reilly?" Maggie asked when they reached the parking lot.

Brinna told Maggie about the abduction and rescue of Jessica and the similarities to her own abduction.

"Do you think it's a copycat?"

"I don't know what to think." She groaned and stretched. "I just don't want this guy to hurt any more kids."

"He doesn't have a chance with the Kid Crusader on his trail."

Brinna managed a chuckle. "I hope you're right, Sister Mary Sunshine."

"I am. Try not to be so pessimistic. I've got your back."

Brinna stopped at home to pick up Hero, knowing he'd appreciate a trip to the beach. Besides, it felt good to hug the furry dog, whose tail wagged furiously because he was happy to see her.

At least somebody was.

The dog bounded out to the truck, and Brinna felt her spirits lift. Maggie's words about her father's approval had struck a nerve and she worked hard to push the confrontation with him from her thoughts.

Her phone rang twice on the way to Second and Bayshore. The first was from Janet Rodriguez, telling her that the shooting board had picked a time and date to convene.

"Umm, okay," Brinna said. "I know it's better to get it out of the way, but I've got so much on my mind."

"Once all the facts are reviewed, it may stick a sock in Hester Shockley's mouth. Monday night after squad meeting."

"I'll be there."

The second call brought even more sobering news. It was from Milo's son, Will.

"Brinna Caruso. This is Will Milovich, Milo's son. I wanted to call and tell you about the memorial service for my dad. His wishes were clear. He didn't want a dog and pony show. So we're just going to have a small service out at that park near his house in Santa Clarita. It'll be on Sunday, about noon. I hope you'll be there."

"I wouldn't miss it, Will. Thanks for the call." She bit back the why questions she wanted to ask Will, deciding to wait until they were face-to-face.

When she reached Second and Bayshore, the sight of Tony and his granddaughters had the same calming effect on her that hugging Hero did. She stepped out into the warm sunshine, enjoying the smell of the ocean and the sounds of people out splashing in the water. Jack wasn't there yet, and she wondered what possible news he could have about a man who'd been dead for ten years.

47

Nigel first saw them on Friday afternoon. He was picking up trash along Bayshore, just past the Second Street bridge. They were playing in the water near the bridge. They were the right age and they were perfect. He felt his face flush with pleasure and anticipation.

He caught himself staring and took a quick inventory of people on the beach to see if anyone noticed. Strolling to a Dumpster to empty his bag, Nigel felt as though he'd been hit by a jolt of electricity that energized his entire body.

This was the something special he'd been searching for. Never had he anointed more than one Special Girl at a time. Now, in front of him, were two identical girls, perfect for his anniversary present to the dog cop. This would definitely rock her world.

Again, the elation and excitement he felt now that the dog cop was in the game surprised him. He hadn't felt this good, this alive, since his rebirth ten years ago. His thoughts drifted back to that hot, dry afternoon in the mountains. He'd believed he was going to die. He certainly wanted to die rather than go to prison. Prison was no place for child molesters.

Nigel thought about how carefully he'd prepared his funeral pyre back then. At first he wasn't going to take anyone with him. Then he decided he didn't want to make anything easy for his pursuers. Besides, who would give a dime about a few worthless drug addicts? Even his cousin was a pathetic loser. Nigel scrunched his nose in distaste. He had his share of twisted predilections, but he never touched drugs, and that knowledge swelled his chest with pride.

At the last minute, before the cops shot the hotel full of tear gas, Nigel had seen an opening. The perimeter cops were pulling back in preparation for the SWAT team assault. He decided in an instant that he could burn in the fire or flee and maybe be cut down by bullets.

Timing was everything. Nigel's grin broadened with the memory. He'd sprinted out the back of the hotel at the same time the cops fired at the front. It was the explosion that probably saved him, he realized later. The hotel had gone up with more force than even Nigel expected. He was in the forest, dodging burning embers, before anyone knew he was gone.

After the escape, he waited for the man-hunt and feverishly prepared to survive for years in the forest. He burglarized several unoccupied vacation homes and had everything he needed to disappear for a long time.

But the manhunt never came. No helicopters, no dogs. Nigel was stumped. After a month he surfaced carefully and found out what had happened.

They had decided that he was dead. At that moment, Nigel was given a whole new life. He was a phoenix who'd risen from the flames.

The elation he'd felt then was now matched by the elation he felt at finding the right present for the dog cop. He'd take those two perfect girls and leave a riddle. This time the dog cop wouldn't be so quick to unravel the mystery, he was certain. *Happy anniversary.*

48

Jack parked across from the water and checked around for Brinna. The sight of the surf and the feel of sand beneath his feet brought on a wash of memories that hit him like a tidal wave. Vicki had loved the beach.

He sucked in a breath as he heard her laughter and in his mind's eye saw her dive into the water. Hands curled into fists as Jack fought the wave of pain threatening to engulf him. *Now is not the time. There is too much to do, too much at stake.* Images of Vicki faded. Breathing deeply, Jack pushed the pain away, turned his thoughts to Brinna, and kept walking, one foot in front of the other.

He wondered how she'd take the news he had for her. Checking his watch, he noted that he was late. Chuck had phoned just as he'd headed for the door, and he'd explained to Jack what a mess the investigation in San Bernardino was. The coroner's records were in a shambles, and Chuck feared they'd never get to the bottom of the shoot-out ten years ago. Jack could only hope they'd dig up something that would help them catch a child killer.

The crowd at the beach was thick, but when Jack located the rental kiosk, he saw Brinna right away. She stood talking to a thin, bald man under the shade of a large umbrella. Hero frolicked near the surf with a couple of little girls.

As Jack approached across the sand, Brinna saw him, offering a nod.

"How's your father doing?" Jack asked when he reached her.

She shrugged. "As well as can be expected." She introduced Jack to Tony DiSanto.

"Pleased to meet you, Jack. While I love Hero, Brinna's other partner, it's nice to see that she has one now who walks on two legs and talks."

"Thanks. I hope I live up to the standard Hero has set." Jack shook the offered hand. "Nice place you have here. It must be great to have your office at the beach."

"It's heaven." DiSanto turned to Brinna. "I'd better go supervise. The girls are going to tire your dog out."

"He's tireless." Brinna smiled and waved

a hand in Hero's direction.

Jack noted a subtle difference in his partner. Though she looked tired, there was something softer in her face. She was more relaxed here on the beach. He wondered about the change.

Brinna faced Jack as DiSanto began some serious play with the little girls.

"So what is this new information you have on Nigel Pearce?" She motioned to two beach chairs and they sat down.

Jack told her about his visit with Gabe Lopez. "Apparently the coroner's office was understaffed and underfunded back then. They got swamped under a big case where as many as thirty old people may have been killed by a nurse. Chaos reigned during the investigation. It seems an unqualified tech might have done as many as a hundred autopsies, unsupervised."

He paused to let Brinna digest the information. Her face betrayed no emotion.

"Anyway," he continued, "this tech found helpful evidence left and right, in order to cinch up weak cases."

"Finding or making up?" Brinna asked.

"Mostly making up, from what the Feds have uncovered so far. Chuck called just as I left the house. He reviewed some copies of the file the bureau has on the investigation out in San Bernardino."

"And this connects to Pearce how?"

"This tech did the autopsies on the bodies recovered when the Rimwood Hotel went up in flames. All five bodies had their hands and feet bound with wire from hangers. And they were shot dead before the fire. None of the wounds could have been self-inflicted." He paused.

Brinna said nothing and Jack continued. "It seems that Nigel Pearce couldn't have been among the bodies recovered. Somehow he escaped that day. He is still out there."

49

Nigel Pearce still alive.

Brinna had had nearly two full days to digest the information, and it still wasn't going down easy. What she wouldn't give for five minutes with the tech who'd made such a thing possible. *Angry* didn't cover what she felt. Not so much for herself but for all the innocent children Pearce had most likely preyed on over the last ten years.

She shoved a stick of gum in her mouth, hoping to remove the nasty taste there, and shifted her attention to the task at hand — Milo's memorial.

I hate funerals, Brinna thought, sitting in her truck at a small park in Santa Clarita. She watched cars arrive and mourners trudge into the park.

Wearing the best cop mask she could muster under the circumstances, Brinna climbed out of her truck and surveyed the gathering of mostly cops. Some guys came in uniform, and several officers from other jurisdictions were present. A few K-9 officers walked around with their dogs.

Thinking of Milo, she imagined how Jack's information would have seized her mentor's attention. He'd have wanted in on the hunt and capture. But reality intruded, and she experienced the shock of his death all over again. Pearce would be captured. Brinna refused to consider any other outcome. Still, the victory would not be as sweet without Milo there to share the celebration.

But Pearce's capture and any victory celebrations were in the future. In the here and now there was the memorial service. *No Kevlar can shut out the finality now,* Brinna thought.

"I'm glad I brought you, Hero," she said as she let the dog out of the truck. Taking a deep breath, she walked with Hero across the lot to the gathering.

Brinna clenched her teeth. "This is respect we're paying. I will not lose my composure."

Though she hadn't seen him in about eight years, Brinna recognized Milo's son, Will, immediately. He definitely resembled Milo. She knew father and son hadn't had much contact for years. Will's mother raised him in Northern California. But Milo was proud of Will, in spite of the fact that he hadn't made an effort to be a more involved father. Milo had few pictures in his house. One favorite was a photo of Will's graduation from law school. Milo bragged about his son the lawyer every chance he got.

Will smiled when he saw her approach. "Brinna, thanks for coming." He extended his hand and she shook it. "Wish it were under different circumstances."

"You and me both. I loved your father like he was my own." The words tumbled out. Brinna couldn't stop them. "Why didn't he tell me he was sick? I would've helped."

Will sighed and put his hands on his hips. "He didn't tell anyone. I got a letter in the mail the day after they told me he was dead, probably mailed the day he killed himself. It said he didn't want his son changing his diapers, so he was checking out. Bye." Will cleared his throat.

Brinna shook her head. She couldn't stop the thought running through her mind: *At least Will got a note.*

"Suicide — quite a cop-out from the guy who said, 'Never give up.' " Will's voice shook and his eyes grew moist as he regarded Brinna. "He may not have called you, but he did leave something for you."

"What?" A glimmer of hope brightened

Brinna's soul. Maybe Milo had left her some answers.

"A journal. Your name was written across it. It's in my car. I'll give it to you after we're all done."

"Great, thanks."

He waved a hand toward the gathering. "Do you want to say anything today?"

Brinna swallowed and hesitated. "No. Thanks for asking, but right now I wouldn't know what to say."

Will nodded. A couple of K-9 officers called to him, and he walked off to start the memorial.

Brinna watched Will approach the portable podium and wondered why she'd told him no. She considered Milo the best influence on her life. The reason she couldn't stand up there and share that with everyone escaped her. As she thought harder, she realized she was still angry. Angry that Milo took what he'd always called the coward's way out, angry that she didn't know how to forgive him.

She sat near the back, nodding to those officers she knew. When the eulogies started, she just listened. The guys who spoke all talked Milo up as a cop's cop. He was tenacious, he worked hard, and he trusted his instincts. His instincts never let him down.

At the end they did, Brinna thought. *His instincts let us all down because they told Milo to take his own life.*

50

Every so often Brinna glanced across the seat at the journal Will had given her. Milo never was one for writing things down. She remembered how he hated writing reports. *What was it that you could write that you couldn't tell me? And what on earth could you say to my mom that you couldn't say to me?*

She pulled into her driveway, exhausted and antsy at the same time. Hero jumped out and jogged for the front door. Brinna followed, suddenly overwhelmed by sadness. The temptation to break down and sob into the dog's neck reached up and grabbed her by the throat. She refused to give in to it.

She tossed Milo's journal on the kitchen table and stalked down the hall to her room to change into shorts. An hour in the water in her kayak was what she needed. Some sweat and hard paddling would provide a good diversion.

The bay and beach were crowded, but Tony was nowhere to be seen. Brinna dragged the yak to the surf and provided her own push-off. She paddled hard, out to the middle of the channel. It wasn't long before her shoulders began to ache from exertion. She kept going, making a circle through Spinnaker Bay, occasionally splashing herself with water to cool off.

By the time she finished, her heart was pumping and she was covered in a sheen of sweat. Humming to herself as she loaded the kayak into her truck and drove home, Brinna contentedly gave in to an exertion-related relaxed feeling.

After a shower, Brinna poured herself a tall glass of ice water. The journal on the kitchen table seemed to taunt her. She grabbed it and took it into the bedroom with her. Opening the book from the back, she picked the dates that corresponded with Milo's last days alive and began to read.

The pages raised more questions than answers in Brinna's mind. Milo seemed to question his whole life.

I've always said you made your luck by hard work. But is Mrs. C. right? There is no luck, only God guiding and providing. Brinna, I fear I made a mistake telling you to ignore your mom. As I contemplate my fate and realize that the end is so close, I think I should tell you to listen to her; she makes sense.

Milo felt his life had no meaning. And he feared what awaited him after death.

Brinna stopped, frowning. She'd always thought the only meaning Milo needed was putting bad guys in jail.

She resumed reading, picking out references to her mother. Milo always called her mother Mrs. C. He merely said that Mrs. C. gave him peace when she talked about God, forgiveness, and life after death.

Unease settled into Brinna as she realized that the man she thought was the toughest man to ever walk the earth, not afraid of anything or anyone, was deathly afraid of dying. He feared going to hell.

Mrs. C. and her Christian drivel gave him hope for life after death. She told him that it was possible to make peace with his Maker.

Brinna put the book down and lay back in her bed. She closed her eyes and tried to remember Milo healthy, big, strong, and fearless. He used to glare at suspects and make them wet their pants. It did not compute that the writing in this book was from the same man.

After a few restless minutes, she fell into a deep, exhausted, and dreamless sleep.

51

"Brinna, I've got news for you." Jack tapped her on the shoulder a couple of minutes before the squad meeting started. "Chuck's here. We'll meet with him and Ben right after squad."

Brinna's eyebrows scrunched, and she glanced at Maggie on her right. "About Pearce?"

"That'd be my guess." He smiled and sat down on her left. This time his smile didn't bother Brinna, but she did wonder about his state of mind. She and Maggie had just discussed Jack's moodiness while they dressed.

"He has too many moods," she'd told her friend. "I figure I've worked with a dead man, a creepy man, and a semi-normal man. Who knows what's waiting for me tonight?"

"Whatever mood he's in, it seems like he's improving," Maggie observed, and Brinna

324

couldn't argue. In spite of the many changes, Jack was getting better and easier to be around and work with.

Now, in the squad room next to her partner as Smiling Man, Brinna worked hard to concentrate on the sergeant at the front of the room. Jack might be a better partner, but he couldn't wave a wand and clear up the turmoil in her life.

By now, the knowledge that Nigel Pearce, the man who'd snatched her off a Palmdale street twenty years ago, was still alive had sunk in. As with her dad's sickness, she didn't know how to feel about this new development.

Ten years ago she'd just gotten her license when Milo phoned to tell her about the arrest of Pearce. He'd never stopped hunting for the creep, though by then the statute of limitations had run out for Brinna.

Pearce had snatched another six-year-old off the street, in the same manner he'd abducted Brinna, but this time he was seen and detained by a couple of gardeners.

"I want you to check out these photos," Milo had said. He was animated, more excited than she'd ever seen him, as he laid a six-pack of mug shots in front of her. She thought Pearce was the guy, but she couldn't make a definitive positive ID. *Thinking* maybe someone was the guy wasn't good enough; she had to be absolutely certain. Now, as she reviewed the facts ten years later, her palms got clammy and she wiped them on her thighs.

Back then, Milo had said not to worry, that Pearce would go to jail for his current crime. Then there was the escape, the manhunt, the siege.

Milo would have been at the siege even though it was out of his jurisdiction, but he'd been needed for a trial in Palmdale. After the fire was the first and — until recently — only time Brinna had heard her mentor mention God without cursing. When he'd heard that Pearce had been identified among the dead, Milo had toasted with a beer, saying, "Maybe there is a God after all."

As the memories rumbled through her mind, it pained her more than she could say to know that Milo's presence now was impossible.

Brinna had another distraction weighing on her mind. The shooting review board. While she believed their findings would only help her with the truth, fear lingered that it still wouldn't be enough to shut Hester Shockley up.

The squad meeting ended and Brinna

doubted she'd heard a thing the sergeant said. Maggie and Rick headed out for patrol while Jack waited for Brinna at the elevator.

"You ready?" he asked when she reached the elevator doors.

Swallowing what felt like cotton, Brinna nodded.

In the homicide office, she saw Chuck and Ben huddled over a computer screen.

Ben looked up. "Hey, is squad over already?" He glanced at the clock.

"Yep. Now what have you guys got?" Jack asked as he took a seat. Brinna leaned against a desk.

"So Jack filled you in on Pearce," Chuck said, facing Brinna, holding a file in his hand.

Brinna nodded. "What a cover he's had all these years. The government declared him dead."

"And he's made the best of it." Chuck held out the file. "I've searched through the past ten years for any crimes that match Pearce's MO. Unfortunately I've found quite a few. It looks like he's left his mark all over the country."

"All because of an incompetent coroner and a 'helpful' tech," Brinna said, a bitter taste in her mouth. "I can't believe no one noticed the body count was off. Someone from the recovery program must've shown up missing."

Chuck nodded. "Someone did. His name was Jared Collins. The agents now investigating the mess in San Bernardino have gone back through everything and concluded that Collins, who was listed as on an approved leave, must've come back early. Somehow he got caught up in the drama. After the smoke cleared, the administrators, not realizing he'd most likely returned, listed him as a walk-away."

"How are they going to prove this? Exhume bodies?" Jack asked.

"They've already dug up quite a few," Chuck answered. "And they'll be digging up a lot more."

"Back to the similar cases." Ben took the file out of Chuck's hand. "We have a total of six cases across the country over the past ten years that we consider an exact match to Nigel's MO. Three victims were found alive, but they were too young and traumatized at the time to describe their attacker." He paused and thumbed through the notes.

"And there are more unsolved abductions of little girls who *could* be Nigel's victims," Chuck continued. "These girls vanished and never resurfaced, but they all lived miles apart, so different agencies never connected the dots or compared the MOs. Our theory: Pearce has been attacking and moving throughout the country."

"In a way, we're lucky he chose to stop here and bait you," Ben added.

Brinna rolled her eyes and said nothing.

"We have a chance to stop him before he moves on again," Jack said. "And we'll have an advantage once we get an age-enhanced photo to flash everywhere."

"Good work checking this out, Jack." Chuck nodded his way.

"Thanks. I trusted my instincts." He cast Brinna a look she couldn't define.

Her feelings about Pearce had ramped up to a palpable need. *He's been an animal hunting freely for ten years,* she thought. *I will stop him if it's the last thing I do.*

52

Nigel quit his job.

He'd be moving on soon — Nevada, Texas, or maybe Florida, and the planning for his next great caper was too important. This one demanded perfection. His actions had to make the dog cop stand up and take notice. Besides, keeping his eyes on the prey he'd decided on was imperative and downright fun.

Twins. Why hadn't he considered twins years ago? he wondered. The possibilities were multiplied by two. He'd followed them. He knew where they lived; he knew their routine; he knew their unguarded moments; he knew everything but when the perfect time to strike would be.

He watched the paper for news on the dog cop's shooting, when the trial would be. At first he thought he'd like to pile on — wait for the trial and kick her when she was down. But impatience got the better of him.

He wanted to strike as soon as possible. And he wanted the press limelight to be centered directly on his handiwork, nothing else.

53

"Why are we always a step behind?" Brinna asked. "It's time we preempted him."

"Working on it," Chuck said. "His picture will go to any jurisdiction where we have a similar crime. We're checking his Social Security number and other things since he must have been earning money all these years. I doubt he kept on using the name Nigel Pearce. Finding his new identity is the key."

"You've got other pressing obligations," Ben observed, concern in his eyes when he turned Brinna's way. "The shooting board."

"Yeah, it convenes in ten minutes."

"So soon?" Jack's eyebrows arched.

Brinna shrugged. "Rodriguez called over the weekend and asked if I minded a rushed one. Hester hasn't officially filed a wrongful-death suit, but all indications are she'll do it this week. The brass wanted to grab a headline before her. Official findings should take the wind out of her sails."

"Bravo." Jack clapped. "Meet her head-on. That's the only way."

"I won't be there," Ben said. "I've been assigned full-time to this kid case. All my other cases were farmed out until we resolve this. You'll be fine."

Brinna wished she had a touch of Jack's bravado and a pinch of Ben's confidence as she took a seat in front of the shooting review board. The board consisted of Commander Cobbley, her division commander; Officer Mitchell, a peer officer from patrol; Sergeant Cannon, the firearms training sergeant and tactics trainer; and Lieutenant Hoffman, the homicide lieutenant, Ben's boss.

"Relax, Officer Caruso." Cobbley smiled. "This is merely a review of your statement, along with the facts we've compiled since the shooting, including the autopsy report on the deceased."

"If you're ready, I'll start the tape, and we'll get this show on the road." Hoffman nodded at Brinna, his thumb poised over the Record button. Brinna returned the nod and he pressed the button.

Hoffman began by stating the date and time and reciting the names and ranks of everyone present. For the next twenty minutes, Brinna answered questions, mostly centered on her frame of mind before, during, and after the shooting.

After the first few minutes, she relaxed. *They're just after the truth,* she thought. The brightest moment in the meeting came when they advised Brinna they'd found a slug, dug out of the side of a house down the street from the crash scene. It matched the kid's gun, and the trajectory was consistent with Brinna's version of being shot at. The autopsy also showed that the kid had ingested enough methamphetamine to kill himself, even if Brinna hadn't.

When they finished up and she left the room, some of the tension she'd felt earlier had eased. The pervasive feeling she got from the proceeding was that evidence proved Brinna had done nothing wrong and the officers on the board knew it. Brinna felt sorrow that the kid had been so young, but the sorrow was tempered by the knowledge he could have just as easily killed her.

The truth of what happened will be out now, Brinna thought, *draped in the official findings of the shooting review board. Trouble is, will the official truth really be enough to douse the fire Hester Shockley has fanned?*

54

"How'd it go?" Jack asked as Brinna joined him in the patrol car.

"Okay, I guess. They didn't hammer me. The autopsy report supports my version of events, and the slug he fired at me was recovered. Plus, the autopsy showed that the guy had enough meth in his system to make an elephant hallucinate. I hope it's enough to put a sock in all the lies media outlets and Shockley keep spouting."

"You'll be fine," Jack assured her as he started the car and backed out of the lot. "I got a call from Tracy Michaels just as I was heading out to get a car."

"Lucky you. Reporters aren't high on my list right now."

Jack chuckled. "Mine either. But she intimated that there might be some interesting information surfacing about that *Times* reporter Gerald Clark and his ethics."

"Like what?"

"She wouldn't say because I wouldn't tell her what we're working on now. I don't want to jeopardize our investigation into Pearce. If we tip our hand too soon, it could cause him to slip away. I figure if Clark is ethically challenged, it will come out sooner rather than later."

Brinna agreed. "And I don't want Pearce to disappear again — not this time. We're chasing my real-life bogeyman." She clicked her teeth. "Though I'm glad I have the opportunity to confront him, it's tragic he's had ten years to victimize other little girls."

"We have the upper hand now." Jack tapped the steering wheel. "When we get his picture plastered everywhere, we'll have him in custody before you know it. This is the Information Age. He won't be able to escape twenty-four-hour news coverage or Amber Alerts."

Brinna grunted in agreement as they settled into the unit and their work shift. The radio was quiet, and Jack drove at a slow patrol cruising speed. This was the kind of night Brinna normally relished. She and Hero could prowl just about anywhere they wanted, to check up on kids or creeps. But tonight she was hard-pressed to feel excited about the shift's prospects. Too much weighed on her mind.

She balled a fist and pressed it into her Kevlar vest, taking comfort in the stiff strength of it. "Do you mind taking a trip up to North Long Beach?" she asked.

"Anywhere in particular?"

"Heather's house." She stared out the window but felt Jack's questioning gaze. "I missed her funeral. I want to pay my respects." *Too many funerals, too much death.*

"Sure."

They made the trip to the Baileys' in silence. Brinna could only guess what Jack was thinking. Her own gut clenched with a grief knot so tight she wondered if she'd be able to stand up straight.

Flowers covered the Baileys' lawn, along with cards and stuffed animals of all kinds. Brinna wished she had thought to bring some Beanie Babies to add to the collection.

"You can wait here," Brinna said as Jack opened his door.

"That's okay. I'll go in. I know what they're going through."

All the way up the walk, Brinna thought of Milo. *I know what they're going through too. And it sucks big-time.*

This time it was Mr. Bailey who opened the door. His face was haggard and his eyes rimmed red. "Officer Caruso."

"Mr. Bailey." She sucked in a breath. "This is my partner, Jack O'Reilly. We came to . . . uh . . . Well, gosh, I feel just terrible." Her throat closed and she stopped speaking, lost for a second in the grieving father's eyes.

Jack held his hand out and Bailey shook it. "We're terribly sorry for your loss," Jack said.

"Thank you both. I'd ask you in, but Emily is sleeping. It's been a rough couple of days."

Brinna swallowed and found her voice. "I, uh . . . Well, I just wanted you to know that we're on it. We'll do our best to catch the guy who did this."

"I know you will. And I know Emily would want to thank you for all your hard work. I just wish . . ." His voice cracked with emotion, and Brinna felt something in her heart rip. Bailey brought a hand to his mouth before he continued. "They can't tell us how she died, you know. I just wish I knew whether or not she suffered."

Jack spoke up as Brinna lost her tongue again. "She's not suffering now, Mr. Bailey; you can be sure of that. She's in a better place."

As he and Brinna walked back to the black-

and-white, Jack felt the Baileys' grief hit as if it were his own. It was as if a tsunami of sorrow rose up and slammed him in the face.

As he pulled the car away from the house, his hands tightened on the steering wheel. All the elation he'd felt about moving forward on the Pearce investigation evaporated like water on a hot sidewalk.

They drove in silence for a while.

It was Brinna who finally spoke up. "Thought you didn't believe in God anymore."

The question jolted Jack. "What? What do you mean?"

"A better place. Heaven," she said. "What you said to Mr. Bailey. According to my mom, God and heaven go hand in hand. Can you have heaven without God?"

Jack shrugged and chewed on his lower lip, wondering why he had said that to the grieving man. "It, uh, it was just the only thing that came to mind at the moment. That man's life has been torn apart. I guess I hoped to mitigate the pain somehow." Jack swallowed. Pain was an understatement. The anguish radiating from Bailey had been palpable, and it had hit Jack like a sucker punch.

When confronted by the grief, he'd reverted to Christian platitudes. Though they never helped him, he wondered if they did anything for Bailey.

"And Christians believe that heaven waits for us when we die?" Brinna asked.

"Yeah, they believe that once absent from the body, present with the Lord."

"Heaven is a perfect place with no crying or pain or evil like Pearce, just the goodness of God, right?"

Jack blew out a breath and glanced at Brinna. The line of questioning forced him to open a door he'd purposely locked. If there was no God, then there was no heaven. So where was Vicki?

"That's what the Bible says. Sounds like you know it pretty good," Jack said.

"I've heard it from my mom often enough. I never really thought much about death."

His partner continued down a road he had no desire to travel. Jack needed quiet to gather his thoughts.

"I've handled murders, suicides, traffic fatalities," Brinna went on, "but never really thought about it past the paperwork. But when it's someone close to you . . ."

Jack stared across the car at Brinna, but she didn't return his gaze. He realized this new train of thought from her came because of the death of her mentor. For some reason that knowledge eased some of the tension he felt. "Ben told me about your friend. I'm sorry. On top of Heather, it has to be very hard."

"It's harder than I ever imagined. Milo was the last person I ever would have thought would eat his own service revolver." Her voice broke and she cleared her throat. "We talked about death a lot but about the physical aspect. He told me what to expect at crime scenes, traffic accidents, that kind of stuff. And he took me on ride-alongs. I saw my first dead body when I was nineteen, two years before I entered the police academy. There was never a thought of anything else after death. Milo's attitude was dust to dust, case closed."

"But now you're wondering?"

Brinna nodded. "Only because he was. He left me a journal. On the last pages he really wanted to believe that there was a heaven, but to him that meant there had to be a God. He was terrified of nothingness, of going to hell. I've always believed like Milo, but now . . ." She turned to stare out the window.

Jack sighed and said nothing. His whole life he'd believed in heaven. The full import of denying the existence of God dawned on him.

Where is Vicki if there is no God?

Jack looked across the car. Brinna's head was still turned away. He felt lost all of a sudden and a little afraid. Swallowing his fear, he tried to focus on his partner and not consider Vicki's eternity at the moment.

Her whole demeanor is different tonight, subdued, he thought. He didn't think it was only because of the shooting board or even because of Heather.

He cruised downtown for a while. Radio traffic was virtually nonexistent. Brinna stayed silent.

After about an hour, Jack broke the silence. "You feel like some coffee?"

"Yeah, that's a great idea. The only place we can get good old-fashioned, bitter coffee downtown is the doughnut shop at Fourth and Orange."

"I'll head right over." Jack chuckled and directed the car to the doughnut shop.

Once they had their coffee in hand, they walked back to the car. Jack leaned against the front fender while Brinna took a seat at one of the outside benches, facing him.

They sipped their coffee for a couple of minutes before Jack spoke up. "Ben said that Milo had cancer and didn't want to hang around and be a burden."

"That's what his note said."

"You don't believe it?"

"It's not that. I wish he'd told me, given me a chance to help or something . . ." She glanced at her coffee cup and then up at Jack.

"When people are determined to commit suicide, they do it." Jack held her gaze. "No one can stop them. Don't blame yourself."

"Harrumph" was all he got in response.

The pair went back to their coffee for a while. The only sound around them was dwindling traffic on quieting city streets.

"Maybe he was afraid he'd lose his nerve if he talked to you," Jack said finally.

"His nerve? Milo was the strongest man I ever knew." Her voice rose as if she tried to convince herself.

Jack watched her gulp her coffee. He gave her time to compose herself.

"In the journal he left me, he wondered if he'd been wrong to deny God and only trust in himself and what he could do. And he talked to my mom. He asked her to repeat all the Christian stuff she's always spouting." She gulped some more coffee.

It appeared to Jack as if she were working up the courage to say something else. "I take it before he was sick, he never cared for your mother — or at least not her religion."

Brinna chuckled mirthlessly. "He thought

343

she was nuts."

"There is a measure of comfort in believing that something better waits for us after we die." *It makes me feel better to envision Vicki in heaven,* Jack thought, *and not rotting in some hole.* A shiver ran through him.

"Seems like that was what Milo wanted." Brinna's voice brought his focus back to Milo and away from Vicki. "He asked my mom a lot of questions and seemed to find peace in her answers. The thing is —" she paused and took a deep breath — "for me, it always comes back to what we talked about before. If there is a God, and if he's so good, why do little kids like Heather get killed by creeps like Nigel?"

She held Jack's gaze. As he formulated his answer, Jack asked another question in his own thoughts. *Why do good women like Vicki get killed by idiot drunks like Gil Bridges?*

He was about to answer when the emergency beep of the radio cut him off. "All units, prepare to copy emergency traffic. . . ."

Brinna and Jack both dumped their coffee and leaped back into the unit. The rest of the night exploded into activity, so the conversation stayed unfinished, their questions unanswered.

55

It seemed like the entire city of Long Beach woke at once and dialed 911. EOW didn't come until almost five o'clock. Brinna and Jack worked the shift through with no time for breaks.

Jack wasn't ready to go home to an empty house with a head full of questions after he'd changed into civvies. He waited for Brinna until she stepped out of the locker room.

"Hey," she said, "you look like death. What are you doing out here?"

He held out a book. "You left this in the glove box. I figured you wouldn't want to lose it."

Brinna shook her head and took Milo's journal. She probably shouldn't have brought it along, but she'd hoped for a chance to read more of it, to find better answers. "Thanks. I guess I'm as tired as you are. This would have disappeared in a heartbeat."

They fell into step toward the parking lot.

"You want to head to Hof's, have breakfast, and talk about this? We didn't get our lunch break."

Brinna took a second to answer. The subdued mood she'd been in earlier when she told Jack about the journal seemed to have dissipated. "Thanks, but I'm beat. Maybe tonight?"

"Sure, bring it. Hopefully tonight will be a little quieter."

Jack watched her truck leave the parking lot, wishing he could shut the questions out of his mind as easily as his partner seemed able to.

Brinna drove home wondering if it was a good idea to talk about all the religious stuff in Milo's journal with Jack — or anyone, for that matter. It was Milo's personal journey. His final journey. *And he gave it to me. I can't ignore the numerous references to my mom.*

Once home, Brinna leashed up Hero and took him out for a run. During his forced inactivity with no patrol time, she noticed he'd put on a little weight.

During the run, Brinna was aware that, for the first time she could remember, missing kids and errant sex offenders were not forefront in her mind. Milo's death and the questions she had about it overshadowed the hunt for Nigel. Catching Nigel was important, but Brinna knew nothing in her own life would be settled unless she could find some answers about Milo.

Why did you talk to my mother and not me?

She knew that the only way she'd get an answer to the question — if there was an answer — was to talk to her mother. And she dreaded that option almost as much as she had dreaded going to the hospital to see her father.

When she got home, Brinna fell into bed, expecting sleep to come quickly, hoping it would quiet her troubled thoughts for a while. But nothing happened. Her ceiling fan sounded like a tornado wind; her pillow felt lumpy; Hero was a bed hog. Every little thing got under her skin. After tossing and turning for an hour, she gave up and hopped into the shower.

The water cooled her off and took away the clammy, sticky feeling but didn't relax her enough to go to sleep. After pacing her living room and downing a tall, cold iced tea, Brinna realized she couldn't put off the talk with her mother. As much as the thought made her cringe, she knew she'd have to go to the hospital.

I'll have to face my father again, she thought and groaned, not wanting any kind of repeat of the last visit. If her dad wanted a fight, she'd just have to bite her tongue and let him vent, she decided.

Once she stepped through the entrance of Long Beach Memorial, she felt the same sense of foreboding that enveloped her the day she'd come with her brother.

Nothing good happens at hospitals.

She'd dressed for the outside temperature in shorts and a tank top and shivered in the air-conditioning. Rubbing the goose bumps on her arms, she stepped into her father's room and heard her mother and Brian speaking in hushed tones. Her gaze traveled to her father's bed. It was empty. Fear shot through her like an electric current.

"Where's Dad?" she asked.

Her mother met her worried gaze and smiled. "He's downstairs having some tests. He'll be back shortly. I know he'll be happy you came to visit again."

Brinna felt a measure of relief that surprised her. She didn't want to face her father, but neither did she want to ponder the possibility she'd miss him when the cancer ran its course. She forced her thoughts to the reason for her visit.

"Actually, I came to talk to you." She sat on the edge of her father's empty bed and looked at her mom.

"Me?" Rose's eyebrows arched in surprise.

"I think this is where I go get a soda or something." Brian stood. He kissed Brinna on the forehead. "Good to see you again."

After he left, Brinna faced her mother's questioning expression. "I wanted to talk to you about Milo."

Rose's expression softened and she nodded. "I should have realized. Brinna, I'm so sorry about Milo. With everything else going on, I just forgot how hard this must be for you."

Brinna felt a lump rise and wished she had a cup of hot, strong coffee to swallow it down with. She cleared her throat. "He talked to you; you knew. Why didn't you tell me?" Brinna hated the emotion in her voice.

Rose left her chair and sat next to her daughter on the bed. "He begged me not to tell you. He said he would, in his own time. I'm sorry he didn't, but I gave him my word that I wouldn't steal his thunder."

"When, uh . . . How many times did you guys talk?"

"Just a few. He called me after he'd been diagnosed. And then once or twice after that. There was no regular pattern to it."

"Why you?"

"Because he knew where I stood on things. As you so often point out, I preach a lot."

Brinna managed a choked chuckle.

Her mother continued. "He knew I believed in God and heaven. He wanted me to explain why I was so sure God was real and that there was a better place waiting after death."

"And you told him? All that stuff you've been telling me for years?"

"Yes, all of it."

"He believed you?"

"That I don't know. The last time we talked, he seemed to have a measure of peace in his heart that he hadn't had before." Rose took Brinna's hand. "I had no idea he was going to take his own life. If I had, I would have done everything in my power to stop him."

Brinna nodded, unable to speak. Her mom had answered her questions but it didn't help. Would she ever understand why Milo made the choice he made?

56

Jack paced a familiar path in his living room. The question of eternity blazed in his mind. Vicki's eternity, Heather's eternity, and his own.

He'd told Heather Bailey's dad that the little girl was in a better place. The consolation was thrown out by reflex, and it kept echoing back to him.

Jack had flipped through Milo's journal before giving it back to Brinna and realized that the man had experienced a true spiritual renewal. Milo found peace with God before his final act. He confessed a belief in a good, merciful, and eternal God. And he was certain he would be in a better place after death.

Brinna had been succinct in her reasoning. It was clear to her: if there was no God, there was no heaven. No better place after death.

Either I believe it . . . or I don't.

Jack picked up a photo of Vicki. He'd taken it while they were on their last anniversary trip. She sat on the beach in Hawaii, smiling toward the camera with beautiful blue water in the background. Jack remembered the smell of her suntan lotion, the temperature of the water, and the feel of the breeze on his skin.

He remembered Vicki saying that Hawaii was probably a lot like how heaven was going to be. She'd told him that she looked forward to the day they could actually sit at the feet of Jesus.

But you went without me.

He felt the tears come and put the picture down to rub his eyes. The foundation of their faith had been Christ's saving grace and the hope of an eternity with him.

Was Vicki really in that better place? Sitting on the couch, Jack pounded his thighs with his fists. He was caught in an impossible situation. He wanted to deny God because Vicki was taken from him so horribly. But to deny God denied heaven and meant Jack could never again gaze upon his wife.

"God, God, God! For so long I believed in you and I served you. But you took the most precious part of my life away!"

He got up and walked to the bedroom and

leaned against a wall, staring at the bed. Fists clenched, biting his lower lip, Jack fought the tears. His back slid down the wall until his butt hit the floor.

I can't cry anymore. I've cried too much. It's time to resolve issues instead of wallowing in grief.

If God wasn't real, if there wasn't a heaven, then where was Vicki? The only image that ever gave him peace was the image of her in a place where he would eventually join her. In his darkest thoughts, when he considered taking his own life like Milo had, the upside of that was that he'd go to Vicki.

He realized that as hard as he tried, there was no escaping God. There had to be a God, and Vicki and Heather had to be at peace in heaven. He didn't want it any other way.

The road to reconciliation with God would take longer than an afternoon of contemplation, but he knew he'd eventually find that road and reconcile with his God. He wanted the peace back, the peace he knew Milo had found. The peace he used to have when he felt the presence of God in his life.

57

Brinna paced her father's empty room, smacking a thigh every so often with an open hand.

"How did I let Mom talk me into waiting around for Dad to get back?" she mumbled under her breath. The memory of their last fight stuck in her mind the same way the antiseptic smell of the hospital stuck in her sinuses.

I may be willing to put the past behind us, she thought, *but I can't picture Dad caving on anything. Rocky Caruso never backs down.* She checked her watch and turned to the door, contemplating flight.

Too late. She could hear the approaching wheelchair and see the turn of the knob. Unclenching her fists, she wiped sweaty palms on her shorts as the door swung open.

"Brinna." The tone of her father's raspy voice betrayed surprise. As the nurse pushed his chair past Brinna to the bed, he smiled.

Brinna stepped back as if pushed and drew in a deep breath. *Is he really glad to see me? Or is this just a product of his medication?*

The nurse helped her father get from the chair to the bed. Brinna looked away, somewhat chastened by his weakness. Once the nurse completed her task, she nodded to Brinna and left the room.

Brinna faced her father, arms folded, but stepped no closer to the bed. "Mom and Brian went to get coffee," she told him, still suspicious of his good humor. "I said I'd wait here until they got back."

His eyes and expression brightened more than she thought possible. "I'm glad." He shifted in the bed, wincing with the effort but flashing another smile when he got settled.

Brinna chewed a thumb cuticle, feeling as uncomfortable as she would if she were in front of an oral board. What could she say to this person before her masquerading as her father? Something in his eyes tied her tongue.

"About the other day . . ." He took a deep breath. "I'm sorry about the things I said. I . . ." His voice trailed off, and Brinna found hers.

"Forget it, Dad. Today is a different day."

Rocky brought a hand crisscrossed with thick blue veins to his chin and nodded. "A different day." He nodded toward the newspaper on his nightstand. "For you, too. Different and better."

Brinna frowned and stepped to the bed. "You mean there's something good in print for a change?"

When he nodded, she snatched the newspaper off the nightstand, wondering if the shooting board's findings had reached the morning edition. "*Times* Reporter Accused of Falsifying Stories," blared the headline.

"That reporter who saw you shoot —" Dad cleared his throat — "guess he didn't really see."

Brinna skimmed the text. "Wow," she mumbled, half to herself. "They're comparing Clark to Jayson Blair." She whistled softly in wonder, feeling tension ease, finally reading good news after days of bad. "He's been suspended, and a lot of his prior work is being reviewed for accuracy and truthfulness."

She folded the paper and slapped her hand with it. "I knew he was off when he claimed the kid never fired a shot. He hid too far under the dashboard to see or hear anything."

Her father leaned back in bed and gripped

his blanket. "I knew you didn't do anything wrong."

Brinna stared at her father. In twenty-six years she couldn't remember his ever saying anything supportive. It was more of a shock than his smile had been. "You mean that?"

"Of course." He closed his eyes and took a deep breath. "In spite of all we've argued about over the years —" his hoarse voice broke, and for a minute Brinna couldn't breathe, much less speak — "I am proud of you. I know you do a very good job."

Maggie's words echoed in her memory, and Brinna knew her friend had been right. All these years she'd wanted her father's approval, and now she had it while he lay dying. Words escaped her. Her throat felt as if someone had just applied a carotid restraint.

"We need to settle things between us, in the time we have left." He opened his eyes, and a tear leaked down his cheek. "You think I never wanted you, that I'd hoped for a boy and was disappointed when you came along. You're wrong. A daughter terrified me."

Brinna blinked back her own tears and fought the burning in her throat. She could feel the solid protection she'd built around her heart cracking. She opened her mouth to say something, but her father waved her quiet.

"I feared I couldn't take care of you or protect you properly." His face was flushed with the effort of so many words, but Brinna couldn't quiet him. "Boys were different — easier somehow, I thought."

Rocky shifted in the bed again and grimaced. "That day, when you were six and they told me what happened —" he choked on a sob and ran his hand across his nose — "my worst fear was realized. I couldn't take care of my baby girl."

Brinna felt paralyzed, terrified that if she moved, she'd lose it. She twisted the newspaper in her hands.

He blinked and more tears fell. "Can you forgive me for letting that happen?"

"I never blamed you, Dad, not for anything," Brinna whispered. She bit her lip and sniffled, not trusting herself to say more.

Rocky went on. "I'm your father. I should have protected you —"

"Dad, stop." She stepped forward and took his hand. *Like I wanted to protect Heather and every other missing kid?* "The only person responsible for what happened to me was Nigel Pearce. I know that now more than ever. You don't deserve any blame."

He leaned his head back into the pillow and squeezed his eyes shut. The strength in his hand as he gripped Brinna's surprised her. "I would have killed him with my bare hands."

Brinna bit her lip as the remaining bit of Kevlar around her heart shattered like ice on concrete.

"I know, Dad; I know," she whispered. "I feel that way every time a kid gets abducted. But we can only take responsibility for what we control."

She sat on the side of the bed gripping his hand and holding his gaze. The warmth she saw in his water-filled eyes erased a lifetime of bitterness and hurt.

58

Nigel knew his plan was perfect. Outside the home of the twin Special Girls, he'd watched enough of their routine that he knew exactly when he'd go in. The anticipation and excitement were unlike any rush he'd ever experienced. Just one more day and he would strike.

In his mind's eye he pictured the girls, and then he visualized the headlines. The dog cop would be dumbfounded. And he'd be gone.

Nigel smiled. As quickly as he'd shown up in her life to celebrate their twentieth anniversary, he'd disappear like smoke. No one would ever catch him; he was a ghost. They just don't hunt for dead men or ghosts.

He giggled like a lunatic.

59

Brinna left her dad's hospital room feeling as if she'd just worked four back-to-back shifts. But some of the tightness in her chest had eased.

My dad really does care. He's proud of me. And he always has been. Realizing how wrong she'd been about her father put a lightness in her step.

She thought about her mother's comment, about how her dad had lived in a bottle for all those years the same way Brinna lived in her work. Both of them trying to avoid the issues and people around them, emotionally unavailable to everyone.

Maybe Mom was right. Dad blamed himself for my abduction; I blame myself every time I can't save a missing kid. I guess I can see how I hide in my work sometimes. Just like he hid in a drunken haze.

Yawning every couple of minutes, she walked slowly through the hospital toward the exit, taking the stairs down to the main floor. The morning's events had taken her by surprise, sapped her strength, and left her wondering why she'd spent so many years angry.

Shortly after she and her father finished reconciling, her mother and brother had returned. She'd sat and listened while Mom and Brian chattered. Apparently her father had done what her mother had prayed for all these years, and he was "saved," whatever that meant. It made Mom and Brian very happy.

Brinna listened. This God thing apparently led her father to do what he'd done, admit how he'd really felt for so many years. It had also given her father the courage to face his fate, unlike Milo. Dad claimed not to fear death; he said he had peace. He believed he would end up in that better place Jack had talked to Mr. Bailey about. Milo had written that he had peace, but he couldn't face the cancer. Was he in a better place?

Now, standing in the hospital parking lot next to her truck in the early afternoon sun, Brinna wondered about peace. *I've never felt lacking,* she thought. *I have a mission, and it keeps me going.* The only time she didn't feel peace was when some maggot

got away with something. Like the dirtbag who killed Heather. She still didn't see how believing in a God you couldn't see and who let some pretty awful things happen could give you peace.

But so many questions nagged. *How do I stop hiding in my work? Saving kids is my mission. It's not destructive like alcohol can be. But if I let it consume me, am I oblivious to life like my drunk father always was? Maggie thinks I'm missing out on life — am I?* Shaking her head, she shrugged, too tired to think about it anymore.

She hopped in the truck and headed home, finally feeling like she could sleep. The journal could wait until tonight. Maybe she'd ask Jack later about this idea of Christian peace.

When she got home, she fell into bed fully clothed and was instantly asleep.

Jack scanned the street in front of the coffee shop and then checked his watch. Half an hour before squad. He rubbed his face. On one hand, he hoped Ben would show, while on the other hand, he berated himself for even calling his old partner.

"Sorry I'm late." Ben walked up behind Jack and slapped a hand on his shoulder.

"Thanks for meeting me. Especially after

our last meeting, I didn't think you'd show." Jack extended his hand and smiled.

Ben returned the smile. "What's past is past. I'm just happy to have the old Jack back. You are back, aren't you?"

"Getting there."

"Great. What's on your mind? Pearce?"

"No, this isn't about him. I actually wanted to talk to you about God."

Surprise flashed across Ben's face.

Jack directed him to a table, where they both took a seat. "I don't think I or anyone else will ever be able to explain why God took Vicki from me." Jack took a deep breath. "But I can't deny God anymore either. All my life I was raised to believe the Bible was truth. It's as much a part of me as Vicki was. Though I haven't picked up a Bible in a year, verses keep running through my head."

"Which verses?"

"Ones about trusting God . . . about how his thoughts toward us are for good, not evil." Jack paused and studied his hands, rubbing a callus with his thumb. "Bottom line, I can't deny him any longer because the only hope I have left is that Vicki is with him, and one day I want to be with both of them."

Jack wiped his eyes and cleared his throat

before going on. "I'm angry, Ben. Angrier than I've ever been. God let me and Vicki down in a big way."

"Well, last time I checked, angry is allowed. How can I help?"

"I guess I want you to keep praying. Pray that somehow, someway, I'll be able to see some good in this. Maybe someday I'll understand. And pray for Brinna. She's got a lot on her mind right now, and I get the feeling she'll be coming to me with questions. Pray I'll have the right answers."

"I'll keep praying for you both, buddy. I promise. And it's good to have you back."

"How's your dad?" Maggie asked breathlessly as she rushed past Brinna to her locker.

Brinna was just buckling her belt keepers. "Same. I saw him again today."

"That's good. Did you make up over what happened the other day?"

"Yeah, we did. And we talked for a while." She checked her image in the mirror. "He actually apologized for being an absent father all my life."

"Great." Maggie patted her shoulder. "I knew he wasn't as bad as you thought all those years."

Brinna shrugged. "Maybe you're right.

But I wish he'd opened up to me a long time ago, not now, just as he's dying."

"Sometimes it takes a crisis for people to reveal their true feelings."

Nodding, Brinna leaned against a locker. "Question: Am I really like my dad? I mean, Mom says he hid in a bottle all these years and I hide in my work the same way."

Maggie latched her gun belt. "Your mom is a smart woman. What have I been telling you for years? Your life is the kids and Hero. Most of the time you shut everything and everyone else out."

"What about you? I never shut you out."

"That's because I don't let you. I'm a pushy broad. And I always figured something would crack your shell eventually. I wish it hadn't been Milo's suicide and your father's cancer that opened your eyes." She closed her locker and faced Brinna.

"How do I stop? The kids are so important to me."

Maggie smiled. "Look around you. There are a ton of blue suits who do the same job you do. The fight is not only yours. Let some of that burden roll off to the rest of us."

Brinna rolled her eyes. "I'll give it a shot; thanks. And thanks for hanging in there with me."

"That's what friends are for. Let's get to squad."

60

As soon as Brinna stepped in the squad room and saw Ben with Sergeant Klein, she knew something was up. "To what do we owe the honor?" she asked.

Ben grinned and held up a wanted poster. There, four computer-enhanced photos of Nigel Pearce — tweaked for various hairstyles, glasses or no, facial hair or no — stared back at her.

"Wow, you got him." Brinna took the poster and read it with Maggie peering over her shoulder.

"We got his likeness," Ben agreed, "and some solid ties to Heather and another little girl. It was like putting a puzzle together. We had some pieces; other agencies had pieces. Once we got together, everything started to fit. He's been using the name Paul Norton. A drifter with that name matching Nigel's description was questioned in two different abductions in two different states, hundreds of miles apart. In one case DNA had been recovered. Chuck rushed it through the lab and compared it to a blood sample taken from Pearce ten years ago. It matched."

Brinna looked up from the image of the monster. She didn't recognize him today any more than she had ten years ago, but her instincts told her this was the guy. His face was now burned into her mind, and she vowed to catch him.

"This is great. I assume you have a trail to follow now."

Ben nodded. "I'm giving everyone the information at the squad meeting."

Brinna and Maggie sat down as Jack rushed into the room very nearly late.

"You seem rested today," Jack whispered as he slid into the chair next to hers.

Brinna nodded and handed him the poster. Jack whistled low as Klein started the meeting.

When it was Ben's turn to speak, he explained about the Pearce investigation and handed out bulletins. He didn't mention Brinna's possible connection but emphasized that Pearce was a suspect in the Heather Bailey slaying. He also said that Pearce's wanted poster had been given to the press and would be all over the Internet and on the airwaves on the five o'clock news. A tip line was in operation and would be manned twenty-four hours a day for the time being.

Brinna glanced around at her coworkers. Everyone studied the poster. It made her smile. Pearce didn't have a chance. And it didn't depend entirely on her.

"I'm ready to go tonight." Brinna clapped her hands when the meeting ended and she and Jack were heading to their car. "It'll just be a matter of time before someone sees his picture and calls with information."

"This is outstanding," Jack agreed as he took the passenger seat.

Brinna was up to drive first, and she hummed as they rolled along. She'd reconciled with her father, watched a vicious, inaccurate campaign against her start to falter, and now was certain she'd eventually put a monster out of commission. Life was good.

Except for Milo. She frowned. She was no closer now to understanding his suicide than she was the day she'd heard.

"You remember the journal I talked about last night?" she asked.

"Yeah," Jack said.

"I had a talk with my dad today. He said a lot of the same things about God and peace that I read in the journal."

"Did he?"

"Yeah, he's a changed man. A couple days ago I would have said that the change was only because he's in the hospital and he can't drink. But it's more than that. He now believes all the stuff my mom is always preaching about God. He's at peace."

"Reconciling with God is a life-changing experience."

"Is it?" She glanced across the car at Jack. "Sounds like your attitude has changed as well."

"It's changing; let's just say that."

"My mom would take me and Brian to church when we were kids, but my dad never went." Brinna chewed on her lower lip and looked away from her partner, remembering the family unit back then. Brian enjoyed church like her mother did, but Dad was always indifferent. *Do I take after my dad?* The question made her frown, but she didn't have time to think any more about it.

Just then the computer beeped with an incoming message. Jack pushed the button and read the message. "It's from Chuck. He's got something. He wants to meet us at the convention center parking lot."

"Hope he's got something for us to check

out," Brinna said as she made a U-turn and headed for the convention center.

"Great news," Chuck exclaimed as Brinna pulled her black-and-white up to his plain car. "We got him."

"Someone turned him in?" Brinna tried hard to keep her voice neutral.

"Not quite. But as soon as the photo aired, someone called in. Until two days ago Paul Norton, aka Nigel Pearce, was employed by the city of Long Beach."

"What?" Brinna and Jack exclaimed simultaneously.

"Yep. We didn't find it right away because of the Social Security number he used. He's been working a part-time seasonal position in beach maintenance. Makes sense considering his transient lifestyle. Anyway, SWAT is staging as we speak. Norton/Pearce gave an address out on the west side of town as his home. Want to join us?"

"Lead the way." Brinna gave a wave of her hand as adrenaline surged. "Let's go catch a killer."

61

Nigel choked on his dinner and bolted from his chair. Coughing and gagging, he stepped close to the TV and stared in disbelief at his face on the screen. Or what they thought was his face now, ten years from the last time he'd been photographed.

It was close enough. He ran a hand over his head, then jerked a drawer open, grasping for scissors. When he found some, he raced into the bathroom and began cutting in a frenzy. After a few minutes he stopped and took a deep breath, slowly exhaling. "Don't panic; don't panic," he told himself. "You can't think if you panic."

It was then he realized he'd been living on borrowed time for ten years. Whatever mistake had set him free in the mountains had just been rectified.

"I'm still free," he declared, putting the scissors down. "And I will not go to prison."

He tossed the hair he'd cut into the toilet

and flushed. Wiping his hands and face on a towel, he studied his reflection in the mirror. He saw a sun-bronzed man with a spiky haircut. *Stylishly spiky,* he thought.

Calmer now, he went back into the living room and shut the TV off. *I have to move on. To stay here would be foolish.* But on the kitchen table sat his favorite pictures of the two Special Girls. Picking one up, he ran a hand over their faces.

He didn't want to leave without them. He knew it would be best just to run now — to go far, far away and disappear in some remote area. Peeking out the window at his neighborhood, he thought it inevitable that even though he'd made no effort to be friendly to anyone, sooner or later someone would put two and two together and call the tip line.

Grabbing his photos off the table, he tossed them in a travel bag. He'd run, he decided. But he wouldn't be running alone.

62

"Who's watching the house?" Brinna asked Chuck when she and Jack arrived at the staging area.

Nigel lived in a depressed area of West Long Beach. It was a neighborhood of cheaply made and poorly maintained 1950s bungalows. A good hiding place. People in this neighborhood minded their own business. SWAT would have no trouble getting inside the shabby building.

"Ben, in a plain car, in front. A couple of West Division patrol guys in the back. Ben can see that the TV is on, but he hasn't seen anyone inside." Chuck frowned and checked some paperwork in his hand.

"Why the frown?" Jack asked. "It sounds as though things are going as planned."

"No van. Not in front of the house or on adjacent blocks."

Brinna sucked in a breath. Fear that Nigel was again one step ahead of them caught in her throat.

"It could be in storage," Jack offered. "There isn't a lot of parking on this street. He could have a second car."

"He didn't list any other car on his job application." Chuck held out the paper in his hands.

Brinna took the application. "But now we have a license plate on the van."

"Yep, it's been added to the media information."

The SWAT sergeant stepped up and indicated everything was a go. While the black-suited men headed toward Pearce's house, Brinna tuned her handheld radio to the frequency they were using and listened carefully, fingers crossed.

The wait was excruciating. Just when Brinna thought she couldn't take it anymore, the team leader came on the air calling it code 4, all clear.

The house was empty.

There wasn't much left in the house to sift through. It was starkly furnished and obvious that Pearce had scooped up most of his personal belongings before he fled.

But what he left in the bedroom took Brinna's breath away. One wall was plastered with all the newspaper articles written about her over the last month, starting with the profile Tracy had done about the anniversary of her abduction.

"You've got a fan," the SWAT sergeant said as he walked past her.

"Creepy" was all Jack said.

Brinna stared at the wall and stifled a curse. She left the bedroom and walked through the other rooms, smelled Nigel's cologne, and tried to get a sense for where he might have run. She picked up some papers scattered on the floor and gasped when she saw what they were.

"He can't have gotten far," Jack said.

"Look what else he's been collecting," Brinna said. Walking into the living room, she showed Jack what she'd found.

Jack grunted and handed the papers to Chuck. "He's been taking pictures of little girls."

All the papers were photo sheets, various candid shots of little girls at the beach. As her stomach turned, Brinna knew she and Jack would have no choice but to go back into service to wait and hope Nigel would be caught before anyone else got hurt.

Waiting was the last thing she wanted to do. Pearce had skirted justice for too long already.

■ ■ ■ ■

Brinna spent the rest of the night on pins and needles. Chuck promised to get back to them if there were any Nigel sightings or solid tips from the tip line. Jack's presence was a plus, and Brinna was glad to have a two-legged partner to talk to.

"I was so hoping this nightmare could have ended at that house," she said as they both seemed to wait with their own individual styles of quiet impatience.

"I think everyone who saw that house hoped the same thing. But the night is still young."

"So are too many little girls." She had to blink away the image of Heather that came to mind.

"You're afraid he won't surface again until he's snatched another kid."

"Yes, I am. He taunted me with Jessica. That's why we found her. What if he doesn't taunt? What if he just takes and disappears?"

"Something tells me this guy is going to want you to know when he makes his next move. He's obsessed with you. You saw the articles. Just like you have your Wall of Slime, he had his Wall of Caruso. When he does make a move, just do what you do best."

"What's that?"

"Trust your instincts."

"You're not going to tell me I have to believe in God and pray?"

Jack chuckled. "No, but I will tell you that I think your instincts are God-given. He's helping you in spite of yourself."

"You mean even if I don't really believe in him, he'll still help me?"

"I think he's been with you for a long time. You just don't know it."

Brinna frowned. "I think I liked you better when you were depressed and quiet. Especially the quiet part."

The rest of the evening passed painfully and quietly. The partners assisted on a few calls. It was close to 11 p.m. when Brinna's cell phone rang. She checked the display and saw Tony DiSanto's name and number. Brows furrowed, she flipped the phone open, hoping there was no emergency and he was calling to chat, although that would be odd.

"Tony, my good —" She never finished the sentence.

Tony's hysterics cut her off and had her holding the phone away from her ear. "He's taken them. That lunatic has taken my book-ends!"

"Tony, calm down. I can't understand. What's happened?"

"The molester. He came in and took Carla and Bella. *My granddaughters. They're gone!*"

63

You can't catch me; I'm a ghost. I faded away once. I'll fade away again. This time I have traveling companions — two of them. And I know you're green with envy.

The words of Nigel's latest taunt seared Brinna's mind as she watched her friend Tony. He alternated between anger and fear. His wife, Connie, simply sobbed. The twins' parents didn't even know yet; they were on vacation in Hawaii. The twins had been snatched from their grandparents' home.

"This time we have a huge advantage. We know who he is." Brinna struggled for the words to put Tony and Connie at ease but knew that such words didn't really exist. And she had her own problems keeping it together. This was too close to home. *Not Carla and Bella!*

The DiSantos' house filled quickly with cops and FBI agents. By now it was close to midnight. Nigel's picture had been posted online and airing on all news channels for hours. The license plate to his van and Carla and Bella's information flashed on every computerized freeway screen in the state as an Amber Alert.

Brinna left Tony with Connie and found Sergeant Rodriguez in the front of the house conferring with Ben and Jack about the contents of the note.

"If it's a riddle, it makes no sense," Ben said.

"It's a taunt." Brinna blew out a breath. "I can't sit around here. I have to be out and doing something."

"You're about end of watch." Janet checked the time.

"He left the note for me." Brinna smacked a doorjamb. "I have to find him and stop him once and for all."

Janet put a hand on her shoulder. "He's got a good hour head start. He could be anywhere."

"But that's why it's important we get going right away. He needs to feel the heat," Brinna insisted. "What kind of statement is he trying to make today? Is this tied to what happened twenty years ago or ten years ago?"

"Climb inside the head of a psychopath." Chuck shook his head. "Let's try to stick with the basics of his MO. He leaves kids in remote locations. And that van will take him almost anywhere. With all the mountains and deserts in Southern California, we've got thousands of miles to cover."

"A needle in a haystack," Jack observed, thumbs hooked in his gun belt. "But his picture is plastered everywhere. Someone is bound to see it and give us the tip we need before he gets the chance to lose himself somewhere."

"But I can't sit here and wait for it." Brinna started for the driveway. "Come on, Jack."

"Where are we going?"

"I'm picking up Hero. I plan on being ready if we get that call."

"Brinna," Janet protested.

"I know. I'm EOW. Don't worry. I often use my free time to search for kids. Why should today be any different?"

They sped to Brinna's house and quickly loaded Hero into the back of their police car. Once they were under way, Brinna drove to the freeway.

"You move like a woman with a plan. Do you have somewhere in mind?" Jack asked.

"Just a feeling, a hunch." She glanced at him. "When we get the call, it will be best to be on or near the freeway. Wherever he is seen, I want to head that way."

"I agree with you, but I wonder if you want to take a chance." Jack tapped on the MDT screen with a thoughtful expression.

"What kind of chance?"

"I've been thinking. Pearce grew up in the San Bernardino Mountains. I remember Lopez telling me his parents were survivalists." Jack tilted his head, cocking an eyebrow. "And there are some pretty remote places up those mountains that would be perfect for him."

Brinna chewed her lower lip. "It would make sense for him to head someplace he's familiar with. But if we're wrong, we could be miles in the wrong direction."

"But if we're right, we're miles in the right direction."

She glanced at her partner, and he smiled. She liked his smile now. And she liked the fact that, at this moment, he was a partner.

"Well, I'm up to take a risk. Maggie always tells me I'm a glass-half-empty person. Today I'll be a glass-half-full type. San Bernardino, here we come."

Brinna shot down the 405, hit the 22, and before long she, Jack, and Hero were on the 91 freeway, speeding down the carpool lane.

They'd just reached Corona when

Brinna's phone rang. She pulled it off her belt and flipped it open.

"Brinna." Chuck's voice greeted her. "Pearce was spotted in Fontana at a 7-Eleven. Local citizens recognized him, confronted him, and he ran."

"Anybody see the girls?"

"No, sorry. But they saw him flee in a van. The girls would be easy to hide inside that thing."

"Which direction? Fontana is east of us, off the 10 freeway." Brinna sat up, tapping her fingers on the steering wheel.

"He's headed farther east. He could be shooting for the San Bernardino Mountains or Palm Springs. San Bernardino County sheriff has a helicopter up, hoping to get an eye on the van. CHP is also on alert."

"Mountains or desert." Brinna glanced at Jack and gave a thumbs-up signal. "Our bet is the mountains. We think he's going to dump the girls up there somewhere," she postulated.

"All right, I've got you heading to the mountains. I'll inform the sheriff. There is a lot of ground to cover," Chuck said.

"Jack and I are halfway there." Brinna flipped the phone closed.

"We've got a problem."

Brinna stared at Jack and noted the concerned frown on his face. "What?"

"Message just came over the computer. The watch commander has ordered us back to the station."

Brinna inhaled and swallowed a curse. "We're too close. Do you want to quit now?"

Jack shook his head. "I don't want to quit, but when this is over, you know we'll be in a lot of trouble."

"I'm kinda used to being in trouble. Anything is worth finding Carla and Bella." She reached across the car and shut the MDT off.

Before long, the 91 freeway turned into the 215 and Brinna's phone rang again.

Brinna tossed it to Jack so she could concentrate on her driving. It was Chuck again. After a few minutes Jack closed the phone and filled Brinna in.

"Chuck says the sheriff's chopper thought they had him. The van was headed up Highway 330; you know, the route that goes up to the mountain resorts?"

Brinna shook her head. "Santa Monica Mountains, Angeles Crest — those mountains I know. I've never spent any time in the San Bernardino Mountains."

"I have. We came up here every summer when I was a kid. Trouble is, there are hundreds of campgrounds and thousands of nooks and crannies for him to hide. Chuck said the Chippies are stretched thin and don't have a unit close yet. The sheriff has two units in Running Springs. One will watch the road toward Big Bear Lake, and the other will watch the road toward Lake Arrowhead."

"Is that where this highway goes?" Brinna asked as she took the ramp for Highway 330, mountain resorts.

"Yep. It turns into Highway 18 in Running Springs, and —" Jack paused.

"What? What is it?"

"Well, it's a long shot, but the place where Nigel was raised is called Green Valley Lake. It's just above Running Springs, on the way to Big Bear."

"But Running Springs was where he disappeared ten years ago. He said he's going to disappear again. Maybe he'll try what worked ten years ago," Brinna said.

"Maybe. But Green Valley Lake would be a better place to hide. It's off the beaten path. There's a campground and several dirt roads, old forest-service firebreaks. One back road will take him all the way up to Fawnskin. It could be he's trying to get off the main roads."

"Seems like there'd still be a lot of people up there this time of year."

"Yeah, but even with a lot of people there enjoying the summer, Pearce could lose himself. A couple of years ago a kid went missing there. Remains weren't found for eleven months."

Brinna shrugged, chewing on her lower lip as she worked to maintain control of the car while speeding up the hill as fast as possible. "I've never heard of Green Valley Lake. But it is usually a good bet that bad guys flee to the familiar."

The phone rang again. Jack only got to speak to Chuck for a moment before they rounded a curve and lost the cell signal.

"All I got from Chuck was that the sheriff's deputy picked up the van just outside of Running Springs heading toward Big Bear Lake."

"Did they stop him or are they following?"

"I don't know; he got cut off."

Brinna flipped on lights and sirens, determined to be there when Nigel Pearce was stopped.

64

Brinna and Jack hit the small town of Running Springs twenty minutes later. Her phone rang immediately.

"Service again, great," Jack said as he flipped the phone open.

Jack gave Chuck an update on their location and, when he hung up, filled Brinna in on what Chuck had to say. "Chuck says the sheriff lost the van a few miles from here in a place called Arrowbear Lake."

"How do you lose a van on a two-lane road?"

"Apparently a head-on collision occurred between two SUVs as the van and the sheriff's unit drove past. Cops are stretched thin up here. The sheriff had to stop and render aid. No sign of the van between Arrowbear and Big Bear."

He'd just finished speaking as they rolled by the accident scene. Brinna slowed. There were two ambulances, and Brinna could see the deputy had his hands full. He saw her and pointed north. As soon as she was able to speed up again, she did.

"The turnoff for Green Valley Lake is coming up," Jack said. "There are sheriffs behind us and sheriffs in Big Bear. You want to take the gamble and head up to the lake campground?"

She tilted her head in the affirmative. "Yeah. My instincts are humming right now. It makes sense for him to flee to an area he knows. He's going to try to fade out of the public eye as soon as he can."

Brinna made the turn to Green Valley Lake. The sign said four miles. The road wound through the forest and had Brinna leaning into curves and Hero sliding back and forth in the backseat.

"The campground is at the end of the road, so keep going," Jack said when they reached the small town of Green Valley Lake.

"What if he takes the back road to — what did you say it was called? Fawnskin?" Brinna asked as she sped past the lake and tiny hamlet, her lights flashing, but she killed the siren. Traffic was minimal to non-existent, but in the predawn darkness the small lake was lined with fishermen.

"That should answer your question." Jack

pointed and Brinna slowed. A yellow forest-service gate was pulled shut across the road to Fawnskin. A sign said the road was closed due to storm damage. "If he came this way, the last stop is the campground."

In minutes they were at the end of the road and the campground host was visible.

"Stop at the host site. I'll find out if Pearce has pulled in here." Jack unsnapped his seat belt and jumped out of the car as soon as Brinna stopped.

As Jack talked to the camp host, Brinna turned to pump Hero up. "Hero, this is the biggest search of your life. We have to find Carla and Bella. We have to."

Hero whimpered, tail wagging, ready to be out of the car and searching.

"He's here." Jack slammed the door. "Fifteen, twenty minutes ago, number sixteen, last campsite on the right." He picked up the radio to give dispatch the information. The dispatcher would contact all the agencies that needed to be advised of the developments.

Brinna shut down the light bar and headed up the narrow campground road slowly.

"How do you want to handle this?" Brinna asked. "He's cornered. I don't want a hostage situation, but then again, we don't have time to wait for the troops."

"He's held hostages in the past. And he already knows he's been spotted." Jack rubbed his chin. "I say confrontation is the best thing, hoping and praying we catch him off guard."

"Me too." Brinna made the last right, and the van came into view. It appeared to be deserted. She stopped the unit, but her stomach felt like it was still doing the curves. "I'll wait to get Hero out of the car."

Jack nodded. They both unsnapped their guns and approached the van. Brinna took the left side and Jack the right. Jack tried the door, found it unlocked, and jerked it open, quickly illuminating the interior with his flashlight.

"Empty." He turned to Brinna. She blew out a breath and shook her head. Jack punched in Chuck's number and made sure their exact location and situation would be broadcast to assisting units.

"Chuck says he'll be here in thirty minutes and wants us to wait."

Brinna frowned. "No way. I'll run this creep into the ground if I have to." She stuck her head inside the open door of the van and searched for any sign of the girls. Other than a few stuffed animals on the floor, there was no indication they'd been in the vehicle.

"How far could he get with two small girls in tow?" Brinna asked. She surveyed the forest surrounding the campground. The sky was pink in the east as the sun brightened it over hills thick with tall pines and cedars.

"Depends on how familiar he is with the area. He didn't hesitate coming up here, knew right where he wanted to be. I'll bet he has a particular hiding spot in mind."

"You're right," Brinna agreed as a wave of helplessness flowed over her.

Where are Carla and Bella?

65

Nigel had nearly screamed when the lady at the convenience store pointed at him and said, "It's him!" He'd run away from the place as if someone had lit his pants on fire, dropping groceries as he fled. The stupid woman followed, all the while jabbering on her cell phone. He'd been tempted to run her over but didn't want to damage his van.

After he got back on the freeway and saw the chopper, it didn't take a rocket scientist to know that it was after him. Except for that day ten years ago, Nigel had never felt cornered in his entire career. He hated being rushed. It was all wrong.

Somehow, someway, they'd figured him out.

At first he cursed and pounded the steering wheel. But after he eluded the helicopter and then avoided a couple sheriffs' units, a serene feeling of invincibility settled over him. *No one's career lasts forever,* he told himself. He glanced back at the twins, tied up on the floor of the van, and euphoria coursed through his veins like a strong drink.

I can go out with a Fourth of July–type finale, he thought. *I've already made more bold moves than anyone else, I bet. My last caper will be the pièce de résistance — something that will make all the talk shows and the major newspapers.*

A tiny spike of fear crowded in as he left the van to check in with the camp host. He debated just driving by. It was still mostly dark out. But their lights were on, and passing them by might arouse more suspicion. He relaxed when he saw that they had neither TV nor computer. They knew nothing about him and the twins. He filled out a registration card with false information and headed for the campsite.

Now he was home free. This was his backyard. He'd mapped these forests in his head when he was a kid, and those maps were still vivid in his mind. *No one will ever find me or the girls,* he thought, smiling for the first time since he fled the convenience store.

When he parked, he untied the twins and calmed their crying by telling them he was taking them to their grandpa. They just had to be quiet as mice, he said, or they'd never make it to him. Along with his camera bag, he filled a small backpack with food, extra clothing, and money. Nigel knew he'd never be back to the van. The most important thing to do right now was get lost in the forest, finish his business with the twins, and disappear.

He grabbed the little girls, one of their hands in each of his, and they headed into the dark fringe of pine trees.

66

With Hero at her side and some of the twins' clothing that Tony had given her, Brinna stood by the van and took a deep breath. There was an early morning chill in the air, and she hoped the girls were warm. She blinked away the image that flashed in her mind of Pearce with the twins.

"Are you back on good terms with that God of yours?" she asked Jack.

"I think so. I've made my peace."

There was conviction in Jack's voice, she thought, and she took note of the change in the man. The weak, creepy guy of last week was now all cop and all confident. The kind of guy she'd want to work with. A guy she could trust to cover her back.

"Good. Pray. If I never find another kid my entire career, I have to find these two. Alive." Her throat thickened and she paused. "They're like members of my own family."

Her father came to mind, and suddenly Brinna knew how he must have felt twenty years ago. Maybe she couldn't excuse the drinking, but after all this time, she knew why he drank. The situation she now found herself in illustrated in painful detail what her father had dealt with.

She bent to one knee and held the clothing under Hero's nose. "Find, Hero; find." Once the leash was unclipped, Hero took off into the forest, testing the air with his sensitive nose.

The sunlight filtering through the trees brightened the trail as Jack and Brinna charged after him. The path was a well-worn firebreak that followed an old logging road.

"He's got at least a twenty- or thirty-minute head start," Jack noted.

"Yeah, but he's also got two little girls to drag or carry, and he started in the dark. I know he hasn't killed them. I know it." Brinna spit the words out, wanting to convince herself that being cornered would not change Nigel's MO drastically. She tried not to think of Carla and Bella being dragged along against their wills, probably cold and most certainly frightened.

Hero eventually came to an unmarked trail that cut off the firebreak and wound upward through the trees. It was a narrow trail, well worn by hikers and coated in a layer of pine needles with pinecones scattered here and there. Because of a fire a few years ago, the forest on this hillside was a sparse mixture of tall old pines, older spread-out oaks, charred trunks, and an occasional cedar. Nothing here caused Hero to pause; he just kept his nose to the air on his way up the trail.

"Pearce isn't even trying to cover his tracks," Brinna noted.

"Why would he? He evaded a helicopter and a sheriff's unit. By now he's probably feeling pretty cocky."

Brinna grunted as she forged up the trail. After about twenty minutes of climbing, the trail leveled off, and they hiked across a ridge. Though the morning was still chilly, Brinna wiped sweat from her brow. The trail was visible ahead, eventually winding up and disappearing into a thicker forest, one that the fire had skipped.

Hero suddenly stopped and stood still, sniffing, ears alert.

"Did he lose the trail?" Jack asked, catching his breath.

"No." Brinna shook her head and tried to quiet her own breathing. "He hears something." She knelt next to the dog and grabbed his collar. Holding her breath, she strained to hear what the dog heard. There it was.

Faintly Brinna heard a little girl crying. "Did you hear that?" She turned to Jack. His expression told her he had. The sound came from below them and echoed across a canyon.

Brinna clipped the leash back on Hero but let him lead them as he cut down, off the worn trail. Here the ground was soft with a thicker mat of pine needles, and Brinna had to step over sticker bushes. Every so often she sank into a gopher hole. The dog turned right, into the forest, and the cries became stronger. Brinna turned to Jack and motioned for him to circle around on her left. He climbed back on the ridge trail and paralleled her.

She and Hero stayed straight, angling down into a gully. Brinna's head snapped up at the sound of a man yelling. A string of obscenities followed, the words carrying from far away. The crying sounded closer, as if it were coming her direction.

Dodging around some trees and hurrying toward the sound, Brinna could clearly hear two girls wailing. Hero whimpered, and she silenced him with a hand gesture. Stepping through some small bushes, she saw them. Carla and Bella were running on her right, sobbing as they ran.

Hero barked, and the girls turned in Brinna's direction. She jogged toward them, all the while searching frantically in the direction they'd run from. Where was Pearce?

"Carla, Bella, come here!" She knelt to scoop the girls close with one arm but kept her other hand on her duty weapon. Both the girls sobbed, the kind of crying that leaves kids stuttering. It was minutes before Brinna could get anything out of them.

Finally Carla wiped her nose and seemed ready to talk.

"Where's the bad man, Carla? Where is he?" Brinna asked, eyes darting around the area.

"He fell, Aunt Brinna. He fell."

"And we ran," Bella added with a sniffle and a hiccup.

Brinna pulled out her handheld radio and hailed Jack. "The girls are with me. Any sign of Pearce?"

"I'm still looking. I'll head back your way in a minute."

Brinna hugged both little girls tight. Eyes closed, thankful and relieved, she considered her mother's God. *Will I ever be able to reconcile the happy endings and the tragic ones?* she wondered. And she knew then, like Milo, she had a lot of questions for her mom.

"Don't worry," she told the girls. "You'll be back with your grandpa before you can say Jack Russell."

They calmed down slowly as Hero nuzzled and licked their faces.

A few minutes later, Jack came crashing down the slope. "There's no sign of him. I found this." He held up a camera bag.

For a brief moment, Brinna went back in time twenty years. The tears were hers, out in the vast expanse of desert. In front of her, Pearce had spread out a blanket and set up a camera.

She bit her lip and brought herself back into the present. "We've got to get these kids home." Standing, she reintroduced Jack to the girls and vowed to herself she'd be back to hunt the creep down.

Jack scanned the bright horizon and directed Brinna's attention that way. "He won't get far. When you're on top of the ridge, all you can see is forest for miles. I didn't want to get lost and become part of the problem. Sheriff's search and rescue will be all over the area before you know it."

"He won't get away this time; he won't," Brinna said through gritted teeth as she picked up Carla. Jack took Bella and the group headed back the way they'd come, to the campground.

67

Sheriff's units already had the van cordoned off with yellow police tape when Brinna and Jack returned with the girls. First order of business was to make sure the twins were okay, then fill in the search unit on where they'd lost Pearce. Brinna was about to ask a deputy where the medics were when she saw a pair huffing up the campground road. They set up quickly and took the girls from Jack and Brinna.

Aside from being hungry and thirsty, Carla and Bella were unhurt. Pearce had had no time to violate them. While Jack phoned Tony, Brinna studied a map the deputies gave her and planned a search grid. She'd find some of Pearce's clothing in the van, and she and Hero would be off. The sound of a helicopter approaching from the south was audible, and she knew that would be a help.

"Congratulations." Chuck extended a

hand to Brinna. "You found them safe."

Brinna shook his hand and sighed. "Not just me and Hero. Jack was a great help. But Pearce is still out there. No little girl is safe as long as he's at large. I'm betting he heard us coming and let the twins go to stall us, so he could get away."

"Where's he going to go?" Chuck held up a clipboard with Pearce's wanted poster and tapped it. "His face is plastered everywhere." He waved the board at the San Bernardino County sheriff and their operations. "These guys know the area better than Pearce does. And search techniques have improved over the last ten years. He'll be in custody before you know it."

"And I want to be there." Brinna crossed her arms.

"I don't think that will happen."

Chuck and Brinna turned as Jack walked up, frowning.

"Why?" Brinna asked.

"I just got off the phone with Scranton," Jack said. "He's at the DiSantos'. We are officially ordered back to Long Beach. Brinna, this is serious. We can't ignore him again."

"No, I've come this far! Pearce is close. Hero can find him; I know it." She clenched her fists, her gaze bouncing from Chuck to Jack. In both men's faces she saw empathy,

405

but she also saw common sense. She'd only just escaped the fire with the shooting. Did she really want to jump back in the frying pan?

Chuck put a hand on her shoulder. "Listen to Jack. We'll get Pearce. Don't put your career in jeopardy over him."

Brinna started to protest, but Jack cut her off. "Brin, we have the girls. You aren't the only cop in the world who can find people." He added the last gently.

Brinna held his gaze and tried to be angry. His weird, empty eyes were gone, and all she saw in them now was genuine concern.

She turned toward Carla and Bella sitting on a gurney, munching food that the paramedics had given them.

It wasn't fair that she had to leave now, so close to the end.

But Jack was right; the girls were safe. That was the most important thing.

Taking a deep breath, Brinna scanned the now-bright forest borders. "You're right." She looked at Jack. "Let's see if the medics will let us transport the twins home."

It was difficult for Brinna not to break down into tears with Tony and his wife as they grabbed the twins in bear hugs. The joy and relief in the room reminded her of something very important. The reunion with her family had been much the same that first day. But it was also that same day when something started to fester inside her father, something that built the wall and impaired their relationship for twenty years. When Tony came up for air, she pulled him aside.

"Thank you, my good friend," he gushed as he grabbed her in a hug. "How can I ever repay you?"

Brinna pushed back and held him at arm's length, smiling. "You don't owe me a thing, my good friend, except maybe this." She nodded to Carla and Bella. "Love the girls, keep them close, but never blame yourself for what happened. The only bad guy in this is Pearce. Don't let anger, guilt, bitterness, or unforgiveness come between you and those two precious girls. Those are destructive emotions. Don't let them ruin what you have."

"You speak from experience." Tony smiled and blew his nose.

"I do. I'd bet my life that it's easier not to build the wall than to try to tear it down later."

68

"I think we stayed one step in front of the reporters," Brinna noted as she and Jack pulled into the station parking lot. It was close to noon. They'd been given the official okay to go home and sleep; their follow-up reports could wait.

"Won't be easy to do in the coming days, especially after Pearce is in custody." Jack parked the unit, and he and Brinna climbed out. Brinna let Hero out and turned toward where her personal truck was parked. Jack reached out and placed a hand on her shoulder. "You've been awfully quiet about Pearce. Are you okay with everything?"

Brinna yawned and stretched. "The girls are home and safe. Do I want to catch the creep? Yes. But I've realized I'm not God. Other cops can catch crooks too." She held Jack's gaze and realized something else she kept to herself. She liked him, and if it weren't for Hero, she wouldn't mind being his partner.

Jack chuckled. "That's quite a concession. I guess I realized something too."

"What?"

"Life goes on. There are some battles worth fighting. Sound corny?" He gave her a sheepish smile that Brinna couldn't help but return.

"Yeah, but I won't tell anyone. Go home and sleep. I don't want a tired partner tonight."

She got to her truck and shed her gun belt, uniform shirt, and vest. "I'm too tired to even kayak," she said to Hero as she started the engine. Brinna thought about calling Maggie but didn't want to wake her. When she pulled into her driveway, she saw she needn't have worried. Maggie was dozing in her porch chair.

Grinning, Brinna let Hero out of the truck. He rushed to Maggie and nuzzled her awake.

"Nothing like wet dog kisses." Brinna laughed as her friend woke up and hugged Hero.

"I have to agree with you. Hero kisses better than my last boyfriend."

"Why are you loitering on my porch?" Brinna asked as she stuck her key in the lock.

"Because I wanted to share the paper with you." Maggie opened the local paper so Brinna could read the headline: "Local Cop Cleared of Any Wrongdoing in Shooting Case."

"Unbelievable," Brinna said as she took the paper from Maggie. "But welcome."

"Yep. Shockley concedes that she'll have to go with the shooting board's official results. That sleazeball reporter Clark has proved unreliable, and the physical evidence supports your story." Maggie snapped both fingers. "Voilà! And Clark may be on the hot seat soon. The *Times* fired him, and the DA may file charges against him." She held her arms out for a hug.

Brinna grinned and hugged her friend. "Thanks for being the bearer of good news."

"I told you it pays to be a glass-half-full-type person. I bet you'll be the subject of another headline," she said as Brinna pushed the door open and they walked inside.

"I don't care about headlines. I'm just glad the kids are okay."

"And Pearce?"

Brinna dumped her stuff on the sofa, then sat to take her boots off. "Pearce." She frowned and pulled on the laces. Maggie sat across from her in the recliner. "He's as good as caught. Even if it's not me doing the catching."

Maggie chuckled. "Good for you. Let the rest of us help you with your mission. Your shoulders aren't broad enough to carry it all."

"Great job, Brinna, great." Janet Rodriguez's call woke Brinna up, but it was a welcome awakening.

"Thanks. I'm glad the girls are safe. Any word on Pearce?"

"Not yet, sorry. But there are search teams from all over the county on his trail. He's on borrowed time. But that's not why I called."

"Am I in trouble for ignoring Scranton?"

Janet laughed. "No. He tried, but eventually he ended up having to shred the letters of reprimand he wrote for you and Jack. Seems the chief is so happy with all the good press you brought the department by finding the twins, Scranton didn't want to be on the wrong side."

"Does that mean I'm back with Hero?"

"Soon. You have twenty hours to finish with Jack. Can you handle twenty more hours?"

"Piece of cake." *It will be too.* She listened as Janet explained why she'd called, then

411

hung up, yawning. Jack had turned out to be a better partner than she'd ever dreamed possible. With that thought in mind, she got out of bed to start coffee. The phone rang before she finished pouring her first cup. Caller ID said it was her mother.

"Morning, Mom," she said as she answered the call.

"I knew everything would turn out well for you; I knew it." Her mom went on to gush about the girls, the shooting, and everything printed in the paper that morning.

"Thanks. How's Dad?"

There was a pause, and Brinna hoped that didn't mean bad news. While the jury was still out on her mother's God stuff, she knew she really wanted to see her father again and share as much time as possible with him.

"Not much change. You'll come by later?"

"Yeah, I will. I have a lot to tell him." Brinna's thoughts drifted back to the happy reunion between Carla, Bella, and their grandparents.

Now she'd tell her dad she really understood. Hopefully all the wounds Pearce had caused her family would now be free to heal.

She'd only just hung up when the phone rang again. This time Brinna's eyebrows arched in surprise. It was Jack.

"I just wanted to call and congratulate you. I read the paper. You and I are in an elite group of cops. We both beat Hester Shockley."

"Yeah, it almost feels as good as finding Carla and Bella. You're up early."

"I've got places to go. How's your father?"

"Same. I'm headed over there soon. Thanks for calling."

"No problem, partner. By the way, that speech you gave Tony DiSanto . . . I want you to know that it touched me, too."

"About destructive emotions?"

"Yeah. It reminded me of Gil Bridges and something I have to do. I have to forgive him. I have to put that all behind me. It won't be easy and it won't happen over-night, but Vicki would have wanted it that way. Thanks for reminding me."

"No problem. You ever need a good slap, give me a call."

69

On the drive to the hospital, Brinna reflected on her father and Milo. All this time she'd thought her father was the weakling and Milo had all the strength. Turned out she was wrong about her father. Dad now faced the end of his life with a courage Brinna never would have thought possible. It wasn't that Milo had been a coward. It was just that she realized he wasn't as perfect as she'd always thought. But was anyone perfect?

When Brinna stepped into her dad's room, it twisted her heart how much weaker he'd become. Though her mom said there hadn't been any changes the last few days, it was as if Brinna was seeing her father for the first time . . . and he was no longer strong or capable. While she regretted the short time they had left, she vowed to make the most of it.

Brinna took his hand and sat on the edge of his bed. "I want you to know I just realized something. When I was searching for Carla and Bella, it was like I'd lost my own kids. I know now what you went through all those years ago. I understand a lot more than I did even the last time we visited."

He nodded but didn't speak. After a few minutes he faded off to sleep.

Rose stepped close and placed her hands on Brinna's shoulders. "It makes me so happy to see you've made peace."

"I only wish we could have hashed this out years ago. There really is a lot more to Dad than I ever considered." Brinna turned to her mom. "And I promise not to shut everyone out by burying myself in my work. I'll find a balance."

The two women shared a hug. "I thank God for that," her mother said.

70

Sitting in the back of the courtroom, Jack watched everyone take their places in preparation for Gil Bridges's sentencing. Bridges's attorney led the defendant to his place at the defense table. A woman Jack recognized as Bridges's wife led two small children to seats directly behind Bridges.

District Attorney Rivers walked in past Jack without seeming to see him and took his seat at the prosecution's table. Besides Jack and Bridges's family, there were no other spectators. After a few minutes the bailiff entered and placed some paperwork on the judge's bench. He then took a seat at his desk, obviously waiting for a call that the judge was on his way.

As Jack studied the back of Bridges's head, the pain and anger were still there. But now he felt free to move on. He could envision a day it wouldn't hurt so much. It dawned on him that right at this moment,

Bridges's sentence didn't matter to him. After all this time he didn't want to start another countdown. He just wanted to get back to his life and live it in a way that would make Vicki proud.

He stood, stepped out into the aisle, and thought about approaching the counsel table but stopped. God was in control of the sentencing. *And of my life,* Jack thought. *I can leave this here.*

He took a deep breath, turned, and left the court just as the bailiff called everyone to order.

Jack normally enjoyed sunrise at the cemetery. But today, because of the sentencing, he'd gotten there later and the sun was high in the sky. He took a seat on the grass next to Vicki's headstone. His heart felt lighter than he could ever remember. D-day had passed and, with it, Jack's burden of unforgiveness and hate.

"I'll always love you and miss you," he said, "but I'm thankful for the five years we had together. The way you died will never make sense to me, at least not until I'm in heaven with you and I can ask God face-to-face. And I have that hope now. I will see you and our baby again." He took her cross out of one pocket and a container of Krazy

Glue from the other. Very carefully he applied the glue to the back of the cross and stuck it to the headstone, centered under Vicki's name.

He traced her name with an index finger and smiled. *When it's my time, I'll be there. Hang tight until that day.*

On the way home Jack punched in a number on his cell phone that he hadn't called in a while. His mom cried when she heard his voice. It was several minutes before he could get the words out, but eventually they made a date for lunch.

71

"Hey, welcome back!" Maggie gave Brinna a hug as soon as she stepped into the locker room.

Two weeks after Carla and Bella were rescued, Brinna found herself sitting in church with her mother and brother at her father's funeral. He'd died peacefully in his sleep, and Brinna was relieved that he no longer suffered. She had taken a week off after her father passed.

"Thanks." Brinna released her friend. "Don't tell me you came in early just to welcome me back?"

"You bet. I missed you." Maggie stood with arms akimbo, looking up and down Brinna's cotton K-9 jumpsuit. "You're back with Hero, but please tell me you miss Jack at least a little bit."

Brinna laughed. "I'm with Hero, where I belong, and Jack is back in homicide, where he belongs."

"He's still every bit a hunk." Maggie tsk-tsked.

Brinna shrugged. "I'll admit that Jack turned out to be a great partner, good instincts. We worked well together." She sat while Maggie finished dressing.

"Any hope you might be seeing more of the man?" Maggie shot Brinna a leer.

"Settle down. I like the guy, but who knows where he's at where his wife is concerned."

"He's got to move on sometime. I read that the drunk who killed his wife was sentenced, five to ten. I'd think that would close the book."

"Whatever." Brinna waved a hand.

"Well, no outright dismissal. At least that's a good sign." Maggie closed her locker.

"I've decided to make some changes in my life," Brinna said as they left the locker room and headed for squad. She'd been asking herself questions since her dad's passing. *Are you in heaven, Dad?* she wondered for the hundredth time. She wasn't entirely convinced of the answers, but she'd promised her father she'd diligently search for them. As diligently as she ever searched for a missing child. Sometimes her mother's preaching still annoyed her, but there were times she listened.

Maggie clapped her hands. "Goodie. You're not going to bury your head in chasing down sex offenders and finding abducted children anymore?"

"I won't go so far as to say that. Those things are still important to me, but you could say that from now on I'll try to be a glass-half-full person. How's that?"

Maggie grinned. "It's a start."

EPILOGUE

Nine Months Later

Brinna was contemplating a trip to the beach to spend some time kayaking when she got a call from Chuck Weldon. "You sitting down?" he asked.

"Yep, what's up?"

"What's surfaced would be a better question."

"You found him." Brinna felt as though her heart stopped.

"Yeah, but not the way you think. A couple hikers stumbled across some remains in the San Bernardino Mountains. Turns out our friend Pearce has been dead for almost as long as we've been searching for him."

"He never made it out of the mountains?"

"Nope, and he never victimized another kid. From the look of things, he took a fall, broke a leg, and most probably died of exposure. And animals helped the decomposition some."

Brinna chuckled. "For once the punishment fit the crime." After she hung up the phone, she sat in her recliner and pondered Nigel's fate.

There is a God after all, she thought.

DISCUSSION QUESTIONS

1. Brinna Caruso's own kidnapping as a young child is the driving force behind her crusade to rescue abducted children. What is admirable about her quest? In her earnestness, what does she fail to recognize? Is there something in your own life that has triggered a desire to act or make a positive difference?

2. At the beginning of *Critical Pursuit,* Jack O'Reilly is consumed with hatred for the man responsible for his wife's death — even to the point of denouncing his faith in God. Have you ever experienced such an extreme situation or felt unable to forgive someone? What does Jack do — good and bad — to move past his feelings? What should he have done?

3. In what ways — physically, emotionally, spiritually — are both Brinna and Jack

"lost" in this story? Who or what rescues them? What can you learn from that?

4. What did you think of Nigel Pearce? How does having scenes from his point of view add to the story?

5. When Brinna and Jack are partnered up in patrol, Brinna worries that Jack doesn't care enough about his job. What does each character bring to this working relationship? How do they ultimately help and support each other?

6. What are some of the reasons that Brinna's relationship with her father is difficult? How have both Brinna and Rocky Caruso contributed in negative ways?

7. Both Rose and Brian Caruso tell Brinna that she is like her father, though she doesn't see the similarities. What evidence in the story supports Rose and Brian's claim? Why might Brinna want to deny any likeness?

8. Throughout the story, Jack wrestles with his unbelief — that if he says there is no God, there must not be a heaven, either, though he wants to believe his wife is in a

better place. Have you ever had similar doubts or encountered someone who has? What would you say to someone like Jack?

9. Brinna's mentor, Milo, struggles with poor health and depression after retiring from the police force and turns to God for answers. Though some characters believe he finds peace, Milo still chooses to take his own life. Do you believe Christians who commit suicide go to heaven? Why or why not?

10. Though Brinna attended church as a child, she struggles with the idea of a God who allows evil in the world. What will it take to convince her of God's sovereignty? What answers would you give for her questions?

11. What did you think of how the story ended? How does Brinna's reaction to news in the epilogue make you feel? Is she too coldhearted or is she justified in her feelings?

ABOUT THE AUTHOR

A former Long Beach, California, police officer of twenty-two years, **Janice Cantore** worked a variety of assignments, including patrol, administration, juvenile investigations, and training. She's always enjoyed writing and published two short articles on faith at work for *Cop and Christ* and *Today's Christian Woman* before tackling novels. A few years ago, she retired to a house in the mountains of Southern California, where she lives with three Labrador retrievers, Jake, Maggie, and Abbie.

Janice writes suspense novels designed to keep readers engrossed and leave them inspired. *Critical Pursuit* is the first book featuring Brinna Caruso. Janice also authored the Pacific Coast Justice series, which includes *Accused, Abducted,* and *Avenged.*

Visit Janice's website at www.janice

cantore.com and connect with her on Facebook at www.facebook.com/JaniceCantore.